DARK HUMOR AND SOCIAL SATIRE IN THE MODERN BRITISH NOVEL

Dark Humor and Social Satire in the Modern British Novel

BY
Lisa Colletta

palgrave
macmillan

52806057

1-25-05

First published 2003 by
PALGRAVE MACMILLAN™
175 Fifth Avenue, New York, N.Y. 10010 and
Houndmills, Basingstoke, Hampshire, England RG21 6XS.
Companies and representatives throughout the world.

PALGRAVE MACMILLAN is the global academic imprint of the Palgrave Macmillan division of St. Martin's Press, LLC and of Palgrave Macmillan Ltd. Macmillan® is a registered trademark in the United States, United Kingdom and other countries. Palgrave is a registered trademark in the European Union and other countries.

ISBN 1–4039–6365–7 hardback

Cataloging-in-Publication Data is available from the Library of Congress.

A catalogue record for this book is available from the British Library.

Design by Newgen Imaging Systems (P) Ltd., Chennai, India.

First edition: October, 2003
10 9 8 7 6 5 4 3 2 1

Printed in the United States of America.

For Stephen, who has always known the importance
of a good dark joke

TABLE OF CONTENTS

ACKNOWLEDGMENTS

Many people deserve thanks for helping me during the writing of this book. Marc Redfield at Claremont Graduate University and Audrey Bilger at Claremont McKenna College gave me excellent suggestions and direction during the very early stages. I am deeply grateful to Wendy Martin at Claremont Graduate University for being a wonderful mentor and friend and for her constant encouragement and consistently sound advice. I must also thank Regina Barreca, whose lively and humane scholarship inspired me from the beginning. I owe a great deal to Kristin Bluemel for her careful readings, generous advice, and unfailing support; she not only listened to my frequent whining but also reminded me to laugh.

For special friendship, I would like to thank John and Sarah Fowles who taught me a lot about British humor and continue to keep me laughing. Thanks also go to Leonora Smith, the lioness, for her unique insight into Dame Ivy.

A version of the chapter on Ivy Compton-Burnett was previously published in *And in Our Time: Vision and Revision in British Writing of the Thirties*, edited by Antony Shuttleworth, Bucknell University Press. I am grateful to the publisher for permission to include this work. Finally, I wish to express my special gratitude to Ella Pearce and Michael Flamini at Palgrave Macmillan for all their help and support.

Introduction
Modernism and Dark Humor

The increasing seriousness of things, then—that's the great opportunity of jokes.

Henry James

Humour is not resigned; it is rebellious. It signifies not only the triumph of the ego but also of the pleasure principle . . .

Sigmund Freud

In the final chapter of Evelyn Waugh's grimly funny novel *Vile Bodies*, the feckless protagonist, Adam Fenwick-Symes, has finally caught up with the man he has been chasing throughout the entire work, the drunk major who owes him 1,000 pounds. They meet in a scene of utter devastation, on the "biggest battlefield in the history of the world," and though Adam at last receives the money that earlier in the novel would have allowed him to marry his lady love, the pound is now worthless, and the sum is only enough to buy him "a couple of drinks and a newspaper."[1] The two retire to the major's (now a general) car, a Daimler limousine sunk to its axles in mud, and drink a salvaged case of champagne with a prostitute named Chastity, as the violence inevitably engulfs them. Ironically titled "Happy Ending," the chapter represents Waugh's apocalyptic vision of the future of Western culture, aptly symbolized by the absurd image of the limousine foundering in the mire of a senseless war. It is at once horrific and hilarious, the only fitting end to a novel that comically bears witness to the turmoil and tragedy of British life in the wake of World War I.

Like Waugh's *Vile Bodies*, the comedic works of many British novelists between the wars are haunted by a sense of anxiety and powerlessness, marked by feelings of loss and uncertainty and shot through with the trauma of violence and the threat of further brutality. However, despite the violent events and unhappy endings, many works from the period insist on being funny, exploring the central themes of

Modernism—alienation, uncertainty, instability, mechanization, and fragmentation—through a grim form of comedy that, according to Virginia Woolf, leaves readers "laughing so hard they feel as grave as corpses."[2] In this work, I suggest a framework for reading what I call Modernist dark humor in relation to the more familiar histories and categories of Modernism, satire, and the twentieth-century comedic social novel. The dark humor of so many social comedies written between the wars offers a valuable way of reexamining the Modernist novel, which is certainly more diverse than traditional definitions of Modernism have allowed. Critical interpretations of Modernism generally exclude most of the social comedies written during the 1920s and 1930s—works by writers like Waugh, the early Huxley, Compton-Burnett, Anthony Powell, Michael Arlen, and Ronald Firbank—assessing them as satiric and therefore conservative, reinforcing the very cultural values they set out to critique, and thus too engaged in social correction to qualify as Modernist, with its ideal Joycean god-artist objectively paring his fingernails. However, dealing as they do with the trauma and confusion of post–World War I life, these satirists employ a deeply ambivalent humor, and just what is being satirized is never entirely clear, making their humor distinctly darker than is generally presumed. Like conventional satire the setting of these novels remains the social world of the privileged classes; however, the humor offers none of the optimism of conventional social satire that suggests correction of vice will lead to the reintegration of the individual into society. Thus, in the dark humor of Modernist satire, the social content remains but its social purpose all but disappears.

Dark humor is characterized by the very concerns of Modernism. It is generally defined by ambivalence, confused chronology, plots that seem to go nowhere, and a conflicting, or even unreliable, narrative stance. It presents violent or traumatic events and questions the values and perceptions of its readers as it represents, simultaneously, the horrifying and the humorous. Like Modernism itself, dark humor defies any system that does not match with personal experience or intuition, whether that system is political, ethical, religious, or even narrative. At the same time it imposes a comedic order on the chaos and oppression represented in the text and refuses to endorse an all-encompassing ideological or philosophical view of the world. The object of the humor makes little difference; it can be the strict hierarchies of English country-house culture, the horrific slaughter of the World War I, the loss of unified identity, or the numbing effects of modern technology. I argue that dark humor is an important characteristic of Modernism, and the satire of these writers is characterized by its dark humor, therefore creating a new form of Modernist social satire. Though Modernist social satire may lack some of the formal experiment of Modernism—or it may not foreground formal experiment—its humor revels in the nonrational, the unstable, and the fragmented, and it resists easy definition and political usefulness. Works as different as *Mrs Dalloway* and *Vile Bodies* are connected not by narrative experimentation but in the way comedy is used to make sense out of an increasingly senseless world. This way of reading allows for a more inclusive discussion of Modernist literature that can include writers as different as Woolf and Waugh.

The term Modernism itself is imprecise and contested. It generally refers to writings that are self-consciously avant-garde and that attempted to break with literary and aesthetic forms inherited from the nineteenth century. But as Nancy Paxton points out, "English Modernism had, in fact, more than one 'face' and the traditions eclipsed by it were also various and multiple."[3] Even the canonical works of Joyce, Eliot, Pound, Stein, Woolf, Lawrence, Forster, and Conrad present the scholars of Modernism with a problem of definition. Whether it is in Malcolm Bradbury and James McFarlane's influential *Modernism: A Guide to European Literature* (a staple in many college courses in Modernism), or in any number of dictionaries of literary terms, the definition of Modernism quickly becomes vague and hard to pin down. Critics often resort to statements such as: "Modernism is less a style than a search for a style in a highly individualistic sense," or "Modernism becomes the movement which has expressed our modern consciousness, [and] created in its works the nature of modern experience at its fullest."[4] Recent critical reappraisals of the period are often recovery efforts, unearthing the contributions of authors who may have been overlooked based on their race, class, or gender. However, attempts to revise the canon do not fundamentally change the way we look at Modernism and have resulted, more often than not, in merely defining the "minor" writers of the period against the major ones, requiring a view of all writers' works through the lens of identity politics.[5]

Comedic writers historically have been of little use in questions of politics and ideology, though of course many humorous writers throughout the centuries are read this way: Shakespeare, Fielding, Swift, Austen, Dickens, to name only a few. But by and large these writers were working within a stable system of values, where ideas about ethical behavior were assumed to be shared, and analyses of their humor were generally used to shed light on their more serious observations about human foibles and failings. Throughout history ethical norms were probably much less stable than is generally assumed, but in the twentieth century even the assumption of stability was overturned, and the satire of the century becomes increasingly difficult to use as a corrective. As Patrick O'Neill notes, dark humor has "an emphatic lack of belief in its own efficacy as an agent of moral education," and most of the social satire between the wars is suspicious of "causes," political, religious, and even artistic.[6] And in their focus on the upper class they suggest that if individuals backed with the power of money and prestige are unable to successfully negotiate the chaotic and threatening forces of change in the twentieth century, there is little to expect from a reshuffling of the deck, which would create merely a different system, equally incapable of addressing the needs of the individuals functioning within it.

Much of the Socialist-inspired literature of the period, also deeply affected by the brutality of World War I and interested in exposing injustice, saw itself as moral and didactic, and there is a difference in motive between the work of writers like the early George Orwell, Sylvia Townsend Warner, Patrick Hamilton, or Henry Green and that of Evelyn Waugh, the young Aldous Huxley, Compton-Burnett, and Anthony Powell. Whether considered in terms of a literary history that emphasizes either the "redness" of the decade or its reactionary tendencies, it is especially important to register the dissenting, skeptical, social vision of the writers of dark comedies.[7] For example, underpinning Orwell's *Burmese Days* (which is dark, satiric, and, at times, funny) are an indictment of injustice and a hope in moral action and social transformation. Flory's undoing is that he is too engaged and too ambivalent, too thoughtful to accept the arrogant brutality of empire and too weak to reject it. As a result, acutely aware of his moral failings, his only recourse is suicide. In dark humor satires, injustice is mocked but so too are personal despair and the ideas of moral action and social transformation. Characters' moral qualms and feelings of desperation are generally undercut by the use of non sequitur and incongruity, and suicide as a meaningful moral act is often reduced to an absurd farce, whether or not characters actually succeed in killing themselves. In Aldous Huxley's *Antic Hay*, the failed painter Lypiatt sits down to write his suicide note, imaging how the others would find his body, and instead spends the rest of the evening composing a blustering treatise on the tortured artist-as-hero, and in Anthony Powell's *Afternoon Men*, the dejected Pringle decides to drown himself in the ocean but changes his mind only to find that his neatly folded clothes have been removed from the beach. In *Vile Bodies*, the aristocratic Simon Balcairn ludicrously dies by putting his head in an oven after learning that he has lost his job as Mr. Chatterbox, the gossip columnist. As implicated as they are in their own societal group, the characters are still thwarted and circumscribed by social hierarchies and the loss of meaning, and the fiction of this world suggests that there is little hope for all individuals to find meaningful roles to perform. Granted, it is somehow easier to laugh at the senseless death of a besotted and idle aristocrat than at the senseless death of an exploited and brutalized coal miner. But in the dark comedic universe there is no more meaning attached to one than the other, as both are reduced to parts functioning within a vast mechanism.

Unlike the social satire produced in the eighteenth and nineteenth centuries, Modernist social satires, like *Vile Bodies*, *A House and Its Head*, and *Afternoon Men*, disallow easy identification with protagonists and do not ridicule cultural values or societal vice with the hope that they may be corrected. Alternative ideas are never offered, as in, for instance, Swift's "A Modest Proposal" or in Fielding's benevolent humor, and they do not assume the successful integration of the individual into society. Instead, they propose nothing in the form of social change and view all ideological systems—from religion and domestic hierarchies to political power structures—as essentially the same, oppressive to the individuals within them because of the inability of any system to adequately address the complex nature of human existence.

Attention to the complexity of experience makes Modernist satire deeply ambivalent; indeed, it is no longer satirical in the traditional definition of the term. Satire is conventionally defined as having "moral norms that are relatively clear" and "assum[ing] standards against which the grotesque and absurd are measured."[8] Traditionally, satire has demanded at least an implicit moral standard or it was not seen as particularly effective. In much of the literature of the twentieth century, the post Enlightenment assumptions about the rational, scientific ordering of the self and the world are viewed as ridiculous. As scholars of traditional high Modernism have observed, the grotesque and the absurd become the "moral" standards. One of the implications of this shift of standards is a need to distinguish traditional ideas about satire from ideas about dark humor and a need to expand our repertoire of terms and gain critical tools for more subtle analyses of Modernism, whether serious or comic. Without faith in meaningful moral development, comedy no longer serves a corrective satirical function but instead offers the pleasurable—if only momentary—protection of laughter in the face of injustice and brutality. As Robert Polhemus asserts, comedy evolves and "what people laugh at and why shows the direction of their lives and the course of their world."[9]

In Modernist dark humor, social arrangements have become too fractured to offer the necessary conformity from which social generalizations can be extracted, and Modernist social satires abandon any hope of understanding the world. In novels like *Vile Bodies*, *Afternoon Men*, and *Antic Hay* there is no progress and no relationship between cause and effect, and the actions of the most benevolent characters often result in tragedy and suffering. In the post-Nietzschean, modern world, the *Weltschmerz* of dark humor clearly has a different motivation than does satire. For example, what are we to make of Compton-Burnett's satire when at the end of *A House and Its Head* Nance Edgeworth comments on the death of her mother and her father's brutality, "We were fond enough of her to want her to have her life, even though it had to lived with father. It shows what we think of life"?[10] To the dark humorist, social aberration—or even antisocial behavior—is only a small fraction of the chaos intuited in a vast indifferent universe; indeed, in the literature of Modernism, social aberration is more often celebrated as useful, protecting the individual from the hostile forces of a monolithic social machine—or a seemingly antipathetic universe—that distrusts difference and crushes individuality.

Dark humor and satire share certain formal characteristics, however, and the deflationary wit and lacerating use of irony and derision of dark humor has much in common with satire. Though it is perhaps awkward to suggest, as Bruce Janoff does, that what dark humor "satirizes is the man's position in the universe,"[11] it can be argued that satire has evolved, as Polhemus suggests comedy does, in the object and purpose of its attack, still retaining some of the formal characteristics of conventional satire but now better reflecting the existential and philosophical crises that characterize the modern world. Writers of the era practice a distinctly Modern type of satire with a purpose that has more to do with the coping devices of gallows humor than with the corrective function of exposing wickedness or foolishness.

Dark humor tends toward the distopian and presents a grim and even hopeless picture of the historical moment between the wars in Britain, but with comedic aggression the texts refuse to be overwhelmed by the absurdity and hopelessness they represent. The crystalline quality of Waugh's satiric style resists the chaos presented in his early novels, and the verve and energy of Huxley's *Antic Hay* belies the dark message embodied in Myra Viveash's final assessment of life at the end of that novel: "Tomorrow will be as awful as today."[12] The comedic defiance of these authors, their insistence on being funny in the face of the distressing subject matter they represent, is humor "on a grand scale,"[13] according to Freud, for it acknowledges pain, suffering, and futility but displays a "magnificent superiority over the real situation."[14] Though this form of comedy does not afford the confidence of change, it does offer the reader momentary protection from feelings of powerlessness and existential unease. In Modernist dark humor, all seems absurd, all seems inscrutable, and, therefore, there is little else to do but laugh. This response may appear resigned, but it is in fact a powerfully assertive and aggressive reaction, for the dark comedic imagination casts off pain and suffering and refuses them their power to overwhelm and destroy. If humor can no longer be used for a moral purpose, it can be employed as a defense and a weapon, a formula of personal survival that suspends the consciousness of death and dissolution and strengthens, if only momentarily, a hold on life.

Freud claims that the grandeur of humor lies in "the triumph of narcissism—the victorious assertion of the ego's invulnerability."[15] According to Freud, the individual ego, embattled by forces that would annihilate it, refuses to "let itself be compelled to suffer"[16] and uses instances of pain and trauma as occasions to gain pleasure in humor. Dark humor is "grand" because it celebrates the protective capacity of the individual by its insistence on making comic sense out of over-whelming non-sense. It takes on our greatest fears and makes a joke out of powerlessness, loneliness, ignorance, authority, chaos, nihilism, and death, allowing them to be mastered for a moment. All the forces that would reduce the individual to nothingness are transformed into a source of pleasure. Narcissism is often discussed as a characteristic of Modernism but it has generally meant a preoccupation with interior subjectivity or individual consciousness. The narcissism of humor protects the individual from threat and pain. Narcissism is aggressive; it reduces everything to the service of ego. Looked at through the lens of comedy, Woolf's representation of the subjective, internal musings of Clarissa Dalloway and Compton-Burnett's rigidly objective observations of social injustice are both narcissistic because they both mock and belittle the traumatic situations the characters find themselves in and allow the reader to feel superior to those circumstances.

Psychological protection and pleasurable experience are equally important in dark humor. The modern psyche is bedeviled by a disturbing awareness of impotence and the oppressions of authority and restraint. The arts, Freud argues in *Civilization and Its Discontents*, are among the palliative remedies the individual uses to cope with excessive disillusionment and suffering.[17] Since the "substitute gratifications" offered by the arts in general allow an escape from the pressures of reality, the comedic arts, which provide both the aesthetic pleasure of the joke and the psychological pleasure of fending off suffering, are especially powerful.[18] The assertive stance of dark humor is particularly apposite in Modern social satire because humor is an inherent social activity, and the negotiation of increasingly confusing and conflicting group identities is the source of much of the comedy and the trauma presented in the texts. Modernist dark humor satire examines the individual in society and reveals the seemingly hopeless struggle to fit in, simultaneously drawing on recognizable group experiences and undermining the possibility of having a truly shared experience. The often savage indignation and scathing irony of Modernist dark humor are important developments in the history of comic prose fiction because they are not only aimed at the injustices of social orderings but at the idea that any kind of order is simply an illusion, and yet the effects of these illusions are damaging—if not murderous.

Freud, of course, is not alone in his valuation of comedy as one of humankind's most important coping devices. Speculators of the comic from Kant, Schiller, and Nietzsche to Baudelaire, Breton, and Bakhtin have all argued that the comic experience was important because it suggested the truth about the basic antinomies of existence, offering a way out, the possibility of understanding and then living with the anxiety of the human predicament.[19] Beyond this, recent scholars, such as Regina Barreca, Nancy Walker, and James Kincaid, have persuasively argued that the disenfranchised and marginalized, that is women and minorities, have always included humor as one of the most important weapons in their arsenal to protect themselves from psychological damage and to subvert the power of those in authority.[20] But Freud's work remains one of the most provocative and useful analyses of humor because of its multiple layers of meaning and its complicated examination of the site of the comic. Though much of twentieth-century comic theory depends on Freud's work in *Jokes and Their Relation to the Unconscious*, as does much of his later psychoanalytic theory, the work is very often dealt with superficially in studies of comic literature. Passing references are made to the idea that all humor is aggressive or to his paradigm of joke-work, but often the nuances and complexities of his theories are overlooked altogether.

Jokes and Their Relation to the Unconscious is a peculiar book. It is an uneven and difficult text and many scholars of Freud find that it raises more questions than it answers. Samuel Weber, who likens the work to a shaggy dog story, concludes that *Jokes* arrives "not so much at [an] organic whole . . . as at its shaggy fleece," and argues that "instead of baring the essential characteristic of a joke," Freud leaves us with "a patchwork quilt."[21] Though the book does appear to lack a certain coherence, even after numerous readings, what felicitously remains, is not a unified whole that uniformly defines humor (for over and over scholars of the comic have proven that is impossible) but complicated examinations of the process of humor that can be extended, augmented, and applied to both comic behavior and comic literature.[22] Freud forever changed the questions we ask about humor and remains important because he examines both the external conditions for humor and its internal functions, its intimate connection to reality and its distance from it, and its immense power to subvert authority and protect the individual.

Not all of the characters in dark comedy use humor in a self-protective fashion, but the narrative stance of the texts is aggressively humorous and allows the reader protection from the traumatic circumstances presented by examining these circumstances from a safe comedic distance. We may feel sympathy for the plight of Adam Fenwick-Symes in Waugh's *Vile Bodies*, but we do not share his pain. The reader, more often than not, identifies with the narrator, implied or otherwise, who is in control than with the character who is not. The historical realities these authors examine are tragic, but they are appraised humorously, an appraisal that is both defensive and aggressive, for as Freud has argued, "Humor is not resigned; it is rebellious. It signifies not only the triumph of the ego but also of the pleasure principle, which is able here to assert itself against the unkindness of the real circumstances."[23]

The real circumstances between the wars were shockingly unkind. Violence on a grand scale, the loss of identity, and the increasing mechanization of society left the modern individual in a dilemma. Traumatized by recent historical events, there was the fear that some incalculable and horrible catastrophe awaited, yet, deprived of a sense of forward movement, there was the equally terrible prospect that nothing at all would happen. Why did certain authors in the interwar period in Britain represent this troubling impasse and the disturbing sense of powerlessness comedically? Many writers of the period—Joyce, Woolf, Beckett—turned inward, choosing to explore individual consciousness and to extend the possibilities of the literary forms inherited from the nineteenth century to better represent alienation and fragmented identity. But others, like Compton-Burnett and Evelyn Waugh, engaged Modernist concerns from a rigidly objective comic perspective, creating characters who consistently find themselves in traumatic circumstances yet who, for the most part, are revealed to the reader through their actions and words rather than their internal stream of consciousness. In dark humor novels, readers cannot be tricked into thinking they "understand" a character in the traditional way. As Winston has observed, "Even when characters are relatively complex, it is difficult to understand motive, and we may know what they do but not why they do it."[24] Just when we think we understand a character, he or she will do something ridiculous or outrageous, and our expectations are undermined. The inability to understand comfortably the relationship between motive and action among the characters reflects a larger uncertainty about meaning and existence, an uncertainty that is at the root of dark humor. If traditional forms of literature assume that human character is knowable and implies that cause and effect can be discerned, in effect, that problems are resolvable, then dark humor supposes, as Matthew Winston argues, "that the patterns one may perceive are arbitrary, that our selection of what is important and what is not has no inherent validity . . . that the crucial questions have no answers, and that mystery is not a particular obscurity in an otherwise known and ordered world but is the very nature of existence."[25] This dark view speaks to the Modern era's concern with instability, nihilism, and alienation and implies a broader more subversive attitude toward the structures of authority than has been previously understood.

Dark humor suggests that there is really only established disorder. Sometimes it examines alienation and absurdity through the intensely subjective individual perceptions of characters, but more often it makes an aggressively objective evaluation of chaos and fragmentation. The canonical Virginia Woolf employs both of these strategies in *Mrs. Dalloway*, but reading her in the context of dark humor not only sheds new light on her work but also reveals its connections to other writers of her time. Rethinking Modernist humor is important not only because it allows for canonical and noncanonical writers, but it also claims a tradition of dark humor for all of them. Dark humor is generally seen as an American phenomenon, and nearly all of the texts dedicated to it discuss American and European writers.[26] Individual writers in English have been looked at in this tradition, notably Samuel Beckett and more contemporary authors such as Muriel Spark and Martin Amis. However most studies of humor in British literature, such as Alice Rayner's *Comic Persuasion: Moral Structure in British Comedy from Shakespeare to Stoppard* or Robert Polhemus's *Comic Faith: The Great Tradition from Austen to Joyce*, read it as redemptive or transformative, as Regina Barreca does women's fiction in *Untamed and Unabashed: Essays on Women and Humor in British Literature.* More recently, Margaret Stetz in *British Women's Comic Fiction, 1890–1990: Not Drowning, But Laughing,* questions the transforming power of comedy in women's writing and interrogates not only its ability to effect change but to guarantee survival. She argues, "When British women writers have weighed the power of comedy and found it wanting, it is because they have discovered its limitations in guaranteeing survival."[27] In dark comedy, rooted as it is in gallows humor, change—even survival—is beside the point. The point is to wrest from pain a momentary victory in laughter; it makes no other claims. The only triumph available is momentary and individual; it allows for pleasure even in the most unpleasant situations because it insists on a humorous appraisal of circumstances that often runs counter to material reality.

Clearly, the political and ethical uselessness of dark humor has profound implications for Postmodern literature. Claiming a tradition for dark humor in the British novel bridges the gap between Modernism and Postmodernism, a gap that is arguable in the first place. The work of Postmodern British writers—Martin Amis, Ian McEwan, Salman Rushdie, et al.—is characterized by ambivalent humor, a delight in incongruity, and a preoccupation with the fractured nature of consciousness. They suggest very little in the way of change, and their work is not a break with the past as much as it is a continuation of it. Kirby Olson argues, "the curious phenomenon of humor is central to the postmodern enterprise."[28] I would argue that the phenomenon of humor was central to the Modernist enterprise as well, and that perhaps the categories "modern" and "postmodern" are too limiting. Though it took Gilles Deleuze and Jean-François Lyotard to make the "positive enjoyment of asymmetry, incongruity, hilarity, and irrationalism" traits associated with philosophy, they have always been traits associated with comedy.[29] In *Toward the Postmodern,* Lyotard observed, "Humor says: there is no correct point of view . . . Humor does not invoke a truth more universal than that of the masters; it does not even struggle in the name of the majority by incriminating the masters for being a minority. Humor wants rather to have this recognized: there are only minorities."[30] Olson is correct and persuasive in his argument that Deleuze and Lyotard champion work that cannot be pressed into service of a given metanarrative, but the comedic literature of Modernism had shown that already.

Of course, not all comedies of the era were dark. Social comedies were popular in the early decades of the century, and writers such as E.F. Benson, Stella Gibbons, Elspeth Huxley, and P.G. Wodehouse (just to name a few) all wrote novels that mock English manners and expose hypocrisy. Their work also partakes of a certain comedic ambivalence and, I would argue, is much less conservative than is generally assumed.[31] However, their comedy rarely deals with the death, destruction, isolation, and loneliness that marks the humor of Woolf, Compton-Burnett, Waugh, Powell, and others who wrote from a position of privilege but were aware of the irrational nature of that privilege. These writers savage their own social set without any expectation that their satire will materially change anything. For the most part, the writers of dark humor satire all write about similar circumstances— sometimes with radically different styles—and behind all the humor lies acute feelings of alienation and isolation. Writers as different as Woolf and Powell share a ruthless observation of the social system and a concern with how individuals are damaged by it yet seemingly survive within it. For example, in *Mrs. Dalloway*, Woolf gives us both Clarissa Dalloway and Septimus Smith, two characters who have performed their duties and have done what is expected of them. Both are thwarted and victimized by the "virtues" of "proportion" and "conversion"; yet Septimus sinks beneath them while Clarissa, "a thorough-going sceptic" aware "that the whole thing is a bad joke" does her part, knowing that "the Gods, who never lost a chance of hurting, thwarting, and spoiling human lives were seriously put out if, all the same, you behaved like a lady."[32] The common thread is not aesthetic form but a darkly comedic stance that confronts the complexities of the modern world and the psychological difficulties of negotiating them.

The role of the individual in society was still of profound importance in Britain during the decades of the 1920s and 1930s, despite the increasing interest in subjectivity of experience. As a result, many writers had an abiding concern with how the individual negotiates increasingly complicated social arrangements and the performance of social roles that no longer corresponded to stable meanings or values. Wife, daughter, "Lady of Fashion," aristocrat, soldier, writer, or lover are simply roles to be inhabited for a moment, no longer tied to identity and subject to change upon a shift in social circumstance. Even traditional expectations of gender performance elide and "masculine" and "feminine" behavior are no longer viewed as necessarily distinct and fixed. The breakdown of stable social categories and the proliferation of social roles to be performed results in an anxiety about the ability of the individual to "sanely" exist (to use Woolf's term) within a social system that is increasingly hostile to the people within it, requiring them to perform roles that do not adequately correspond to ideas of personal identity.

Wylie Sypher has argued that twentieth-century social satires are "a sign of desperation," ghastly comedies of manners that reveal how the "awkward and hopelessly maladroit hero . . . struggles vainly somehow to 'belong' to an order that is impregnably closed by some inscrutable authority."[33] Throughout the literature of the period, characters reflect the anxiety that results from the individual's inability to "fit in." Most of the comedy arises when they attempt to adapt to the perpetually changing roles required of them, applying values and beliefs that worked in one situation to circumstances that continually change and require a different set of values and beliefs each time. Of course, one can never catch up, and the "through-the looking-glass" absurdity of the Modern world leaves the characters who do not succumb to death or madness with the unsettling feeling of stasis that prompted Waugh to cite Lewis Carroll in the epigraph to *Vile Bodies*: "it takes all the running you can do, to keep in the same place."

Engaging in activity that can no longer be seen as informed by meaning beyond that of the moment leads to a painful awareness of life's inanity, and as Sypher claimed, "wherever man has been able to think about his present plight he has felt the suction of the absurd."[34] Indeed, in the twentieth century it would appear, as Sypher has claimed, that the absurd, "that is the irrational, the inexplicable, the nonsensical—in other words, the comic," is more than ever inherent in human existence.[35] Comedy is the language of the absurd because it deals in contradictions, and the modern individual lives amid the incongruities and irreconcilables that is comedy's domain. Dark humor admits disorder, incoherence, and instability and yet resists being overwhelmed by them. Imposing a certain absurd logic, it takes potentially devastating meaninglessness and turns it into a joke. When external reality threatens the stability of the individual from all sides, dark humor allows for the triumph of narcissism, the protection of the individual, and the pleasure of laughter.

Chapter 1 looks at comedy theory in relation to social comedy and discusses the characteristics of dark humor and the way joke-work functions. Using Freud's psychoanalytic theories of humor, it examines the self-protective nature of jokes and humor and how they allow for the assertion of the individual and the release of aggression when outright protest is prohibited by external circumstances or internal prohibitions. Throughout the works in this study, many of the characters retain a hold on their "customary" selves, even when the hostile reality of a situation requires a different response.[36] In Freud's discussion of gallows humor, he argues that herein lies the magnanimity of humor; it allows the individual self to resist the provocations of cruel reality. According to Freud, humor involves at least three participants—the teller of the joke, the hearer of the joke, and the object of the joke; though, the teller may frequently make himself the object of the joke, as well. Since humor generally requires an audience, I will also examine the relationship between the reader and the text and show how the implied narrator in these texts functions as the joke teller, creating in the reader the same pleasurable response and protective laughter that occurs in the joker.[37]

Chapter 2 examines how Virginia Woolf comedically explores the possibilities of sanely negotiating the social system in *Mrs. Dalloway*. Woolf's ambivalent presentation of Clarissa Dalloway has led many scholars to either condemn her as a vacuous lady of fashion or praise her as an artist, creating beauty and order in her parties. Clarissa is, of course, both. She protects herself from the traumas of illness, war, and a passionless marriage, by engaging in social customs from which she wrests momentary pleasure, and she is implicated in the injustices of the society she participates in and is the object of much of the narrative's humor. The vacuity of her social world is ridiculed, but her participation in it, despite her intuitive and uneasy awareness of its meaninglessness, is also represented as heroic, protecting her from the loss of self that drives Septimus to suicide. Her absurd and incongruous identification with Septimus, a man who has been terribly wounded and has lost everything, is admitted within the dark comedy of the novel because it refuses a judgment of her. Clarissa's engagement with social customs is at once silly and serious—as Woolf has said elsewhere with regard to society, "It is all an illusion (which is nothing against it; for illusions are the most valuable and necessary of all things, and she who can create one is among the world's greatest benefactors)."[38]

Chapter 3 looks at the disturbing domestic comedy of Ivy Compton-Burnett's *A House and Its Head*, showing how, in the microcosm of the family, abuses of power, hypocrisy, and greed warp the characters of all family members, both victims and victimizers alike. Compton-Burnett's tyrants are all-powerful in their control of their families, and this oppressive atmosphere spawns crimes of murder, incest, and will tampering. Those unable to psychologically protect themselves sink under the weight of cruelty—some die, some become unstable and cruel themselves—but those who endure, defend themselves with wit and sharply aggressive word-play, which mocks the authority of the domestic despot but never overturns it in open revolt. Open revolt is rarely an option in the rigidly controlled hierarchy of Compton-Burnett's households, and the dependents of Duncan Edgeworth rely on him entirely for their material well-being. Freud has argued that people are so often prevented by external circumstances from openly challenging authority that "jokes are especially favoured in order to make criticism possible against [those] who claim to exercise authority,"[39] and Compton-Burnett's characters use this form of humor wickedly. Her dark comedy plays out amid traumatic events and unhappy people, and, though power rarely shifts and all the characters' lives are blighted, a few survive to grimly joke about their circumstance.

Waugh's early satires have been described as striking the perfect pitch for the interwar years, capturing the headlong activity of the 1920s yet lamenting the passing of the last century's gentlemanly code of values.[40] However, chapter 4 argues that Waugh's early fiction, here examined in *Vile Bodies*, is much darker and more ambivalent than this analysis allows for. Waugh's critique of Victorian culture is as vicious as his assessment of Modern society, and his dark comedy suggests that all of Western culture's constructs, from religion and government to codes of gentlemanliness, are bankrupt, offering nothing but sham principles that have no correspondence to real meaning. Like the limousine mired in mud, which may have been elegant and nimble in a different historical terrain, the past's values are now ridiculous and useless, and there is little to do about it but draw the blinds and have a drink. In *Vile Bodies* modern life is presented as hopelessly violent and absurd, and traditional ethical categories of good and bad no longer obtain. Characters are distressingly unmoored from any meaning that would inform their breathless activity, left alone to negotiate confusing and constantly changing demands on them. The characters within the novel have little recourse to the protective qualities of humor, but Waugh's humorously cranky narrative style makes them and their difficult situation the object of its joke, causing the reader to laugh at misfortune that can cut very close to the bone. Though denied the comfort of a critique of identifiable error, the reader joins with the narrative stance of the text and laughs at distressing events; thus, an absurd type of comedic order is imposed upon the chaos.

Anthony Powell's first novel, *Afternoon Men*, is examined in chapter 5. Known primarily for his epic *Dance to the Music of Time*, Powell presents in *Afternoon Men* a grim comment on a world similar to that of *Vile Bodies* and reveals slowly, repetitiously, and inexorably the numbing routine of social life in the interwar years. Caught in an endless cycle of parties and dead-end work, the protagonist, William Atwater, is so engulfed by ennui and so disassociated from the activities that make up his life that he generally seems to be viewing his existence from an uninterested and bemused distance. The novel is marked by a profound melancholy, but Powell's understated dialogue and deflationary wit defend the novel from being overwhelmed by sadness. Powell's use of repetition adroitly captures the tedious daily realities of his characters' lives and in doing so he creates a humor that reflects the anomie and non-sense of modern life. The conversations and pursuits of Powell's characters rarely have a point and always wind up back where they began. Bergson has argued that "really living life should never repeat itself," and when it does we suspect that something mechanical is at work behind the living.[41] This mechanical encrustation on the living results in humor because when human beings act like machines, they are behaving incongruously. Freud has also argued that repetition is humorous because it frustrates the demand of our conscious reason for advancement. Powell's use of repetition is therefore pleasurable and disturbing; the reader laughs at the narrative technique but is unsettled by what it says about the meaninglessness of modern life. As in all the works this study examines, the humor results in a very dark comedy of manners that elicits laughter at the absurdity that serves for life in the social world of the modern novel.

At the end of his work on Rabelais, Bakhtin asserts, "All the acts of the drama of world history were performed before a chorus of laughing people. Without hearing this chorus we cannot understand the drama as a whole."[42] Comic derision, which the authors in this study aim at an antipathetic and painful world, is rooted in the "popular laughter," which Bakhtin argues is an important legacy in the development of literary fiction.[43] The dark social satires of the interwar years in Britain rely on the pleasures of laughter to subvert presumed societal, comedic, and even rhetorical norms, presenting readers with the range of human experience and allowing for the momentary triumph over that experience.

CHAPTER 1
COMEDY THEORY, THE SOCIAL NOVEL, AND FREUD

A sense of humor develops in a society to the degree that its members are simultaneously conscious of being each a unique person and of being all in common subjection to unalterable laws.

W.H. Auden

In his essay, "Laughter," Henri Bergson declared, "Our laughter is always the laughter of the group,"[1] and, because of his insistence on the social function of comedy, he is an appropriate place to begin an examination of the humor in the social satires studied here. Bergson is interested in gesture and the social manners that people adopt when playing a role in society, roles that too often become rigid and mechanical. Though Bergson's theories do not engage the psychological uses of humor, near the end of his essay on laughter he suggests, "comic absurdity is of the same nature as that of dreams,"[2] a claim that he does not fully develop but treats as a bit of a digression. It will be Freud's work on jokes that fully develops a theory connecting dream-work and joke-work and focuses both on the process of humor and its role in overcoming both internal and external obstacles that would stand in the way of laughter.

For Bergson, humor is essentially corrective; the natural environment of laughter is society, and any utility that laughter has rests in its "social signification,"[3] its ability to comment on certain requirements of life that are common and shared by the social group. He argues that what life and society require of the individual is flexibility, "a constantly alert attention that discerns the outlines of the present situation"[4] and the ability to adapt in consequence. The inability of the individual to adapt to circumstances forms the foundation of Bergson's comic theory, and his notion of mechanical inelasticity argues that laughter arises when a rigidity in character or behavior precludes individuals from responding to changing situations in a living, vital way. Truly living beings, contends Bergson, adjust their behavior to fit varying circumstances; when individuals do not accommodate themselves to the exigencies of social circumstances, relying on the "automatism of acquired habits,"[5] they become inflexible and mechanical. This "mechanical inelasticity, just where one would expect to find the wide awake adaptability and the living pliableness of a human being"[6] is incongruous and therefore inherently humorous; for, when experience of the world leads us to expect one reaction to familiar situations and we perceive another, the surprise generally results in laughter.[7] Mechanical inelasticity results in eccentricity, which is antipathetic to the social group, and the group laughter that arises from the perception of rigid behavior chastens errant individuals and brings them back into the fold.

Bergson follows in a long tradition of philosophers—from Aristotle, Plato, and Cicero onwards—who described comedy as the humorous representation of inferior people and who held that humor arises from delight in witnessing the suffering of other people.[8] The classical view of laughter as essentially the product of derision, ridicule, and self-satisfied mockery is perhaps the oldest and most tenacious general theory of humor we have, according to Patrick O'Neill.[9] It may have been stated most forcefully by Thomas Hobbes in 1651, who explained that the individual is hit with the "*Sudden Glory*" of laughter when "the passion which maketh those *Grimaces* called LAUGHTER... is caused either by some sudden act of their own, that pleaseth them; or by the apprehension of some deformed thing in another, in comparison whereof they suddenly applaud themselves."[10] Humor, then, is essentially a function of perceived superiority, and we laugh when we see someone slip on a banana peel and suddenly, gloriously, realize that it could have just as easily been ourselves.* This is the laughter of power, directed at those perceived as inferior, which has for centuries ignored the humor of women, minorities, and the marginalized because they were quite often perceived as the inferior butt of the joke.

Bergson's view of humor clearly accords with traditional notions of satire, which assumes stable societal values and agreed upon notions of moral and ethical behavior and uses social satire to mock and correct individuals or groups who have deviated from those values. The difference between Bergson and classical theorists, though, is that for him incongruity is the primary key to humor, and though laughter may be seen as punishment inflicted on the unsocial or at least castigation for stupidity, both of these errors arise from the incongruity of individuals

---

* See Patrick O'Neill's discussion of Hobbes in "The Comedy of Entropy" 35.

responding mechanically to social realities. Because we are both in society and of it, Bergson regards society as a "living being" that requires vitality and spontaneity from its members, and he claims, "there is no essential difference between the social ideal and the moral."[11] What is damaging for individuals is damaging for society, so emotional or moral ossification in individuals is harmful to the vitality of society, resulting in a "mechanical tampering with life"[12] that is in need of correction.

Bergson's emphasis on the mechanical and his analysis of its warping influence on the vital and flowing consciousness of individuals and therefore the "living" life of the society reveals a profound anxiety about the increasing mechanization of life in the early decades of the twentieth century, an anxiety of which even he himself seems unaware. His use of the jack-in-the-box to examine the humor found in mechanical repetition is telling. The child finds the mechanized inhumanity of the toy humorous as it pops up again and again, no matter how many times it is crushed back into the box, because it is incongruous with real, living life. However, Bergson seems not to realize that the child must continually push the jack back down for the toy to repeat its motion. The child's behavior becomes as mechanical as the toy's. Though there may be humor in action that "recurs several times in its original form and thus contrasts with the changing stream of life,"[13] the humor is unsettling when we perceive that the individual is effectively reduced to the same status as that of the mechanism, endlessly performing his role just as the jack does. His very participation in the activity requires him to adapt to the machine (all of this reminds us of the famous *I Love Lucy Show* episode with the candy on the conveyor belt, not to mention the comedy of Buster Keaton and Charlie Chaplin). If the mechanical is no longer seen as something "encrusted" upon society but indeed the primary characteristic of social organization, then the individual's role within that society is fundamentally different from what Bergson envisioned. Being in and of society now creates and requires mechanical behavior, and the moral, ethical, and psychological needs of societal members are sacrificed to the functioning of the machine.

This view opens a way for examining a new, darker, form of social satire that moves away from corrective critique and the comfort of stable values. Though mechanical repetition and inelasticity may still be a source of humor, the focus of the comedy is now the rigid and mechanical ordering of society, and it does not attempt to correct individuals' behavior as much as it reveals the way complex individuals negotiate the various roles they perform within the social structure. The needs and goals of individuals and society are no longer in concert but are seen in the modern period as conflicting, and the utility of laughter is no longer in correcting errant behavior but in offering human beings a pleasurable defense against forces that would reduce them to interchangeable mechanical parts in a vast machine.

In "The Work of Art in the Age of Mechanical Reproduction," Walter Benjamin asserts, "the authenticity of a thing is the essence of all that is transmissible from its beginning, ranging from its substantive duration to its testimony to the history which it has experienced."[14] Of course, Benjamin is discussing the work of art, but, as he comments, the process of mechanical reproduction has significance, which "points beyond the realm of art."[15] Mechanical reproduction "detaches the reproduced object from the domain of tradition," resulting in a diminishment of what he calls the work's "aura," the authority resulting from the work's unique engagement with history and tradition.[16] Reproduction substitutes "a plurality of copies for unique existence," reactivating the reproduced object in each individual's particular situation but leading to a "tremendous shattering of tradition."[17] In the increasingly mechanized modern world, anxiety arises from the disturbing awareness that people are reduced to the roles they play, reproducible and interchangeable, and requiring not individual uniqueness but merely the ability to perform expected behavior. They are therefore subject to a similar kind of "withering" that Benjamin suggests for the work of art, and though the "liquidation of traditional value and cultural heritage"[18] is revolutionary in the experience of the artwork, it is nonetheless profoundly traumatic for the individual, who is unmoored from stable, historical and cultural conceptions of value and is now alone responsible for creating meaning within his or her life.

In *Comic Faith*, Robert Polhemus argues that the comedic literature in the nineteenth century offered a way of finding meaning and structure in the absence of beliefs and institutions that once provided purpose to individual lives and suggests that it performs, "in secular and hypothetical fashion, many of the conventional religious functions of the old 'divine comedy.'"[19] Whereas institutional religion offered immortality in the promise of an afterlife, the comic sense allows for the belief that the world is "both funny and potentially good" and implies the assumption "that the basis for believing in the value of life can be found in the fact of comic expression itself."[20] Equating the will to laughter with an act of faith is provocative, but what is interesting is that Polhemus's own argument tends to break down as he moves into the latter years of the nineteenth century and into the twentieth. He wants to find progress and hope for the future in the human ability to laugh; "People need to believe that the limits and terrors of reality can be changed, that the future can be different and better, that wonderful things can happen; if religious institutions cannot do these things, something else must."[21] However, the later literature he examines subverts his premise that in comedy there is "the promise of some form of enduring life in which we have part."[22] He struggles to find the humor of Lewis Carroll and Thackery hopeful. He finds that the successful integration of the individual into society becomes increasingly difficult, if not impossible, and that there are only momentary triumphs through laughter.

The loss of faith Polhemus discusses extends to all social and personal constructs in the twentieth century and defines the literature of Postmodernism. However, the literature of the interwar years also is full of characters struggling not only to find a stable role in society that corresponds to ideas of an authentic self but with the disturbing awareness that a definite, unified self may not even exist. Unsure of themselves because of the "orts, scraps, and fragments" that lie beneath the surface of consciousness and uncertain about the history to which they are testimony because of the efficiency of big lies and the politics of power,[23] the performance of social roles becomes absurdly both meaningless and all important; meaningless in that they say nothing about the individual who performs them and have nothing "authentic" underpinning them, and all-important because they can construct the foundation on which a conscious sense of identity rests and can hold chaos at bay.

The literature of the decades following World War I reflects an apprehension that the social system, and indeed all of history, is a betrayal, "a repeating mechanism, with reversible action and interchangeable parts."[24] In Modernist fiction, characters perform roles that have little correspondence to the idea of an authentic self, "the Captain self, the Key self," as Woolf refers to it in *Orlando*.[25] Yet, these roles seem to take on a reality of their own, regardless of their superficiality or meaninglessness, and they become the primary way individuals are defined by the society they participate in. Additionally, in a complex and changing society, there are an increasing number of roles to perform, and they are often conflicting and unstable. As Mathew Winston noted, much dark humor arises from the perception of "inseparable complexities" and "unresolvable antithesis" that characterize modern life,[26] and in many social comedies characters attempt to keep up with demands on them by taking one set of actions and relations and applying them to another set with which they partially coincide. Therefore, inadaptability is still presented humorously but for psychological reasons that Bergson's theory does not permit. Inadaptabilty enables the individual to retain a hold on what Freud calls, the "customary self,"[27] and affords a defense against the confusing and traumatic assaults on identity. Conversely, adaptability frequently results in a confusion of self-identity that can prove costly, resulting in madness or even death, as is the case with Septimus in *Mrs. Dalloway*, Sibyl in *A House and Its Head*, and Agatha Runcible in *Vile Bodies*.

The humorous refusal to adapt to societal expectations is a technique that women writers have long employed in resisting and subverting a dominant order that has left them at the margins, and, as Mary Douglas points out in *Purity and Danger*, "all margins are dangerous."[28] The serious study of comedy has tended to neglect the humor of women writers, and dark humor has been seen as an almost entirely masculine endeavor.[29] The history of women's humor has begun to be more fully examined, and thanks to scholars such as Regina Barreca, Judy Little, Nancy Walker, and others, a tradition of women's humor is finally being written.[30] Writing of the often overlooked humor in works of writers such as George Eliot and Charlotte Bronte, Barreca argues that "women's comedies have often been misread since they often do not adhere to... essentially conservative conventions of comedy."[31] Certainly, it is only in the last decade and a half or so that Virginia Woolf has come to be seen as a writer who employs humor as a weapon against hypocrisy and social injustices. And when Ivy Compton-Burnett was writing the critics focused on the crimes and cruelty of her characters rather than her savagely funny unmasking of the brutality of the patriarchal Victorian household.

Barreca argues that unlike the classical understanding of the comedic impulse described earlier, which is motivated by feelings of superiority, the comedy written by women is "more likely to make fun of those in high and seemingly invulnerable positions."[32] And Nancy Walker asserts that because women have been largely excluded from power, "their humorous writing evidences a different relationship with the culture, one in which the status quo, however ludicrous, exerts a force to be coped with, rather than representing one of a number of interchangeable realities."[33]

Of course, not all masculine humor adheres to the rigid definition of classically aggressive humor and mocks those seen as inferior, and women's comedy frequently mocks those perceived as inferior. Certainly, no one is safe from the scalding wit of Ivy Compton-Burnett, and Woolf takes great pleasure in mocking the pinched intellect of the poor Miss Kilman. Indeed, in the twentieth century, feelings of powerlessness and exclusion are characteristic of the comedy of both genders, and the darkly humorous novels of men and women often share similar themes.[34] The want of real power and the denial of the possibility of meaningful action are hallmarks of dark humor, and though the male writers still write from a position of privilege, their humor evinces little confidence in the potential for change, and both genders produce a comedy in which protagonists are caught in a system with mysterious rules from which they are barred any understanding. However, it is a fact that women have lived with these social realities for centuries, and I also would argue that women have a long and thorough acquaintance with the dark comedic muse, which has historically been ignored. Clearly, the outsider humor of their writing has not only been funnier than previously admitted but darker, demonstrating not only a tradition of women's humor but a tradition of dark humor as well. Women, as Barreca notes, have always been funny, and, as Helene Cixious describes, they have been violently funny, and they have long engaged in a dark form of comedy that has enabled them to defend themselves against an oppressive social order.[35]

Just as women have been ignored in discussions of dark humor, British writers of comedic literature have long been associated with a gentle form of social comedy, considered too "good humored" to write true dark comedy, and examinations of dark humor have usually focused on American and European writers. Examinations of black humor almost always begin with the theories of Nietzsche, Baudelaire, and Breton, and then move to the literature of American and Continental writers, such as Joseph Heller, Kurt Vonnegut, Thomas Pynchon, Franz Kafka, Louis-Ferdinand Céline, Günter Grass, and Vladimir Nabokov.[36] Mathew Winston, in his landmark essay on black humor claims, "The notion of humor as dark, meditative, self-doubting, and full of the incongruities that are its special focus is alien to the English, who tend to equate humor with good humor, but it is at home on the European continent."[37] Seriously misreading some of the most disquieting aspects of Dickens's humor, Patrick O'Neill states, "in the English-speaking world...there is a well-established tendency to associate humour as a concept with notions of Dickensian good cheer and *bonhomie*, the expansiveness and good-natured tolerance of postprandial laughter over the old port and cigars."[38] William Keough, though he acknowledges the aggressive comedy of Swift, Pope, and Monty Python, underestimates the dark and disruptive power of British humor: "We must agree that the English sense of humor, on the whole, has been, as Harold Nicolson describes it, 'kind, sentimental, reasonable and fanciful.' "[39] Keough argues that American humor is simply too nasty for English tastes, and refers to some carefully gleaned comments by a handful of British writers to support his claim. Mrs. Trollope and Dickens, Keough relates, returned to England "shaking their heads," discomfited by the fact that Americans simply go too far in the brutality of their humor. W. H. Auden and V.S. Pritchett are "astonished" by the frightening assortment of child-beaters, cowards, con men, and cutthroats who people the world of the stoical Huck Finn. "How unlike Oliver Twist," he remarks parenthetically, missing, like O'Neill, the nuanced humor and disturbing representation of social realities in Dickens's fiction. Even Martin Amis, skilled in the use of humorous brutality and obscenity, is read only at face value in his judgment that "the cynical wise-cracking of the reporters covering Ronald Reagan's 1980 campaign was all savage and sad, since 'like so much American laughter, [it] did not express high spirits or amusement but a willed raucousness.' "[40]

Keough's rather selective and superficial readings of comments by British authors clearly are meant to serve his argument, but they reveal the tenacity of the misguided view that English humor equates with good humor. He is correct that particularly in the twentieth century, American humor does indeed seem outraged, and it is typically discussed as a reaction to the disorientation and uncertainty generated by a badly disintegrated American dream. Though no one ever speaks of the "English" dream and the individual sense of loss and outrage that might result at its failure (however this could be discussed in relation to the "angry young men" of the 1950s), in Britain there was the dream of Empire, which disintegrated throughout the twentieth century, unleashing a collective anxiety about social orderings in general and the roles people play within what had been thought to be a stable and coherent structure. If British dark humor tends to be more "social," it is no less brutal and savage—though it may indeed be more glittering and crystalline. With a pellucid style and keen eye for social absurdities, British authors of dark social satire both reveal and obscure the unsettling understanding that superficiality *is* historical reality, and, as Polhemus states, "appearances must be taken at face value and rejected too. The 'truth' is that conditions may be both tolerable and intolerable, statements true and false, our beliefs and assumptions some-how wrong and right at the same time."[41] This is not a gentle, good-natured comedy but one that engages some of the central problems of the flux of modern existence by revealing how individuals negotiate a social order that is important precisely because it is meaningless, unstable, senselessly violent—and more importantly—understood to be all there is.

Because the social realities represented in many British social comedies pose such an absurd existential dilemma for the characters, the "gallows" humor outlined in psychoanalytic theories of comedy reveals more about the humor than do other theories of social comedy. Freud argues in his essay "Humour," that gallows humor is based on the displacement of psychic energy that would be expended in the expression of feelings of anger, pain, or horror into humorous pleasure when the person who is most intimately concerned with the unpleasant circumstances "expresses no affect, but makes a jest."[42] He uses as an example the situation of a criminal being led to the gallows on a Monday who remarked, "Well, the week's beginning nicely."[43] As Freud discusses in *Jokes and Their Relation to the Unconscious*, the man's statement is actually a joke, partaking of certain aspects of joke-work such as condensation and displacement; however, the joke is "misplaced in a nonsensical way, since for the man himself there would be no further events that week."[44] The dark humor rests in the psychological reasons for making the joke, that is, "in disregarding what it is that distinguishes the beginning of this week from others, in denying the distinction which might give rise to motives for quite special emotions."[45]

The economy of expenditure of effort is the explanation of the pleasure, according to Freud, and his ideas about saving psychical energy are deeply rooted in the idea of play.[46] Central to Freud is the idea that wit conceals serious meanings, and play is not detachment and the pure sense of freedom but one of the most basic characteristics of the unconscious. Play is therefore of the greatest importance and the deepest significance, and the joke, a literary form with origins in childhood play and in unconscious mechanisms, is equally important.[47] Jokes, like dreams, reveal the unconscious to be governed by play, and Freud's concepts of jokes, the comic, and humor are tied to the physical but also make a new connection to the internal life of individuals. Just as dreams are purposeful in playing with the real in a nonphysical reality, so are jokes, and both defend the individual from repression, inhibitions, and other forces that threaten the ego. However, if jokes and humor are the contribution of the unconscious to conscious thought, then humor is an aesthetic creation in a way that dreams are not, and Freud's theories of the comic probably say more about the role of art than do critical and aesthetic theories based on his ideas of dream-work.

In *Jokes*, Freud finds all forms of the comic rooted in play, and humor is the victory of pleasure and play over the most threatening aspects of reality. Therefore, the concept of triumph is built into Freud's concept of the comic, and this is particularly true in his discussion of gallows humor. In Freud's example of another criminal on the way to the gallows who requests a scarf to protect his bare neck so as not to catch cold, he gives us one of the most extreme examples of the pleasure principle triumphing over the reality principle.[48] This concern for one's health would be laudable in another context, but in view of what is imminently in store for that neck, the remark appears "remarkably superfluous and unimportant."[49] The humor does not lie in the statement itself, but in the man's reaction to his circumstances, his insistence on pleasure in the face of threatening reality. Thus, the joke-work involved in both the creation and appreciation of this grim form of humor cannot be separated from the historically specific moment. If the man were being freed rather than led to the gallows, the statement might retain a trace of humor in its understatement, but it would cease to be darkly humorous in that it does not challenge the hostility of external reality with a response that runs counter to the expected expression of emotion.

Freud argues that this type of humor is liberating, possessing "grandeur and elevation":

> The grandeur in it clearly lies in the triumph of narcissism, the victorious assertion of the ego's invulnerability. The ego refuses to be distressed by the provocations of reality, to let itself be compelled to suffer. It insists that it cannot be affected by the traumas of the external world; it shows, in fact, that such traumas are no more than occasions for it to gain pleasure.[50]

The creation of pleasure in the face of distressing circumstances is a fundamental feature of dark humor, as Winston has summed up in his examination of black humor, "The contents provide the blackness and the style mitigates that blackness with humor."[51] It is in the tension between form and content that the joke is created, and the humor does not point a way to improving the situation, but it allows for the possibility of pleasure in decidedly unpleasant circumstances. What makes the joke is the form, "the contribution from the unconscious," for once the joke is summarized and reduced to merely its content, the humor disappears. As Freud explains, if the criminal being led to the gallows had responded to his situation by saying, "It doesn't worry me. What does it matter, after all, if a fellow like me is hanged? The world won't come to an end because of it," his attitude would still display the same "magnificent superiority over the real situation," but it would not display a trace of humor.[52] Humor resists an appraisal of the real circumstances as they are and insists on an appraisal of the situation based on the concerns of the "customary self," adhering to the role one performs in quotidian life as if the circumstances had not changed.[53] Humor also imposes form on unruly experience and insists that even the most serious material be treated in a way that enables us to retain the capability of exchanging it for playful pleasure.

In Freud's paradigm of joke-work, there are at least three participants: the object of the joke, the teller of the joke, and the hearer of the joke. The teller of the joke may make himself the object of the joke, but this does not essentially change the way the joke-work functions. The teller treats himself with the same kind of distance he would treat any object of his joke, disassociating himself from his own experience in order to arrive at a humorous appraisal of the situation, the pleasure of which both the teller and hearer share. In dark humor, a person who is most at risk in a potentially traumatic situation dismisses the affective emotional response with a jest, he "obviously affords himself a certain sense of satisfaction," but the hearer, "affected as it were at long-range by this humorous production," feels, like him, a similar "yield of humorous pleasure."[54]

This has important implications for humorous literature that deals with difficult or disturbing events, and Freud argues that when a "writer or narrator describes the behaviour of real or imaginary people in a humorous way," the reader experiences humorous pleasure in the same way the hearer of a joke would.[55] There is no need for the characters themselves to display any humor, for "the humorous attitude is solely the business of the person who is taking them as his object; and, as in the former instance, the reader or hearer share in the enjoyment of the humour."[56] In the novels studied here, some of the characters knowingly display a humorous attitude, particularly in the work of Compton-Burnett and Anthony Powell; however, a good many of them are presented as disturbingly powerless and sometimes even unaware of the potentially disastrous circumstances they are in. This is where the humor is perhaps the most unsettling, as is, for instance, the death of Agatha Runcible in *Vile Bodies*. But throughout these works the narrator insists on viewing the lives of the characters with the comic distance that allows them to be laughed at; whether overt or implied, the narrator functions as the teller of the joke, colluding humorously with the reader and refusing to assess serious situations seriously. Because of the comedic narrative stance of the texts, the works resist being overwhelmed by the events they present, and the reader is saved from the trauma of a painful affective response. Disturbing events and unhappy people are the subject of the works, but the humorous attitude of the narrative resists pain and suffering, and the reader, adopting the same position as the teller/narrator, is moved to laughter rather than to tears.

Freud's theory of the function of joke-work, while by no means the final word on humor, comedy, and jokes, still remains one of the most useful examinations of the comic because it is concerned with the process of humor and not a definition of it. As contemporary feminist and Postmodern critics begin to question ideas about the political and/or ethical efficacy of humor, Freud's observations about the processes of humor seem even more apposite. Though he devotes a significant amount of time to joke technique and characteristics, Freud's emphasis is not on what jokes say but on what they do, and features of the comic are examined in light of psychological and social processes, which manipulate and rearrange the material with which they are concerned. Darkly humorous novels do precisely the same thing; they rearrange what is typically tragic material and present it in a comical way. Thematic or plot characteristics that have been used to define dark humor are not funny in themselves but are made funny by being subjected to the processes of humor. Reliance on caricature, subjecting people, things, and events to comic and even grotesque distortion, an almost maniacal celebration of nonsense, ineffectual protagonists, and other characteristics so often present in darkly humorous novels can all be seen as participating in the process of joke-work rather than simply being viewed as features that make comedy different from tragedy or functioning solely within the service of satiric correction of behavior.

Freud begins his analysis in *Jokes and Their Relation to the Unconscious* with an examination of the techniques of joke-work. Like dream-work, the major features of the joking process are condensation and displacement, but unlike dreams jokes foreground these characteristics. Condensation, for Freud, means that the material to be processed experiences a startling compression in which more than one idea of representation is condensed into a single idea.[57] Brevity is indeed the soul of wit, and Freud argues that it is essential to a good joke: "A joke says what it has to say, not always in few words, but in *too* few words—that is, in words that are insufficient by strict logic or by common modes of thought or speech. It may even actually say what it has to say by not saying it."[58] Condensation, packing multiple levels of meaning into a word or thought, is at the heart of the witty dialogue in Compton-Burnett, Waugh, and Powell. Displacement is a shifting of emphasis that serves to disguise the joke's point, whereby the joker can sneak the punch line past the listener, allowing it to be revealed at the moment of maximum effect.[59] Displacement sets up the hearer or reader to expect a certain response—usually a traumatic one in dark humor—and then shifts the emphasis on to something else, subverting those expectations. Displacement is particularly important in dark humor, because the content in these texts is very often disturbing, threatening, or violent, and in order for them to remain funny the reader cannot have the expected reaction to events.

However, the site of humor is complicated, and the pleasure found in comedy comes not only from its technique but from the satisfaction of an instinct in the face of an obstacle—either internal or external—that stands in pleasure's way. Freud divides jokes into two groups: innocent, or nontendentious, jokes and hostile, or tendentious, jokes. Nontendentious jokes are pleasurable for the enjoyment of technique involved; this type of joke is purely aesthetic, "an aim in itself."[60] Tendentious jokes are directed against someone or something, "serving the purpose of aggressiveness, satire, or defence,"[61] and are pleasurable because they "make possible the satisfaction of an instinct."[62] Freud contends that the construct of joking finds a way of placating aggressive or socially unacceptable desires by circumventing the obstacles to desire that civilization and education have erected. Even a brief examination of these two categories reveals that jokes and humor are more complicated than these categories allow for. His "innocent" jokes frequently have undertones of aggression, and his hostile jokes usually exhibit clever joke technique. These two observations prompt Freud to qualify his division of jokes into the two categories of innocent and hostile, and lead him to conclusions that are important for the examination of dark humor: "We do not know what we are laughing at" and "Jokes...are in fact never non-tendentious."[63] This very important concession by Freud has led most scholars merely to the conclusion that joking and humor are always aggressive. However, if we are unsure what we are laughing at, humor is therefore deeply ambivalent and, more importantly for the purposes of dark humor, not particularly socially useful. A joke, Freud explains, is the celebration of irrationality that serves rational purposes, a return to the childhood pleasures of play that helps preserve the sanity of the adult. Though some jokes may seem innocent or even nonsensical, they are really subversive and anarchic in that they promote thought which reason cannot use: "they are once again expressing their original nature by setting themselves up against an inhibiting and restricting power—which is now the critical judgement."[64]

As I have argued, dark humor transgresses against societal norms yet offers no corrective or alternative to them other than laughter. Like tendentious jokes, dark humor allows for rebellion against oppressive circumstances and liberation from pressure. It even rebels against reason and critical judgment, which are generally suspect in most novels of the twentieth century, given that these attributes are frequently seen to be in the service of violence and oppression. As Freud asserts, humor is "a psychical factor possessed of power," because it is pleasurable as well as rebellious and aggressive, making it "psychologically... more effective" than either of those qualities without humor.[65] It is for this reason we admire those who laugh and joke in the face of threatening circumstances. In the case of the rogue on the way to his execution, Freud remarks, "there is something like magnanimity in this *blague*, in the man's tenacious hold upon his customary self and his disregard of what might overthrow that self and drive it to despair."[66] Freud emphasizes the importance of the onlooker—or reader as the case may be—experiencing the same feelings of pleasure and mastery, despite the threatening nature of the situation, because he is spared the need to call up his own emotional impulses of despair, fear, or horror and participates in the same "assertion of the ego's invulnerability."[67] The triumph of narcissism is linked to the two main features of joke-work: the pleasure principle and the idea that overwhelming emotions are displaced into the structure of the joke. In doing this, the humorist uses "customary" concern to assert the pleasure principle, the outward sign of which is laughter, at precisely the moment when the reality principle would seem in total command.

Though pleasure does momentarily triumph over pain, the reality of the victim is never denied, as Freud makes clear in the numerous Jewish jokes that run throughout *Jokes*. The symbolic action of the joke does not deny the real conditions of oppression but simply finds a way of adapting to conditions while maintaining an acute awareness of them. This, of course, is the position represented by many modern writers, and Freud's theories at the beginning of the century offer a way of reading comedic literary responses to violence and brutality. He indicates that this dark species of humor is diverse and always changing, suggesting that it can only really be examined within its historical context: "The kingdom of humor is constantly being enlarged whenever an artist or writer succeeds in submitting some hitherto unconquered emotions to the control of humorous pleasure, in making them... into sources of pleasure."[68] While laughing into the gaping maw of grim reality is only arguably a sign of psychic good health, we cannot forget that comedy, like tragedy, began its existence as part of a fertility rite, and though it may be born of despair, skepticism, and disorientation, the dark humor in the following novels takes great pleasure in language, design, and structure, as well as in laughter itself. Echoing Zarathustra, Ionesco wrote, "To become conscious of what is horrifying and to laugh at it is to master that which is horrifying."[69] And in the controlled narrative of the novels studied here, the horrifying is mastered through laughter and form.

However, some critics have charged that making horrible events merely the object of laughter creates social satires that effectively end up reinforcing the values and beliefs of a society that has victimized its members.[70] Terry Eagleton has argued that British novelists between the wars had, for all intents and purposes, lost the ability to creatively interpret "the interaction between particular commitments and the structure of a whole society" that was active and vigorous in the work of novelists of the nineteenth century.[71] The twentieth-century British novel, according to Eagleton, diverged along two viewpoints: the lower middle-class fiction of Gissing, Bennett, Wells, and later, Orwell, and the upper-class fiction of Forster, Woolf, and Waugh. The first examines the seedy, drably detailed realms of routine social existence beneath the conventions of "polite" society, and the second displays the intense but narrow concerns of an elitist and enclosed group, "marooned from the world of working relationships and wider social institutions."[72] The lower middle-class novel saw "its own audacious realism as an assault on bourgeois conventionality," and the upper-class novel "stood counter to that conventionality either in its liberalism and aestheticism, or, as with Waugh, in its nostalgic conservatism."[73] Both genres, he argues, are to a large extent tied to the "dominant orthodoxy they opposed," and as a result could not transcend the direct pressures of their experience to evaluate British culture as a whole.[74] Thus fragmented, neither genre could effectively comment on the social turbulence and sense of impending or actual collapse that threatened English culture.

Eagleton suggests that the social comedies of the upper-class novels present the reader with the view that society is a game, and the uncommitted satire of *Mrs. Dalloway* and Waugh's early novels prevents the novels from making any real critique of the culture they present. Woolf's ambivalent characterization of Clarissa Dalloway protects the character from the "full force of the damaging charges which might be listed against her," and Waugh's comedically blank characters are so "thoroughly disassociated from their own experience" that they are prevented from articulating anything even faintly resembling a protest.[75] Eagleton's study, though it is not concerned with the uses and techniques of comedy but with the limitations of class on the ability of certain novels to interpret the significance of the turbulent events facing British culture in the wake of World War I, is suggestive for dark comedy. The fragmentation of British culture he outlines, which he argues is the reason for the inability of interwar British fiction to present a unified vision of English society, speaks directly to the anxiety about disintegration and fragmentation with which dark comedy deals but does not presume to answer. The satire is most definitely uncommitted, and that is precisely the point.

The novels in this study capture an aspect of society that, for the most part, no longer exists. After World War II and the Labour government's attempts to dismantle the class system and the abolishment of certain aristocratic titles, the aimless, affluent life represented in these works all but disappeared, and it is only the subject of novels that are more overtly nostalgic, such as P.G. Wodehouse's halcyonian evocation of the daft but endearing social set of Bertie Wooster. Even though Wodehouse began writing early in the century, he continued to write about the decades between the wars well into the 1960s, and in these novels upper-class society of the 1920s and 1930s is frozen in time and blissfully untouched by the turmoil of the era. Social comedy tends to be aristocratic, but the works in this study also are deeply affected by their historical moment, and, though their social milieu is rather enclosed and elitist, they directly engage the concerns with violence, alienation, fragmentation, and disintegration. Indeed, the fact that their specific social world is no longer relevant or even present in British life attests to the anxiety of loss and confusion present in the novels. When an individual functioning within the social structure is made redundant, the effect is deeply traumatic, whether that individual is an aristocratic, a returning war veteran, or a factory worker.

Of course, some would argue that the loss of the social world represented in these novels is no great one, and the novels themselves seem anxiously aware of this. However, this awareness does nothing to alleviate the sense of existential unease and only heightens feelings of meaninglessness and isolation within the works. All the novels studied here are concerned with how people can give meaning to their existence in the absence of traditional structures. However, the inability of all social systems to address the needs of the complex individuals who compose them is inherent in civilized life. In *Civilization and Its Discontents*, Freud comments that though "the question of the purpose of human life has been raised countless times; it has never yet received a satisfactory answer and perhaps does not admit one."[76] Though some would claim that life without purpose would lose all value for them, Freud asserts that this "threat alters nothing."[77] Indeed, according to Freud, it would seem as if one had the right to dismiss the question, as it appears to derive from "human presumptuousness, for one never thinks to ask about the purpose of the lives of animals, unless it is to be of service to humans."[78] The question of the purpose of life seems only to be answered by religion, in Freud's view, so when confidence in religious belief is no longer tenable, the only purpose that can be granted for life is the pursuit of happiness. However, happiness is fleeting, and even when we find pleasure in situations, it wanes after a certain length of time. The capacity for unhappiness is limitless, though, and Freud suggests we are threatened with suffering from three directions:

> from our own body, which is doomed to decay and dissolution and which cannot even do that without pain and anxiety as warning signals; from the external world, which may rage against us with overwhelming and merciless forces of destruction; and finally from our relations to other[s].[79]

Given this unhappy state of affairs, what, then, are people to do? Like Polhemus, Wylie Sypher sees comedy fulfilling a religious function and states, "man has been defined as a social animal, a tool-making animal, a speaking animal, a thinking animal, and a religious animal. He is also a laughing animal,"[80] and the power of comedy to create pleasure amid suffering and impose a certain order on absurdity borders on the religious in his analysis. The comedic and the religious are the only views of the world that admit irreconcilables to exist in tension.[81] In religion one can be both sinner and saved, corrupt and purified, and comedy is built on similar "double occasions, double premises, double values."[82] Though comedy does not afford the existential assurance of religion, it would appear to offer one of the more valuable coping mechanisms for the twentieth century, which views human existence alienated from a divine plan, multiple and fractured, and in the grip of "merciless logic for futile purposes."[83] There are other ways of coping with the trauma of the claims of the real world: "neurosis, madness, intoxication, self-absorption, and ecstasy,"[84] but as Freud suggests, comedy, with its fending off of the possibility of suffering and its insistence on the pleasure of laughter, "places it among the great series of methods which the human mind has constructed in order to evade the compulsion to suffer."[85]

In a century of disorder and irrationalism, comedy seems more germane to the human condition than does tragedy. Comedy admits disorder and absurdity into the realm of fiction and art, and the darkly funny novel embodies what Bakhtin identified as the carnivalesque aversion to all forms of "straightforward seriousness."[86] Tragedy requires a stable set of values and ethics and a noble hero or heroine who struggles with them. Though the dark humor novel subverts stable norms, comedic characters still struggle with values, and even in an absurd universe, robbed of ultimate meaning, this type of humor still suggests that certain ethical positions are better than others. For the most part, it is better to be humble rather than arrogant, tolerant rather than bigoted, and generous rather than mean. However, in the modern world, there appears to be no stable correspondences to these values, and they become largely a matter of perspective. Because of this, the actions of even the best-intentioned characters frequently result in horror or death and morally ambivalent characters are blown from disaster to fortune by arbitrary winds, offering no connection between actions, attitudes, and end results. This has often resulted in dark comedic novels being labeled amoral, but designations of this sort are beside the point. Dark humor, like the carnivalesque, valorizes the subversion of authority, and this of course means political, religious, moral, and rhetorical authority, as well as even the idea of authority itself. Bahktin's analyses of the development novel does not necessarily suggest a rebellion against political or social injustice—though novels often do this—but celebrates the "polyglossia" that defines the form against other forms of writing that convey a "monologic" sense of rhetorical control. Seeing the novel's ability to hold various discourses in radical suspension, Bakhtin argues that it is the most capacious and supple of literary forms.[87] The form and the humor in darkly comedic novels engage the "inseparable complexities" and "unresolvable antithesis"[88] of modern life, holding these in suspension and distancing them through laughter.

"Comedy is the logic of the absurd"[89] claims Sypher, and though some characters succumb to the overpowering forces of absurdity and irrationality, the texts themselves do not. The greatest effects available in comic art, according to Polhemus, is that "it asserts the power of the mind and body over the universe of death. To the sudden flow of mirth, it adds comic structure."[90] Within the dark comedic novel, contradictions and irreconcilables are allowed, but they also submit to the glittering intellectual designs of witty dialogue and the pleasures of raillery, and the narrative structure and joke technique permit at least a temporary feeling of triumph over the chaos of the situations depicted.

The novel has often been described as a form that reflects society and shows us ourselves, and reflective devices have always been central in theories and myths of narcissism. The metaphor of the mirror, important in such works of criticism as M.H. Abrams's *The Mirror and the Lamp*, has also long been associated with comedy. Cicero asserted, "comedy is an imitation of life, a mirror of custom, an image of truth,"[91] and Waugh quotes Lewis Carroll in commenting on the "through the looking glass world" of modern life. Flaubert is said to have told a friend, "Go look in your mirror and tell me you don't have a great desire to laugh. So much the worse for you if you don't."[92] Arguably, the novel is considered the dominant literary form in the twentieth century, and one of the primary characteristics of the modern novel "is that it has ceased to recognize the categories of tragic and comic...and sees life as tragicomedy."[93] The comedic novels examined in this work are then all equally "Modern," and they all represent the triumph of narcissism. They insist on confronting the violence and confusion of the twentieth century and reflect it back to us, and, with astonishing creative tension, assert the pleasure of humor.

CHAPTER 2

CRITICIZING THE SOCIAL SYSTEM: MRS. DALLOWAY, VIRGINIA WOOLF'S DARK COMEDY OF MANNERS

Humor...undermines limits from the inside...In doing so it undermines the law. It makes us feel the uneasiness of living under a law—any law.

Umberto Eco

Virginia Woolf thought that her reputation might well rest on her satiric sensibilities and that she would be remembered merely for being a humorist, and in most of her writing her satirical impulses are evident. However, Woolf was also aware of the importance of humor as a coping device, and in both her life and her fiction, she often greeted injustice, madness, violence, and death with a grimly humorous attitude. In *Mrs. Dalloway* all of Woolf's humorous sensibilities are evident; it is a withering satire of her social set, and it is informed—though not necessarily dominated—by a dark brand of humor. Life's traumas are frequently dealt with comically, and institutions and beliefs, such as marriage, patriotism, empire, and the medical profession, which were thought to give comfort and meaning to life, are shown in reality to oppress and do violence. Socially constructed categories and the values underpinning them, springing from ideas of order and the belief in rational progress for the future, no longer appear viable when confronted with the realities of a cruelly irrational, postwar world. Societal institutions are paradoxically shown to impose too much order and not enough—too much in that they do violence to individuals in the interest of the status quo and a slavish adherence to rules—and too little in that they cannot truly fulfill their functions since they are incapable of dealing with the complexities of human behavior. In *Mrs. Dalloway* the negotiation of the social system is often comical, even while it is set against the backdrop of madness, death, and war.

Though "society" is the target of her satire, throughout her life and writing Woolf disliked the idea of a political agenda in art, and she detested what she called "preaching" in fiction; however, she was deeply concerned with how individuals are shaped, and sometimes warped, by social environment and with how historical forces can impact lives and alter their courses. In her fiction, Woolf is loathe to explicitly endorse political causes or offer correctives to society's ills. Even if she is fundamentally sympathetic to a cause, women's suffrage for instance, Woolf is chary of people anxious to reform society or who feel they are possessed of a message, and she suggests there is a mental obtuseness in their inability to understand how their political ideas serve their personal, psychological needs.[1] As did Freud, Woolf inveighed against the moralizing social control of a Christianized capitalist society. She writes in her diary, "... these social reformers and philanthropists get so out of hand and harbour so many discreditable desires under the disguise of loving their kind, that in the end there's more to find fault with in them than in us [artists]."[2] In *Jokes and Their Relation to the Unconscious*, Freud asserts:

> The wishes and desires of men [*sic*] have a right to make themselves acceptable alongside exacting and ruthless morality. And in our days it has been said in forceful and stirring sentences that this morality is only a selfish regulation laid down by the few who are rich and powerful and who can satisfy their wishes at any time without any postponement. So long as the art of healing has not gone further in making our life safe and so long as social arrangements do no more to make it more enjoyable, so long will it be impossible to stifle the voice within us that rebels against the demands of morality.[3]

Woolf is reluctant to say that anyone is "this" or "that," and she views most systems and ideologies with suspicion, suggesting that they are merely ways of replacing one form of violence with another. She was too conscious of the conflicts between society's often necessary demands and the individual's equally necessary needs to commit herself to a radical or utopian stance. This is where the power of the comic is most salutary: it defies the forces of reaction and repression and permits the powerless to cope with the irrationality and onerousness of authority. To protest oppression and injustice, Woolf scorns and ridicules the powerful for their misjudgments and pretensions; as she suggests in *Three Guineas*, "for psychological reasons," a useful response to the tyranny of those in power is to pelt them with laughter.[4]

Woolf's humor and her social satire are evident, to some degree, in most of her novels; however, *Mrs. Dalloway* is the one novel in which she overtly sets out to critique society. Alex Zwerdling argues that Woolf's satire is given its most complete expression in the novel,[5] and in her often-quoted diary entry regarding *Mrs. Dalloway*, Woolf states, "I want to give life and death, sanity and insanity; I want to criticise the social system, and to show it at work, at its most intense."[6] Her linking of these two intentions suggests a connection between death, insanity, and the social system, a connection that moves her comedy beyond the traditional aims of satire and into a darker brand of humor, which examines the social system and sees little reason to hope for improvement, choosing instead to look at ways of coping with it. In her desire to "adumbrate...a study of insanity and suicide; the social world seen by the sane and the insane side by side," Woolf suggests that there is a "sane" way of negotiating the social system, even at its most oppressive, and, in associating most of the humor in the novel with Clarissa and her "society," it can be argued that humor is the coping device that allows for this "sane" negotiation.[7]

Throughout the novel, Clarissa and Septimus are linked, despite gender and class differences, in their relations and reactions to the constraints placed on them by a rule-bound imperial, patriarchal society that requires gender and class conformity from its members. Clarissa and Septimus have both done what was expected of them, yet remain isolated and alienated from that society which has imposed patterns of behavior on them: Clarissa married well, and, though her marriage to Richard Dalloway is not an unhappy one, it is devoid of passion and intimacy, the kind of "catastrophe"[8] that she and Sally Seton used to think of marriage as being, and Septimus, though he performed his duty in the war and "had won crosses"; he had also lost a loved one and learned "not to feel."[9] Both characters are highly sensitive and imaginative and experience a sense of being overwhelmed and consumed by a society that disallows deviation from the imposed patterns. Both feel "hounded" in their attempts to preserve themselves from "the death of the soul,"[10] and both are "rasped," experiencing physical pain in their spines when faced with "dominators and tyrants."[11]

While their thoughts and feelings have much in common, they respond to their circumstances quite differently. For example, upon recalling Elizabeth's relationship with Miss Kilman, Clarissa experiences intense feelings of agitation that seem out of proportion to the actual circumstances:

> It rasped her...hurt in her spine; gave her physical pain, and made all pleasure in beauty, in friendship, in being well, in being loved and making her home delightful rock, quiver, and bend as if indeed there were some monster grubbing at the roots.[12]

Her reaction to the threat of Miss Kilman and all she represents will be echoed in Septimus's intense response to the confusion he feels when being out in public. A nursemaid's song in Regent's Park, "rasped his spine," and, overwhelmed by the terror of daily life, he creates grandiose illusions of "the birth of a new religion" to cope with his fear.[13] For Septimus, the sight of people carrying on their mundane activities is an outrage, and all human relationships are contaminated, for he "knew how wicked people were...he could see them making up lies as they passed in the street."[14] He must "shut his eyes...see no more," or he would "be sent mad."[15] Unlike Septimus, who retreats from the world, Clarissa declares it all "Nonsense, nonsense!" and busies herself with her party plans.[16] When she eventually encounters Miss Kilman, Clarissa overcomes her "violent anguish" by laughing at "this woman taking her daughter from her."[17] With Clarissa's laughter, Miss Kilman dwindles from a "prehistoric monster armed for primeval warfare" to "merely Miss Kilman, in a mackintosh, whom Heaven knows Clarissa would have liked to help."[18] Rather than shut her eyes, isolating herself further from the world, Clarissa embraces the social world and creates a space for herself within it.

Clarissa responds to society "sanely," and Septimus responds "insanely"; however, as Woolf suggests in her use of the adverb phrase, "side by side," the two responses are psychologically similar. R.D.Laing states, "Schizophrenia is a special strategy that a person invents in order to live in an unlivable situation."[19] Gloria Kaufman argues, "When the social situation becomes so oppressive that madness is a potential survival response, humor is also a possibility."[20] Freud says that humor's "fending off of the possibility of suffering places it among the great series of methods the human mind has constructed in order to evade the compulsion to suffer—a series which begins with neurosis and culminates in madness."[21] With Clarissa, Woolf creates a character who protects herself from the things that would overwhelm her by engaging in societal customs yet remains, for the most part, ironically and even humorously detached from them. She is therefore able to retain a certain "hold on herself" that Septimus is unable to do because of his violent wartime experiences. The war has not left Septimus with an ironically distanced, grimly humorous view of an absurd world; rather, it has left him delusional and paranoid (though—as the saying goes—being paranoid does not mean that the world isn't really out to get you).

Suzette Henke has argued that Septimus "would probably be diagnosed as 'paraphrenic,'" which is a category used by Freud in relation to paranoia.[22] According to Freud, paraphrenics "display two fundamental characteristics: they suffer from megalomania and they have withdrawn their interest from the external world (people and things)."[23] Both of these characteristics can easily be applied to Septimus in his messianic impulses with regard to a "new religion" and his belief that "he knew the meaning of the world,"[24] as well as in his withdrawal from Rezia and their domestic life together. Without the protective armor of humor, Septimus experiences a "disappearance of the normal boundaries between the ego and the world, a cosmic fusion," which is both terrifying and exhilarating but which also leads to "ontological insecurity."[25] While it is unnecessary—and even reductive—to clinically diagnose the psychological anomalies of fictional characters, Freud's ideas on the protective use of humor help to shed some light on Woolf's aesthetic and creative portrayal of individuals negotiating the complex and threatening realities of the modern world, a world where "ontological insecurity" is a major feature of the philosophical and psychological terrain. For, of course, Woolf herself was familiar with both responses to the trauma of violence and oppression.

Though Clarissa is a product of "society" and participates in its rules, she retains the "exquisite sense of comedy"[26] that Peter Walsh recognized in her when she was a young woman and that allows her to manage society "sanely." In the past, he praised her for her ability to create "some absurd little drama" at the spur of the moment, and he admired "her courage; her social instinct; he admired her power of carrying things through."[27] Clarissa has not lost the ability to create comic little dramas—this is basically what her party is—but Peter has lost the ability to recognize her creations as courageous, though he momentarily regains this at the very end of the novel. Her sense of comedy allows her to carry on and create pleasure in a dark and threatening world. Aware of death and the "horror"[28] of the fundamentally isolated existence of the individual, Clarissa does not shut her eyes but rather dons a party dress in her determination to remain creative and to insist on her own subjectivity. Septimus, too, is aware of the death and the horror of isolation, and his madness is another expression of the determination to preserve his autonomous self. Clarissa intuits their connection to each other at the end of the novel when she hears of Septimus's suicide. Musing on his death in defiance of those who would "force his soul," she sees a similar determination in the action of her party and his suicide: "She felt somehow very much like him ... She felt glad he had done it."[29]

Just as important as Woolf's examination of "sane" and "insane" responses to the world is her satire of the society that forces individuals into these polar responses. "Armed with wit," argues Barreca, "women must protect themselves against a world that values neither their inherent nor their acquired talents. Their wit evolves into an essential strategy for survival."[30] Clarissa's "humorous attitude," rests in her use of the manners and customary concerns of society, but she is often presented comically by the narrator's commentary on and shrewd observations of her participation in this world. From Woolf's earliest writings her satire is apparent, and in her contributions to the family newspaper, *The Hyde Park Gate News*, there is evidence of a distanced, comedic observer who examines the trivial, quotidian activities of a large, complicated household to satirize hypocrisy and insincerity. Woolf's juvenilia, like her later work, provided an outlet for her frustrations with the injustices and incongruities she saw around her, and it allowed her to create a place for herself in the midst of a volatile extended clan full of a variety a consuming egoists. Using the daily events and customary activities of the family as fodder, *The Hyde Park Gate News* is ruthlessly satirical. As does *Mrs. Dalloway*, the stories and columns mock everything from romantic love and the "matrimony market," husband/wife relations, and parental tenderness, to class sensibilities and master/servant relations, grief, and embarrassment.[31] Though the publication was a group effort, in its licensed outlet for "rudeness and aggression," and in its unabashed delight in the superiority of being in on the joke, it fostered in Woolf a penchant for social critique and a "lifelong ruthless pleasure in satire."[32] In *Mrs. Dalloway*, Woolf's ruthless pleasure in satire is given full reign in her description of Clarissa's party guests. Everyone is exposed to her keen, satiric gaze; from poor Ellie Henderson "not even caring to hold [herself] upright" and "Dear Sir Harry...a fine old fellow who had produced more bad pictures than any other two Academicians in the whole of St. John's Wood," to Lady Bradshaw, "balancing like a sea-lion at the edge of its tank, barking for invitations," and the Prime Minister, whose presence assures Clarissa's party of success but nevertheless looks as if "you could have stood him behind a counter and bought biscuits."[33]

The early writings mark the beginnings of Woolf as a satirist who is intimately acquainted with the manners and mores of "society," and indeed uses the very qualities of that society, such as a punctilious adherence to ritual and a lack of emotionalism, to critique it and to interrogate how and why societal conventions are used. Like Freud's rogue on his way to the gallows who requests a scarf to protect his neck, Clarissa retains a "customary concern" for the manners of everyday life, even when the realities of the actual situation might require a different response. The concern with catching a cold on the way to a hanging brings into sharp (comic) relief the death sentence under which we all exist and dramatically calls into question the meaning and usefulness of any activity. The "grandeur" and "magnanimity" evinced by the condemned man' s narcissistic assertion of his subjective identity evokes our admiration, and contrary to seeing his concerns as trivial, we see them as heroic. Clarissa, too, is aware of the death sentence under which we all live, and even during the height of her party recognizes "how certain it is we must die."[34] Freud's discussion of gallows humor bears a striking resemblance to what Peter Walsh refers to as Clarissa's "thorough-going scepticism," which he uses to "account for her, so transparent in some ways, so inscrutable in others":

> As we are a doomed race, chained to a sinking ship . . . as the whole thing is a bad joke, let us, at any rate, do our part; mitigate the sufferings of our fellow prisoners . . . decorate the dungeon with flowers and air-cushions. Those ruffians, the Gods, shan't have it all their own way—her notion being that the Gods, who never lost a chance of hurting, thwarting and spoiling human lives were seriously put out if, all the same, you behaved like a lady.[35]

In its engagement with the customs and manners of society, Woolf's fiction simultaneously values those manners for their ability to impose order on chaotic or even purposeless existence and subverts them by exposing them for their lack of any real meaning. Woolf therefore writes about "society" not as an elitist who privileges that world but as a canny and nuanced observer intimately familiar with it, an observer who has an aesthetic admiration for societal manners in their ability to shape and to moderate the difficulties and traumas of life but also an observer who is deeply troubled by the violence and injustice to individual lives resulting from the ossification of those very rules and conventions.

In the hands of Sir William, society's manners and customs become a bludgeon, and Woolf's tone is viciously satiric when she describes the beating individuals receive from the goddesses of Proportion and Conversion:

> Sir William had a friend in Surrey where they taught, what Sir William frankly admitted was a difficult art—a sense of proportion. There were, moreover, family affection; honour; courage; and a brilliant career. All of these had in Sir William a resolute champion. If they failed him, he had to support police and the good of society, which, he remarked very quietly, would take care, down in Surrey, that these unsocial impulses, bred more than anything by the lack of good blood, were held in control. And then stole out from her hiding place and mounted her

throne that Goddess whose lust is to override opposition, to stamp indelibly in the sanctuaries of others the image of herself. Naked, defenceless, the exhausted, the friendless received the impress of Sir William's will.[36]

To submit oneself to the shapers and preservers of proportion and convention is psychologically dangerous, and somehow the individual must resist. Like Clarissa herself, the social world is both "transparent" and "inscrutable," and social customs and manners can be employed defiantly to create order and meaning in a chaotic and meaningless universe, or they can be used violently to crush individuality in the service of the "good of society."

Woolf's social satire explores these seemingly conflicting points of view by allowing characters to summon the protective features of social custom as a response to hostile reality, but at the same time, she creates narrators whose perspective is broader and more inclusive than that of the characters. With this narrative technique, she ridicules social conventions when they are taken as *essentially* meaningful and used to define and circumscribe individual lives. Though Clarissa uses the social world creatively and protectively, she is "a Lady of Fashion"—a title Woolf had considered using before she settled on *Mrs. Dalloway*—and her social world is mocked by Woolf for its pretension and hypocrisy. With comic vengeance, Woolf reveals the disparity between the reputations many of the characters have within the world of the novel and their actions and motivations as revealed by the narrator. The most obvious targets of attack—Sir William Bradshaw and Lady Bruton— represent social norms at their most oppressive: worship of wealth and position, swift and imperious judgments of others, and the subjugation of any individuality to the goddesses of Proportion and Conversion, whether that individuality manifests itself in Septimus's psychological pain and terror or in Clarissa's unique charm and fragile health. Though not an outsider in the same way as Septimus, Clarissa is seen as inadequate by the novel's more powerful figures, and Lady Bruton opines, "it might have been better if Richard had married a woman with less charm, who would have helped him with his work," and "she detested illness in the wives of politicians."[37]

Sir William's reputation for sympathy and "understanding of the human soul"[38] is undercut by the narrator's description of him and his symbolic counterpart, his automobile. The worship of silver and gold by Sir and Lady Bradshaw appears almost biblical as they hypocritically use the medical profession in their pursuit of power and wealth just as corrupt church officials did in times past:

> Sir William Bradshaw's motor car; low, powerful, grey with plain initials interlocked on the panel, as if the pomps of heraldry were incongruous, this man being the ghostly helper, the priest of science; and, as the motor car was grey, so to match its sober suavity, grey furs, silver grey rugs were heaped upon it, to keep her ladyship warm while she waited. For often Sir William would travel sixty miles or more down into the country to visit the rich, the afflicted, who could afford the very large fee which Sir William very properly charged for his advice. Her ladyship waited with the rugs about her knees an hour or more, leaning back, thinking sometimes of the patients, sometimes, excusably, of the wall of gold, mounting minute by minute while she waited.[39]

The appositive, "the afflicted," almost seems like an afterthought, and the narrator, with both grammatical and comical understatement exposes Sir William's low motives at the same time she ironically praises his humility and selfless dedication to his profession.

Throughout Sir William's consultation with Septimus, the narrator parenthetically breaks in, wickedly laudatory in her observations as she attacks him and the society that grants such men power over the lives of others. As the narrator extols Sir William's virtues—his winning of his position "by sheer ability (being the son of a shopkeeper)" and his love of his profession despite the hard work "(the stream of patients being so incessant, and the responsibilities and privileges of his profession so onerous)"—she is expressing an opposing set of values that is not directly stated but is communicated by the ironic tone, which by implication affirms the opposite of what it praises. Melba Cuddy-Keane has explained that the narrator's perspective is "given through negative definition," and that, fittingly, "this entails an absence: the refusal to sum someone up in a few phrases, the refusal to believe in the infallible wisdom of a doctor or indeed in any enshrined authority."[40] These values stand in direct opposition to the values of Sir William, who had Septimus formulated and pinned down "the first moment [he] came into the room," and the society which made him, a society that prizes "lightning skill, and almost infallible accuracy in diagnosis."[41] Commenting on the problematic ambiguity of Woolf's satire, Cuddy-Keane notes, "Other than acknowledging the sanctity and otherness of Septimus's soul, the novel provides no specific answers to his problem."[42] Given, Septimus's mental state, death is the only answer to his problem, and this is precisely why I argue that Woolf's comedy is a much darker form of humor than traditional satire and offers none of its comforts. An ethical norm is only obliquely endorsed by the narrative, and answers to society's ills are never proffered. Indeed, there is no one view that the reader is asked to adopt, and though everyone is satirized, no one is expelled from "the new social vision," as Cuddy-Keane has suggested.[43] Sir William and Lady Bradshaw are in attendance at Clarissa's party—their threat still present—Septimus is dead, and Clarissa's victory is in carrying on. Woolf does not give us a happy ending, but instead, the narrative suggests only a way of negotiating the world and a comic perspective on the trivial and the traumatic, the earnest and the insincere.

As in all satire, there is an ethical norm in *Mrs. Dalloway*—though it is not prescriptive and is profoundly ambivalent—and the reader recognizes it or there would be no opportunity for humor. The sense of the in-joke that can be seen in Woolf's earliest writings is an important aspect of the humor in *Mrs. Dalloway*. As I have argued, much of the humor originates in the satiric observations of an informed and mocking narrator and relies on the collusion between that narrator and the reader. Woolf's narrator exposes to the reader the characters' thoughts and motivations from a vantage point that is at once intensely intimate and coolly distanced, revealing more about the characters and the social forces that have gone into forming them than they themselves could possibly be aware and complicating traditional notions of comedic distance, which demand that the amused observer remain detached from the object of the satire. Thus, despite Woolf's claim to "recording the atoms as they fall," her narrators play the role of the teller of the joke, exposing and ridiculing the hypocrisy, insincerity, and even violence in the characters' actions for the pleasure and judgment of the reader.

Though Woolf presents characters who are obvious targets of attack, even her sympathetic characters are mocked. She simultaneously grants us enough distance to laugh at these characters and also reveals their most private internal thoughts, so we often find ourselves laughing at characters we identify and even sympathize with. Throughout *Mrs. Dalloway* customs, courtesies, and manners form the pivot of the comedy, and unthinking adherence to them becomes the object of her attack; anything can create this lack of knowledge—self-delusion, social illusion, stupidity, pride, or merely the passage of time. Clarissa is frequently mocked for her unknowing, but other characters, such as Hugh Whitbread and Peter Walsh, are also shown to either misunderstand or be unaware of their own motivations.

Clarissa is a part of society, though she feels alienated from it, and, despite the fact that she resists being overwhelmed and defined by her social world, the narrator allows us to see just how much she is a product of it. Though Clarissa is kind and generous to her servants and she prides herself for her enlightened relationship with them, her attitude toward them is defined by hierarchical class distinctions. When her maid Lucy had to miss the end of a play the night before because her companions were required to return to their employers before ten, Clarissa expresses sympathy for her spoilt evening, but the narrator breaks in to add: "(for her servants stayed later, if they asked her)."[44] The paternal aspect of the relationship cannot be missed—her servants do not have control over their own time, and they must ask her permission to come and go. The narrator's praise of Clarissa's generosity is as ironic as her praise of Sir William's devotion to his profession is. Though the narrator's scorn for Clarissa may be less caustic, it is clearly there, mocking what it praises.

Irony is a mode "that springs from a recognition that the socially constructed self is arbitrary and that demands revision of values and conventions," explains Nancy Walker.[45] Clarissa's patterns of identification are aligned with the aristocratic elite: they are arbitrary and unstable and, as such, are as deserving of ridicule as anything else. The rest of the episode maintains this ironic view of Clarissa, as it wryly questions her generosity in sending Lucy off with the present of a cushion for the cook, Mrs. Walker, by noting that it is an "old, bald-looking" one and in her effusive thankfulness to Lucy by adding, "thank you, thank you, she went on saying to her servants generally for helping her to be like this, to be what she wanted, gentle, generous-hearted."[46] And as she sits mending her party dress and praising the artistry of her dressmaker now retired and living in the unfashionable Ealing, Clarissa thinks to herself that as soon as she has a moment she will go and see her, but the narrator ironically exposes the hollowness of Clarissa's sentiments; even if Clarissa herself really believes she has every intention of visiting her old seamstress, the narrator tells us: "(but never would she have a moment any more)."[47] In the final assessment, Clarissa's attitude toward the servant class is not all that different from Lady Bruton and the "grey tide of service which washed round [her] day in, day out," absorbing the knocks and bumps of life and seeing to her every need, while at the same time allowing her to feel generous in her need of them.[48]

The fact that Clarissa is at times unaware of her motivations and values is, for the reader, one of the most disconcerting aspects of the satire in *Mrs. Dalloway*. For unlike Sir William and Lady Bruton, Clarissa is not distanced in the narrative. The reader has the privilege of her thoughts and feelings, and the humorous invective aimed at her is discomfiting, for we have come to understand and even identify with her. As in most dark humor, the psychological safety of the purely satiric stance is violated: "the comic distance is shortened and sometimes nearly removed, thus allowing the naked horror to show through."[49] Our perspective on Clarissa is continually changing, so that we do not know whether to take her seriously and extend our compassion to her or to maintain the distance that allows us to laugh at her. Clarissa is ambiguously a vacuous lady of fashion and a complicated skeptic, standing at the top of the stairs and bravely maintaining her selfhood, and we simultaneously laugh at her and with her. Both ambiguity and simultaneity are important to dark humor, because they keep the reader off balance and prevent them from making a useful moral judgment of the characters. Dark humor laughs at the very norms that would enable a moral judgment and suggests with grim pleasure that because they are created by human beings, who are generally unable to know or understand their own motivations and sink into greed and tyranny with alarming ease, there is really no hope for the betterment of society.

Social satire in the twentieth century tends toward dark humor because lurking behind all the fun is the sneaking suspicion that society and its constructions, which are usually hierarchical, unjust, and deforming to individual subjectivity, are all there is, and underpinning them is the finality of death. Thus, the satire in *Mrs. Dalloway* is dark comedy not only because the humor is juxtaposed against madness, death, and the effects of war but also because beneath all of this is the unsettling belief that the notion of the rational progress of history is merely illusion. Though this aspect of Woolf's comedy will be more apparent in her later works, specifically *Orlando* and *Between the Acts*, it is nascent in *Mrs. Dalloway* in the inaccessibility individual characters have to knowledge of their own natures and motivations and in the narrative's refusal of reconciliation: Septimus commits suicide and Clarissa remains fundamentally isolated. Unlike Northrop Frye's notions of comedy, which posit that it always works toward a reconciliation between the individual and society, dark humor stops short of any such victory, and social satires written by women have often suggested that "reconciliation" usually involves subjugation. Judy Little claims that lack of closure and resolution "characterizes the feminist comedy."[50] And Barreca argues, "The endings of comic works by women writers do not, ultimately, reproduce expected hierarchies, or if they do there is often an attendant sense of dislocation even with the happiest ending."[51]

The social world inhabited by Clarissa is a vexed and troubled one. Though we first meet Clarissa plunging into life, there is a sense of danger and apprehension accompanying her at all times. Even as the novel opens on a fresh June day full of promise, Clarissa is immediately transported to a similar day in her youth at the family home of Bourton, where even then, her enjoyment of life is blighted by something "chill and sharp," and with the awareness that "something awful was about to happen."[52] Clarissa is always aware of death, and, though she perseveres in the face of it, "she always had the feeling that it was very, very dangerous to live even one day."[53] Despite the activities that fill up life: parties, buying flowers and gloves, and the hum of London getting on with its business, the hours pass, "irrevocable," and the "leaden circles" of time and death hang in the air. Even in the midst of her party, savoring the triumph of the appearance of the prime minister, Clarissa thinks to herself, "How certain it is we must die."[54] The awareness of death only occasionally sends her into metaphysical speculation, though. Instead she turns to life and the rather trivial things that make it up. Alone in her room as the party continues without her, Clarissa thinks, "No pleasure could equal . . . straightening the chairs, pushing in one book on the shelf . . . los[ing] her self in the process of living, to find it, with a shock of delight, as the sun rose, as the day sank."[55]

Death is final in *Mrs. Dalloway*, and both the narrator and Clarissa either dismiss or ironize any belief in God or an afterlife. This puts the presence of death in a different light than previous centuries' social satire. In his study of entropy and comedy, Patrick O'Neill suggests that the main attribute of Modernism, the loss of certainty in all systems traditionally seen as giving meaning to the world, creates darkly ludic potential because activity that is repeated but not informed with meaning appears simultaneously funny and tragic (think of Beckett's Watt reorganizing the furniture in his room, or Sisyphus eternally pushing a boulder up a hill only to watch it roll back down again, or the endless attempts to get objects to do what they are supposed to in any one of Charlie Chaplin's films). Carrying on with life, repeating and perpetuating social manners and customs, and continuing "to behave like a lady" despite the lack of any transcendent meaning in life can have this same darkly ludic potential. Therefore, the laughter of dark comedy lacks the untroubled simplicity and unshaken self-confidence of traditional social satire, and the grim comic spirit of the twentieth century takes nothing entirely seriously nor entirely lightly.

In this view Clarissa's preoccupation with the trivialities of her social life manifest the *blague* and magnanimity of gallows humor. Her

admiration for Lady Bexborough's opening of a bazaar while still holding the telegram telling of her son's death in the war, and her simulta-
neous feelings of concern for Evelyn Whitbread's ill health and of regret
at her own choice of a hat, which she self-consciously decides is "not the
right hat for the early morning," reveal a desire to retain a tenacious hold
on the self in the face of death. As she window-shops down Bond Street,
Clarissa's thoughts turn to death and the annihilation of her individual
self:

> But often now this body she wore (she stopped to look at a Dutch
> picture), this body, with all its capacities seemed nothing—nothing at all.
> She had the oddest sense of being herself invisible; unseen; unknown;
> there being no more marrying, no more having of children now, but only
> this astonishing and rather solemn progress with the rest of them, up
> Bond Street, this being Mrs. Dalloway; not even Clarissa any more, this
> being Mrs. Richard Dalloway.[56]

She defends herself against being overwhelmed by a social structure that
insists she become Mrs. Richard Dalloway and by the eventual death
that will reduce everyone on Bond Street to "bones with a few wedding
rings mixed up in their dust and the gold stoppings of innumerable
decayed teeth"[57] by summoning the protective features of ritual and
custom. Curiously repeating to herself, "that is all, that is all," she examines a roll of tweed in the shop "where her father had bought his suits
for fifty years," and, pausing at the window of a glove shop, remembers
that her "Uncle William used to say a lady is known by her shoes and
her gloves."[58] This same uncle had shifted in his bed one morning
during the war and said, "I have had enough." Thoughts of death are
replaced by thoughts of social ritual and custom, and Clarissa humorously returns to thinking about her passion for gloves and shoes at the
thought of this painful memory.

Throughout the novel Clarissa's concerns and preoccupations are
both trivial and all-important, for, in a universe that can no longer
confidently be seen to have ultimate and transcendent meaning, the
daily events of life—bazaars, parties, and flowers—have as much meaning as the affairs of state—the slaughter of thousands of young men in
battles over a few hundred yards of mud, an empire deciding the affairs
of "Armenian or Albanians," and prime ministers who look as if they
should be selling biscuits. Creating parity between what has been seen
as trivial and important has implications for both dark humor and feminist humor. As Barreca has argued, it is generally men who have decided
what is trivial and what is important, and the fact that many women

write about the details of their daily lives has more often than not been used to trivialize their writing.[59] Woolf argued in her 1919 essay "Modern Novels," that "one must not take for granted that life exists more fully in what is commonly thought big than in what is commonly thought small."[60] And in *A Room of One's Own*, she explains,

> It is obvious that the values of women differ very often from the values which have been made by the other sex; naturally, this is so. Yet it is the masculine values that prevail. Speaking crudely, football and sport are "important" and the worship of fashion, the buying of clothes "trivial." And these values are inevitably transferred from life to fiction. This is an important book, the critic assumes, because it deals with war. This is an insignificant book because it deals with the feelings of women in the drawing room. A scene in a battlefield is more important than a scene in a shop—everywhere and much more subtly the difference of value persists.[61]

Thus, Clarissa's championing of the trivial is not only feminist refusal to accept the values of patriarchal culture, but it is also heroic for its defiance in the face of death without meaning. Critics and scholars often discuss the feminist aspect of Clarissa's character, but the aspect of gallows humor in her outlook and actions for the most part has been overlooked. The dark humor has probably been overlooked for the same reasons the subversive nature of her feminism was for so long. Clarissa's complicated and nuanced character also explains why assessments of her have varied widely, and even Woolf feared she would seem too "glittering and tinselly."[62] Elizabeth Bowen remarks that Woolf's fiction often contains characters who appear "conventional and compliant" but who actually contain an "inner strangeness...in the way they think and feel."[63]

The mock heroic that is frequently used in relation to Clarissa serves both to trivialize her activities and to invest them with importance, and Woolf employs the comedic convention at moments when Clarissa is feeling the most vulnerable. One of the earliest examples of its usage comes after Clarissa has been informed that her husband will be lunching with Lady Bruton and that she was not invited. At the snub Clarissa is thrown back on herself, left smarting from the pang of feeling abandoned and that her life was dwindling, "how year by year her share was sliced."[64] However, Lucy "took the hint" and responds with military devotion. She venerates Clarissa's parasol as a "sacred weapon which a Goddess, having acquitted herself honourably in the field of battle, sheds, and placed it in the umbrella stand."[65] Later, during Peter Walsh's surprise visit, Clarissa is again in need of a heroic, defensive posture. Peter, who always has the ability to make Clarissa feel "frivolous; empty-minded; a mere silly chatterbox," menacingly toys with his pocketknife.[66] Clarissa heroically calls on the artifacts of her domestic life, wielding her sewing needle like a lance, and in assertive but awkward grammar:

> But *I* too, she thought, and, taking up her needle, summoned, like a Queen whose guards have fallen asleep and left her unprotected (she had been quite taken aback by this visit—it had upset her) so that any one can stroll in and have a look at her where she lies with the brambles curving over her, summoned to her help the things she did; the things she liked; her husband; Elizabeth; *her self, in short*, which Peter hardly knew now, all to come about her and beat off the enemy.[67]

As before, Clarissa feels herself dwindling, and she resists being made to feel exposed, trivial, and inconsequential by Peter's presence. She insists, "But I, too," and summons to her rescue the customary concerns of her domestic life, armored in the humor of the mock-heroic.

Denise Marshall and others have observed that Woolf's reclaiming of the trivial aspects of life, aspects traditionally associated with women's lives, is a powerful feminist statement.[68] Barreca asserts, "the subjects of women's comedy are far from unimportant, however unofficial their designation within the dominant discourse."[69] Equating domestic realities with affairs of state endows the domestic with power and force at the same time it scorns and challenges the self-interest and violence of patriarchal power. Woolf further accomplishes this by trivializing the professional and political world dominated by men. For instance Hugh Whitbread, facetiously referred to as having "been afloat on the cream of English society for fifty-five years," keeps guard at Buckingham Palace, "over what nobody knew. But he did it extremely efficiently." He doesn't really do anything, he "had not taken part in any great movements of the time or held important office"; however, he is known for having known prime ministers and having deep affections.[70]

Peter Walsh, who had been a colonial administrator, is consistently undermined by the narrator, even as he prides himself in being a "radical," fulminating against the status quo embodied in Richard Dalloway and Hugh Whitbread. Asserting that he "does not care a straw" for their set, Peter (or the narrator) reveals parenthetically that he would have "to see whether Richard couldn't help him to some job."[71] Peter is consistently wrong about people, and his perceptions of the world around him are generally inaccurate. Seeing Rezia and Septimus, who are respectively miserable and suicidal, sitting on a park bench in Regent's Park,

Peter waxes poetic about young lovers and their quarrels. Later, when he hears the siren of the ambulance taking Septimus's body away, his ruminations on the "triumphs of civilization" are heavy with irony. Peter proudly contemplates the "efficiency, the organization—the communal spirit of London," which allows for the sick or the injured to be picked up "instantly [and] humanely."[72] However, it is the efficiency of the killing fields in France, fostered by the deadly communal spirit of nationalism, that has led to Septimus's death. Also damaging, though, is Peter's trivializing of Clarissa's life choices as he aggrandizes his own, even in the face of his lack of accomplishments. As he stares at the statue of the Duke of Cambridge, he identifies with the icon of nationalism and patriarchy and thinks,

> the future of civilization lies in the hands of young men like that; of young men such as he was, thirty years ago; with their love of abstract principles; getting books sent out to them all the way from London to a peak in the Himalayas; reading science; reading philosophy. The future lies in the hands of young men like that, he thought.[73]

Young men such as Peter was thirty years ago, with their love of abstract principles, had administered an empire and led the world to war, and Woolf's ironic tone critiques by implication a sanguine view of the future if it lies in the hands of such men.

While Woolf's satire does not attempt a solution to society's ills, her caustically humorous critique of patriarchal culture is an intellectual protest against the violence and injustice she sees resulting from culture being ordered along patriarchal and hierarchical lines. Denise Marshall argues, "In a patriarchy it is men who order society and impose their version of reality on the rest of society. Women are usually the victims because they have not had a hand in their own definitions."[74] Woolf's fiction is a powerful and eloquent rejoinder to this state of affairs, for, as Marshall has suggested, "In her culture women were not quite human enough to laugh at their condition, as human or woman. And it was a tricky business to laugh at males who share those conditions."[75] However, as Gail Finney notes, "humor does not exist in a vacuum but within a specific sociohistoric context. Depending on the period and milieu producing a text, differences [between male and female comedy] can shade into similarities and vice versa, and the lines of demarcation are not always sharply drawn."[76] Woolf's humor is feminist because she was writing at a time when the laughter of women was not easily heard outside the domestic circle. Her satire dares to expose the arbitrariness of all social constructions that limit the lives of human beings—women,

men, servants, clerks, soldiers, and aristocrats. Unlike the comedy of women in previous centuries, Woolf's satire is aimed at the world at large not just the limitations of the domestic sphere, and even more distinct from the previous centuries' humorous women, Woolf points to a certain "cosmic disarray [that] prompts new facets of dark disquiet in comedy."[77] She satirizes the social world and its injustices not necessarily to promote change or acceptance but certainly to foster recognition of the complexities and contradictions of life in the modern world and then asks us to laugh at the difficulties in negotiating that world. Darkly subversive, Woolf's comedy affords a female perspective on the "important" issues usually reserved for male writers—the push and pull between emotion and repression, self-sacrifice and self-deception, and the self largely created but not wholly determined by social forces.

Woolf's humor, therefore, is serious and even tragic. Her leveling of the trivial and the momentous evokes "deep laughter," a laughter that is also somber because it illuminates the profound ironies of existence.[78] "Deep laughter" more often produces a wince than a belly laugh because the ironies touch upon things of such penetrating humanness that one laughs at the quirky twists of humanity while being at the same time aware of sadness, tragedy, or great seriousness. The great tragedy that informs all the action in *Mrs. Dalloway* is World War I, "that preposterous masculine fiction,"[79] which leads Woolf to interrogate the fundamental values of Western culture even as she is disturbed by the passing of many of them.

Though Woolf would write eloquently about her feminist-pacifist position in *Three Guineas*, she was noticeably silent about the war while it was raging. There are letter and diary entries that reveal Woolf's revulsion for "revolting patriotic sentiment," but for the most part she withheld from public comment about the war. Of course, Woolf was suffering from one of her worst mental breakdowns during the years 1915–16, so perhaps it is no surprise that *Mrs. Dalloway*, a work Mark Hussey has called "a war novel,"[80] deals with war distantly, through the lens of madness and nostalgia for a world forever changed and lives forever damaged. Everyone in the novel is victimized by the war, and Woolf writes with authority about the damage on the home front. Woolf knew about trauma and death, and her characters' symptoms parallel her own feelings of insanity, paranoia, and loss—both of loved ones and of personal autonomy—personal feelings and experiences writ large in the postwar world.

Septimus's shell shock is the most obvious engagement with the atrocities of the war, and Woolf famously used her own memories of madness in creating his character. Her attack on the treatment Septimus receives at the hands of Doctor Holmes and Sir William Bradshaw is no doubt a reflection of her anger at the rest cure prescribed for her during her bouts with mental illness, but it may also be a more public response to a report presented in Parliament in August of 1922 dealing with the appropriate therapies for treating shell shock. *The Report of the War Office Committee of Enquiry into "Shellshock"* and its suggestions for the treatment of shell-shock victims were examined in articles by *The Times*, so Woolf most likely would have been aware of it.[81] Sir William discusses with Richard Dalloway a Bill he wants seen passed by Parliament: "They were talking about this Bill. Some case, Sir William was mentioning, lowering his voice. It had its bearing upon what he was saying about the deferred effects of shell shock. There must be some provision in the Bill."[82] With an emphasis Sir William would have approved of, *The Report* urged self-knowledge and moral control as remedies for shell shock.[83] The irrationality of this approach to treatment would have had personal and political resonance with Woolf, who saw neither of these attributes exercised by the government or society in putting an end to the war sooner. Throughout *Mrs. Dalloway* the very notion of self-knowledge is questioned, and morality in the postwar world is exposed as being a matter of perspective. For example, we learn that the leadership of government and society, peopled by well-meaning, public school men like Hugh Whitbread, is frequently the agent of "evil": "God knows the rascals who get hanged for battering the brains of a girl out on a train do less harm on the whole than Hugh Whitbread and his kindness."[84] As a "good" man in the service of Empire, Hugh Whitbread is as implicated in the system of violence and crime as the murderer on the train, and Polhemus argues "it hardly signifies whether those who strive...are moral or immoral, wise or foolish, benevolent or selfish...a switch in perspective reflects a comic vision" that gives intimations of thorough immorality.[85]

The war's legacy of insanity, irrationality, and death permeates postwar English life from the very opening pages of the novel:

> The War was over, except for some one like Mrs. Foxcroft at the Embassy last night eating her heart out because that nice boy was killed and now the old Manor House must go to a cousin; or Lady Bexborough who opened a bazaar, they said, with the telegram in her hand, John, her favourite, killed.[86]

Woolf seems to question what exactly comprises a "sane" reaction to the loss of a loved one to the "fiction" of a preposterous war, and how one is to react to it. Confusion of emotions and motivations is evident in these grimly funny lines, as Woolf shows characters trying to carry on with customary concerns of living at the same time she simultaneously undercuts any easy identification with their feelings by implicating them in the very values that brought about the war. Woolf refuses to give the reader a "rational" portrait of a mother's grief, and we are both moved by pity for their loss and left with disgust at their concern for property and social position.

The war has left the living in the difficult position of carrying on in a world where the old values and moral certainties no longer work, and there seems nothing with which to replace them. Miss Kilman, another kind of war victim, was fired from her teaching position because "she had never been able to tell lies" and "she would not pretend that the Germans were all villains."[87] Honesty and tolerance are generally virtues admired by a society, but not during a war. Miss Kilman is enraged at her dismissal and "all her soul rusted with that grievance sticking in it."[88] She responds with the "violent and filthy passions"[89] of a reformer that made Woolf so uneasy with "causes," which tended to "dull their [adherents] feelings" and perpetrate the same injustices of which they themselves were victims.[90]

Given its look at the fractured lives and the irrational social conditions occasioned by the war, *Mrs. Dalloway* is quite correctly described as a "war novel"; however, it is also a social satire, and in her combination of these two genres Woolf is setting the stage for many of the grimly comedic novels of the twentieth century. For one of the most salient themes in the darkly comedic literature of the century is how to live in the ever-present shadow of war. In dealing with the absurdly irrational climate created by war, they explore the unsolved and irresolvable moral and philosophical enigmas of life in the modern world. Living in the shadow of war is much like living in the shadow of the gallows; one can have a variety of responses, but there is very little to be done about the actual circumstances. For the most part, the novelists in this study, choose to retain a customary concern with the manners and mores of society—even while they are critical of them and impose comedic order on the chaos and meaninglessness represented in the texts.

As stated at the beginning, Woolf is not generally viewed as a practitioner of dark humor; however, *Mrs. Dalloway*, is an important contribution to the literature of grim humor in the twentieth century. In her presentation of a flawed but humorous protagonist, who is as much a product of the society as a critique of it, her treatment of isolation, death, and violence done to the individual by society, and her reevaluation of culture in the aftermath of a devastating and fruitless war, Woolf engages the issues that will preoccupy the rest of the century, issues that, despite their serious and tragic consequences, appear more and more difficult to treat seriously and tragically. Patrick O'Neill argues that in the twentieth century tragedy as a genre has "beaten a retreat, where we might expect to find it we tend to find comedy."[91] This is not comedy in the traditional sense, either, "but varieties of comic writing whose affinity to tragic writing is so marked as to disorient completely our stock responses to traditional tragedy and comedy and disrupt totally the traditional cathartic reaffirmation of the norms of an ordered societal system."[92] Woolf's use of comedic strategies to confront the pain and oppression of her historical moment sets the stage for the dark and antinomic social satire of Ivy Compton-Burnett, in whose hands tragedy and comedy are so intimately connected as to become indistinguishable and concerns with good and evil become grotesquely, comedically, irrelevant.

CHAPTER 3

THE DARK DOMESTIC VISION OF IVY COMPTON-BURNETT: *A HOUSE AND ITS HEAD*

> Now the world is possessed of a certain big book...the Book of Egoism... Comedy...condenses whole sections of the book in a sentence, volumes in a character...
>
> George Meredith

Ivy Compton-Burnett occupies an unusual space in British literary history, for, like many novelists of her generation, her work is deeply influenced by British literary tradition. At the same time it breaks with that tradition in an attempt to find an aesthetic that more accurately portrays the social and psychological realities of modern life. However, unlike many of her contemporaries, Compton-Burnett generally has not been viewed as an experimentalist, and her work is rarely examined in the light of Modernist artistic aims. Though she was interested in what constitutes the self and how it can be protected against tyrants and dominators, to use Woolf's terms, Compton Burnett chose to investigate these subjects from a rigorously objective perspective. Emerging from the long shadow cast by Bloomsbury, Compton-Burnett's novels afford an opportunity to investigate the complex and diverse nature of modernism. She was every bit as experimental as Woolf was, and as Angus Wilson described, "rigorously adapted form and language to accord with her aims, which is surely the only serious experiment to be considered."[1]

Compton-Burnett created darkly funny social satires that cut straight to the heart of many of the tensions defining British social life in the wake of World War I. With a condensed, abstract style, Compton-Burnett reveals aesthetic sensibilities influenced by the innovations associated with the more impersonal strains of literary modernism such as those of Ford Maddox Ford, T.S. Eliot, and Wyndham Lewis.

Anthony Powell noted that the "ironic despair set against the background of humdrum circumstances" connects her to writers working much later in the century.[2] And in her brittle, deflationary wit and artfully plotted narrative she has much in common with postwar writers like Waugh, Powell, Mitford, and the early Huxley. She eschewed Bloomsbury interiority and embraced instead a pellucid prose style and a dark satirical stance to explore the trauma and uncertainty of life in the first half of the twentieth century and to examine the individual's negotiation of increasingly complex and demanding social identities and affiliations.

Despite the fact that more than a few scholars and fellow writers committed themselves in print to the assertion that Compton-Burnett was "one of the greatest British novelists of the century,"[3] her work remains relatively little-known, and her relentless lack of sentimentality has prompted most scholars to view her work in light of the masculine tradition and ignore her feminist critique of the male totalitarianism that is the hallmark of the Victorian social and domestic arrangements. Regina Barreca's observations about the fiction of Elizabeth Bowen can also be applied to Compton-Burnett: "In disrupting the pattern [of traditional female comedy], she risks being categorized as a writer of 'limited appeal.' When she is misfiled under an inappropriate heading, the woman writer is in danger of being either drastically misread or passed over altogether."[4] Like Bowen, Compton-Burnett is "what happened after Bloomsbury," and she also is a "link that connects Virginia Woolf and Muriel Spark."[5] Her comedy "recognizes experience as arbitrary and subjective, and declares that the ordering of it is illusory," but "only illusion can instill in an inhabitant of the twentieth century a sense that life has any meaning whatsoever."[6]

All of her novels are dated about the turn of the century, for the most part between 1888 and 1902, and set in large country houses inhabited by a complicated array of servants, children, and dependent relatives. Like Virginia Woolf, Compton Burnett recognized that the world changed on or about December 1910, stating, "I do not feel that I have any real or organic knowledge of life later than about 1910. When an age has ended, you see it as it is."[7] She chose to examine this change through the lens of the past, and she ground her lens in new ways that allowed for clarity, precision, and a disturbing degree of magnification. Compton-Burnett's insistence on setting her novels—even those written in the 1950s and 1960s—in the increasingly distant, domestically enclosed, and highly mannered Victorian/Edwardian country house is no doubt the reason for many of the comparisons of her work to

Jane Austen. Compton-Burnett trains her gaze at the circumscribed world of the domestic and pointedly uses a precise vocabulary that is at once plainspoken and sophisticatedly understated to expose greed, hypocrisy, and unjust power relations. Her action takes place under strictly controlled circumstances, but its import reaches well beyond the country-house set.

Like Austen she writes of the "comfortable classes"[8] and her world seems reassuringly distant; however, Compton-Burnett is a thoroughly modern writer who believed that "nothing is so corrupting as power,"[9] and she focuses relentlessly on the economic and institutional bases of social power embedded in family relationships and laws of inheritance. In the microcosm of the family Compton-Burnett examines the misuse of power and the misery and violence that result, and her work, though set in a previous historical epoch, suggests the anxiety over the threat of future violence and the increasing distrust of government and those in power that pervades much of the literature of the 1930s. Maurice Cranston nicely sums up her oeuvre:

> She depicts a world where power counts above all things, a time when the bourgeoisie is at its moment of ripeness, with the rot already there but the disintegration yet to come; she sees all relations in terms of the family, and the family as an institution based on property; the class war is endemic in her novels, and history unfolds itself at once dialectically and inevitably.[10]

Composed almost entirely in dialogue that is brittle, artificial, and chillingly controlled, her novels reveal the disruptive forces seething under the smooth surface of a deceptively calm and well-ordered society, prompting Elizabeth Bowen to liken reading a page of Compton-Burnett dialogue to listening to "glass being swept up, one of these London mornings after a blitz."[11] In Compton-Burnett's hands domestic comedy takes a decidedly dark turn; the inhabitants of her country houses are tyrannized by hierarchical family relationships, murderous concerns with inheritance, and incestuous sexual desire. The acts of domestic tyranny that seem too sordid for polite exposure are presented without remorse in almost grotesquely stilted language that is grim, glittering, and astoundingly precise. Family members play on each other's phrases like university wits and employ their exacting and condensed language on profoundly disturbing themes.

For Compton-Burnett, the family is the focus of both her plots and all the relationships examined in her novels. Though her satire of family life allows for rich analogies to the greater social world, her characters are first and foremost members of a family: fathers and wives, sons and daughters, brothers and sisters; and second they are separate individuals with lives of their own. For her the family is the central meeting place and model for love, hate, greed, ambition, and real affection. It is also where the tension in Compton-Burnett's novels occurs; as family ties tighten around the individual violence and tragedy result, and as the victims attempt to loosen the tie and protect themselves comedy and satire ensue. In a characteristic example of a domestic despot defending power excesses in the name of family, Henrietta Ponsonby muses to her brother in *Daughters and Sons*:

> What is a little impatience, hastiness—tyranny, if it must be said— compared with real isolation and loneliness?
> I am afraid it must be said, and they are a great deal worse.[12]

Compton-Burnett's treatment of the enclosed world of domestic life give her novels what has been described as "a sinister cosiness."[13] Shunning sensational treatment of perversion and injustice, she reveals the dark side of family life through dialogue that is so condensed it is easy to miss just how horrific the subject matter really is. Because of the self-contained and mannered character of the Edwardian household, daughters, younger sons, and dependent relations are unable to protect themselves from tyrannical heads of families except through their intelligence and word play. When crimes such as murder, adultery, will tampering, or incest are finally revealed, it is done through such a controlled use of language that they frequently appear less shocking than the daily cruelty of the breakfast table. With few options and no economic independence, those lacking power defend themselves with darkly funny turns of phrase that are at once assertive and aggressive in the use of the tyrant's own language against him or her and restrained and sophisticated in adherence to the social conventions of country-house culture.

Wilson said of Compton-Burnett's work: "In the age of the concentration camp, when, from 1935 or so to 1947, she wrote her best novels, no writer did more to illumine the springs of human cruelty, suffering, and bravery," for her concealing and revealing dialogue explores the "stuff of personality, its fictions and its onion peelings of reality."[14] Wilson's summation of Compton-Burnett's work is telling and important, for she is not concerned to expose cruelty in order to correct it, and her satire has little that is salutary or corrective. She is concerned with how individuals cope with and respond to violent, threatening, and hostile circumstances, but offers no suggestion that those circumstances will be ameliorated. Indeed, much to the consternation of several of the reviewers of her early books, villains and tyrants in Compton-Burnett novels are rarely punished, and in the end power relationships remain much as they were at the beginning of the works. Though this is also true at the end of *Mrs. Dalloway*, Compton-Burnett is more disturbingly ambivalent, and there is no ethical norm to be found. Her dark comedy is beyond good and evil, and it exposes the arbitrariness of those categories. Compton-Burnett countered criticism of her "amorality" by saying that murder and perversion of justice are frequently the normal subjects of plots, and the fact that her characters do not receive "poetic justice" is simply reflective of life:

> I think life makes great demands of people's characters, and gives them . . . great opportunity to serve their own ends by the sacrifice of other people. Such ill-doing may meet with little retribution, may indeed be hardly recognized, and I cannot feel so surprised if people yield to it . . . I shouldn't mind being described as amoral, but I don't think guilty people meet punishment in life. I think it is a literary convention. I think the evidence tends to show that crime on the whole pays.[15]

Compton-Burnett's technique of writing in dialogue with little narrative description, prevents the reader from unequivocally passing judgment on the characters. As in *Mrs. Dalloway*, there is no one view the reader is asked to adopt, and, although her domestic tyrants are shocking in their despotism, the victims can be equally vicious in their response and in their treatment of those more powerless than they. Compton-Burnett has stated in several interviews that her tyrants never seem to her as monstrous as they seem to others, and she attempts to show in her fiction that most people are capable of cruelty when they feel threatened and of yielding to strong temptation if there is no risk of being found out.[16]

There is a certain "ambiguity of personal values"[17] at work in Compton-Burnett's novels, a characteristic frequently found in works employing dark humor. The melodramatic aspects of her plots—the family secrets of incest, illegitimacy, and the occasional murder—do not serve a didactic function as much as they suggest the instability of personality. The revelation of incest or illegitimacy means that members of a family must readjust definitions of themselves in the most important sense that exists in the family unit; they are no longer sons, daughters, or dependent cousins, or they are not *only* sons, daughters, and dependent cousins, but brothers and sisters of their parents or rightful heirs of their tyrannical uncles as well. And if, as sometimes happens, the revelation was untrue or events take another turn, they must once again redefine themselves in accordance with their former role, all of which involves a rather large degree of psychological trauma. And, as we have seen, one response to psychological trauma is humor, and Compton-Burnett's characters use it with vengeance.

A House and Its Head contains all the classic Compton-Burnett characteristics: a domineering father, possible incest, murder, machinations to ensure inheritance, and intelligent but powerless children. Additionally, it is one of the more social of Compton-Burnett's works, incorporating the local village inhabitants in a function similar to that of a Greek chorus, but as they comment and pass judgment on the occurrences in the manor house, they are exposed as prurient, hypocritical, and jealous do-gooders, who, in ways similar to Miss Kilman in *Mrs Dalloway*, are prompted to charitable action by anything but benevolent reasons.

Briefly, the complicated plot revolves around the towering ego of the head of the household, Duncan Edgeworth, who after shortening the life of his first wife with his bullying, is left with his two daughters, Nance and Sibyl, and his nephew Grant, who has been groomed to take over the estate. Duncan soon marries Alison, a young woman thirty-nine years younger than he. Alison has an affair with the nephew, Grant, and bears a son that is recognized to be Grant's by a telltale lock of white hair that all the men on Grant's side of the family possess. Ironically, Grant's own son, being raised as Duncan's, bars Grant's succession to the entailed estate. Alison, chaffing under the despotism of Duncan, runs off with Almeric Bode, a young man from the village. Grant marries Sibyl, Duncan's daughter, who is an alarming and unbalanced young woman—possibly as a result of incest, but this is never made explicit. She suborns a dismissed servant to murder her small stepbrother/stepson, so that Grant may again be heir. Although Sibyl tries to implicate Cassandra, the former governess and now Duncan's third wife, the family learns of her actions. She is exiled for a short period but manages to acquire the legacy of a rich aunt, and the family then welcomes her and her newfound riches back into the fold just as Nance and Cassandra's brother, Oscar, are about to be married.

Many scholars consider *A House and Its Head* one of Compton-Burnett's most successful novels, and the characters are some of the most complicated and varied in her fiction.[18] The tyrannical Duncan Edgeworth may not be overtly criminal, but the crimes and misalliances in the novel result from the oppressive atmosphere he has generated. He is a patriarch whose family belongs to him in much the same way his estate does, and he uses his family merely as instruments for his happiness, which rests on retaining his power as head of the household for as long as he can. The egoism that Compton-Burnett's tyrants display is an extreme self-protection that must triumph over everything and everyone and sees each new encounter as a threat. Her egoists demand respect, credit for virtue and glories of civilized society, power, eternal life, adoration, and love. The many levels of their egoism creates desires that conflict within themselves, but they also find themselves living in a world with other egoists so every encounter becomes a battle of wills.

Duncan's absolute refusal to acknowledge how his lust for power blights the lives of his family and his selfish demands for sympathy after the loss of both his first and second wives mark him as a supreme egoist and tyrant reminiscent of a host of Victorian fathers, both real and fictive, from Woolf's accounts of her father, Leslie Stephen, to Samuel Butler's portrait of the tyrannical Theobald Pontifex in *The Way of All Flesh*. His behavior, like that of all the characters in the novel, is of course defined by the economic and power hierarchies that create the Victorian household. In an interview with Michael Millgate, Compton-Burnett remarks that she believes "economic forces influence people a great deal, that many things in their lives are bound up with them. Their scale of values, their ambitions and ideas for the future, their attitude to other people and themselves."[13] The problem of inheritance is a primary one in Compton-Burnett, and in her melodramatic satire of the rule of primogeniture and the laws of entail, she is critiquing larger social structures and the institutional frameworks through which authority is granted and power is wielded.

Though Duncan has played more than a small role in the death of his first wife, he feels her loss acutely because there is one fewer person in the household to dominate. Duncan rules supreme at the family dining table, and his insistence that every family member be present at family meals, despite the tension and discomfort he creates, extends to his obviously ill wife Ellen. The novel opens at the breakfast table on Christmas morning, beginning with a banal piece of social cruelty that sets the tone for the rest of the book's action. The first fifty pages of the novel are devoted to the activities of this one day, and, in doing this, Compton-Burnett not only fully reveals the relationships among the family members but also adroitly establishes the links between social and religious authority that create and sustain those relationships. Duncan is annoyed that the young people have slept in a little later than usual, and his suppliant wife, attempting to break the uneasy silence, inquires, "So the children are not down yet?"[20] As in all of Compton-Burnett's novels, tyrants rule through language, and Duncan, in typical tyrant fashion, decides who will be allowed to speak and who will be heard and responded to. Ellen, it appears, is not worthy of a response without an audience present, so he ignores her question twice and then once again after she rephrases her query: "So you are down first, Duncan?" This seems a more "acceptable form" for her observation, as Duncan is now the subject of her sentence rather than the children; however, it remains unanswered. This anxious nonexchange is interrupted by one of the few narrative descriptions in novel in which we learn that Duncan "was a man of medium height and build, appearing both to others and himself to be tall" and possessed of "narrow grey eyes, stiff, grey hair and beard, and a stiff imperious bearing."[21] The dining room itself possesses "the powerful manner of objects of the Victorian age, seeming in so doing to rank themselves with their possessor."[22] In this intimidating space the "small, spare" Ellen, with "large, kind" eyes, seems barely able to register a presence. Indeed, she attempts her question again, "employing a note propitiation," but receives merely a shoulder shrug as a reply.[23] The scene continues with Ellen nervously rambling on, commenting on the Christmas presents and making excuses for the children's dilatory actions. Unwilling to allow them any defense, Duncan finally responds to his wife, pouncing on every word she says and twisting her every sentiment until she grows quiet.

Compton-Burnett carefully crafts the exchange, and in Ellen's inability to defend herself through language her demise is felt in these first pages of the novel, though no mention of her illness is made. At the beginning, her questions are not even acknowledged, and throughout the conversation she is less and less able to respond to Duncan. To his demand "Why should they be late on Christmas Day or any other" "What reason would you suppose," we learn "Ellen did not say."[24] She suggests that the mornings are getting dark, and Duncan responds: "The mornings are getting dark! The mornings are getting dark! Do you mean they are so sunk in lethargy and self-indulgence, that they need a strong light to force them to raise their heads from their pillows? Is that what you mean?" The narrator informs us that "Ellen, uncertain how much she had meant of this, was silent."[25] And when Nance finally is heard on her way down to the dining room, Ellen says with relief, "I am glad that one of them is down." To which Duncan retorts, "Glad? Why?"; for he seems to have been enjoying torturing her in this way, but

"Ellen gave no reason."[26] With Duncan repeatedly badgering her into silence, her death early in the novel comes as no surprise. On the day of Ellen's death, Nance shows that she is aware of the role Duncan has had in silencing his wife by reproving him, "I wish her words were allowed to have some meaning, Father."[27]

Ellen and Sibyl are the two characters in the novel who are unable to linguistically defend themselves against Duncan. Sibyl, as her father's favorite, is less frequently the victim of his verbal attacks. She continually seeks her father's approval and generally responds to his catechisms with answers that please him, and when her replies do not please him, she often makes excuses for his churlish behavior. Duncan uses Sibyl's pliancy to condemn the others' self-possession, and his putative affection for her to torture his wife. Though incest is never explicitly acknowledged, early in the novel, after the miserable Christmas morning breakfast, there is an exchange between Sibyl and her cousin Grant that hints of something sinister in her relationship with Duncan:

> "Poor Father! He is rather one by himself in the house," said Sibyl. "I hope he knows what we all feel for him."
> Ellen raised her eyes with a faintly grieved expression.
> "If he does not know what you feel, it is not for want of being told." said her cousin.
> "He and I have always been friends. I have known his look for me all my life."
> "He cares the most for Aunt Ellen."
> Ellen's eyes filled with tears . . . [28]

Grant's veiled comments, Sibyl's defense of Duncan, and Ellen's grieved response hint at incest—as do numerous other incidents in the novel—and the action of the plot generally bears this suspicion out. Sibyl's behavior becomes increasingly peculiar, and of the three children she is the least able to verbally defend herself against Duncan. Aggressive word play is the only defense in this household and those unable to use it meet with the most unfortunate ends; Ellen dies and the unstable Sibyl instigates the murder of an infant.

Nance is distinguished from Sibyl by her wit, and as Barreca argues, "If the heroines of Victorian novels were separated from their less interesting counterparts by their pronounced intelligence," then the female protagonists of modern novels "are distinguished by their sense of humor . . . [they] claim the witty remark as their signature."[29] Compton-Burnett, however, uses the witty remark to distinguish between victims and survivors, and, unlike Ellen and Sibyl, both Nance and Grant defend themselves through language by using Duncan's own words against him. As Andrzej Gasiorek points out, "The authority exercised by Compton-Burnett's tyrants is always directed at those who are subservient to them. Some succumb, others resist," and one of the primary ways in which those lacking power undermine authority (though it is never overturned in open revolt) is by mocking their superior's words.[30] After everyone has assembled for Christmas breakfast, Duncan requires each of the young people to explain the significance of the day:

> "Nance, will you tell me what Day it is?"
> "The day of the Birth of Christ, Father," said Nance, forcing a natural voice.
> "Yes," said Duncan. "Yes. Sibyl, can *you* tell me what Day it is?"
> "The Day of the Birth of Christ, Father," said Sibyl, in a fuller tone, perhaps feeling confidence in the answer, after his confirmation of it.
> "Grant?" said Duncan.
> "Oh, I agree," said Grant, making a gesture towards his cousins, and causing his aunt to laugh before she knew it.
> Duncan simply turned from him.
> "Nance, I should like to hear you say it as Sibyl did."
> "No, you must pass my individual performance. You asked for it."
> There was a pause.
> "I hope that my allowing you to treat the occasion as a festival has not blinded you to its significance?"
> "It is the usual way of treating it."[31]

Nance defends herself from her father's bullying by holding him responsible for his own language and by very precisely answering his questions; thus, she is not openly defying him but is nevertheless subverting his authority. By creating characters like Nance and Grant, who use Duncan's own words against him, Compton-Burnett illustrates what Barreca calls "the humorous mocking voice that characterizes the woman writer."[32] And she employs her wit, the way female protagonists before her have done, "as an aesthetic strategy for survival."[33]

Authority figures in Compton-Burnett exercise power by controlling access to language, but language can be used as a subtle weapon against the despots who utilize it so viciously. Throughout the novel, Nance and Grant, restate Duncan's words in a context that exposes their vapidity, ask apparently innocent questions in order to expose hypocritical values, and invert trite platitudes in order to challenge the power of those who use them to justify their authoritarian excesses. They are able to fend off

Duncan's assaults while for the most remaining perfectly decorous. For instance, Nance uses her wit against Duncan, who defends his throwing of Grant's Christmas present, a science book "inimical to the faith of the day," into the fire. Duncan pretentiously claims responsibility for the moral instruction of his wards: "I shall really do my best to guide—to force you, if it must be, into the way you must go. I would not face the consequences of doing otherwise." To which Nance responds: "Would not the consequences be more widely distributed?"[34] Duncan interrogates Grant more specifically, and, though he receives truthful and accurate answers to his questions, he does not get the response he is hoping for.

> "Did you remember that I refused to give it to you?"
> "Yes, Uncle. That is why I asked somebody else."
> "Did you say I had forbidden it in the house?"
> "No, or I should not have been given it."[35]

The defensive use of language, which parodies Duncan's statements, succeeds because of Compton-Burnett's condensed style of writing. Indeed, I would argue that the significance of her oft-discussed, condensed style lies in its ability to represent the darkly funny battle between those who use language to bludgeon others into submission and those who use it as self-defense. When Duncan piously comments that he would not face the moral consequences of allowing his wards to read a work of science that undermines religious teaching, Nance counters with a play on the word "consequences," which suggests both that an individual's religious choices are his alone, and, as an individual, each must face the consequences of his own beliefs, as well as, that the consequences of Duncan's bullying and denial of freedom are that he makes everyone miserable, and these consequences are distributed widely throughout the household. Had these statements been explained thoroughly to Duncan there would be nothing humorous in the exchange; however, her economy of language makes the response witty and humorous.

The condensation in Compton-Burnett makes for brittle, caustic—but humorous—dialogue and a subterranean violence that requires a certain vigilance on the part of the reader. Compton-Burnett is often described as a "difficult" writer, or a "writer's writer" (she is praised by the likes of Evelyn Waugh, Anthony Powell, Elizabeth Bowen, W.H. Auden, and Christopher Isherwood, none of whom are strangers to crisp but venomous dialogue), and I suggest this idea is mainly due to the condensed form that makes leaps in meaning and plays at various levels. Compton-Burnett uses this condensed style to slow the action, focus on the psychological realities of each character, and ward off any sentimental response that might arise in reaction to the characters' plight. In dark humor satires, sentimentality is an ally of injustice and oppression, making individuals feel complacent and self-satisfied and prohibiting a defensive gesture.

Condensation is an important aspect to the defensive and assertive nature of jokes because it allows for the expression of suppressed or prohibited thoughts without their having to be openly stated. In Grant's exchange with Duncan, he does not engage Duncan in a discussion about his right to own or read the scientific work under question, nor does he openly denounce Duncan as a tyrant, for Duncan, as head of household, has the power to prohibit whatever objects or activities he chooses. Instead, Grant challenges Duncan's arbitrary use of power by honestly and candidly answering Duncan's questions, without giving Duncan the response he really wants, which was for Grant to admit that he was wrong in requesting the book. In so doing, Grant robs Duncan's words of authority because, though he receives precise and truthful answers to his questions, they are not the responses he is looking for, and no matter how he rephrases his questions, he will not get the desired response from Grant. The anger and resentment felt by Duncan and Grant respectively are evident in the artfully condensed dialogue; however, no insults or invectives are exchanged, for their utterance would trespass against the rules of decorous, country-house culture.

Freud argues that people are so frequently prevented by external circumstances from resorting to invective or to insulting rejoinders that "jokes are especially favoured in order to make aggressiveness or criticism possible against persons in exalted positions who claim to exercise authority."[36] His example, which reads very much like dialogue found in a Compton-Burnett novel, is of a haughty, young prince who comes upon a stranger who bears a strong resemblance to himself: "Was your mother in the Palace at one time?" asks the prince, and the stranger replies, "No, but my father was." Clearly, the stranger could not risk revenge on the prince for casting aspersions on his mother's virtue, unless, as Freud suggests, he was "prepared to purchase that revenge at the price of [his] whole existence. The insult must therefore, it would seem, be swallowed in silence."[37] Compton-Burnett's victims are frequently in situations in which protecting themselves against psychological damage from tyrants would be possible only at extreme cost, for heads of households exercise complete economic control over their dependents at a historical moment when there are little or no career options open to daughters, younger sons, or orphaned nephews. But, as Freud states, "fortunately, a joke shows the way in which [an] insult may be safely avenged"; it alludes to other meanings provided for in the remark and turns the aggressor's own statement against him.[38] The joke then represents rebellion against authority and liberation from its constraint. But as Freud suggests and Compton-Burnett shows, the humor does not significantly alter power hierarchies, nor does it lead to the overthrow of the person in the exalted position, but it does provide for the self-defense of those lacking power and provides them a way of refusing to be silenced, succumbing to vaguely defined illnesses, or losing their grip on reality.

Compton-Burnett's refusal to overthrow her tyrants, which led to cries of amorality from some of her contemporary reviewers, marks not only her desire to mirror reality but also is an important characteristic of dark humor. As I have argued in chapter 1, the social satire in novels employing dark humor is not ameliorative, and all is not well nor does it end well. Dark humor tends toward the distopian; it reveals the unjust and arbitrary nature of societal power structures, but it does not suggest that these structures, with the forces of tradition and economic privilege to sustain them, will be dismantled anytime soon—or, even if they were, that something better would replace them. Dark humor only offers the humorous defiance of those who wield power and the institutions that support them. For this reason, the "morality" of characters, both that of the powerful and the powerless, is generally ambivalent, and Compton-Burnett never suggests that the victims of unjust power hierarchies are in any way more virtuous than their persecutors. Alison Light has noted, in Compton-Burnett's circumscribed, hierarchical domestic world, women are as likely to be "peevish despots" as men are.[39] Women in these enclosed spaces can be just as "attracted to cruelty as to caring, to the satisfactions to be found in hurting rather than helping others," and while literary history is filled with examples of parental despots, "Compton-Burnett attacks the whole shared structure of family life."[40] In *A House and Its Head*, Grant, though a victim of his uncle's authoritarian rule, seduces a maid, who is then fired from her post, an injustice that leads to Sibyl's ability to use the young woman's desire for revenge to murder the baby. These acts of violence are perpetrated by the "victims" in the novel and are possible because of the corrupting nature of power on everyone caught up in the oppressive family structure.

This is not to argue that Compton-Burnett is commenting universally on the dark side of human character, for she is keenly aware of how material reality and the social organization of power based upon this reality—country estates, laws of inheritance, patriarchal power structures—shape people's thoughts and behavior. As Polhemus claims, "The patterns of human inequality may develop naturally in individual minds; but inequalities of class, sex [sic], and wealth, institutionalized and perpetuated by leaching selfishness, must be shown up for the terrible practical joke that they are."[41] Her work does suggest, however, that those with power are likely to keep it, and those lacking power are warped by their powerlessness. Her statement, "nothing is so corrupting as power" implies more than just that the powerful are corrupted, but that in oppressive social relationships all are affected and violence and unhappiness are the inevitable results. Dark humor satires frequently suggest that tyranny and oppression exist not because of the aberrant behavior of one or two selfish individuals but because of the patterns inherent in social existence, which require of all individuals—victims and tyrants—a complicity that is inescapable.[42] Her concern is not to shift the balances of power, for one form of power seems equally as corrupting as another. Some responses allow for a degree of psychological protection and some do not, but the psychological differences alter very little materially and rulers generally retain their rule.

Psychological protection is rarely found in official avenues of "goodness," like the church or philanthropic endeavor, and some of Compton-Burnett's most scathing satire is aimed at religion and its role in legitimizing tyrants. Like Virginia Woolf, Compton-Burnett is highly suspicious of officially sanctioned goodness, for it is generally based on power structures that mirror, reinforce, and perpetuate the economic and social injustices of the larger world and offer no real comfort to individuals. Compton-Burnett stated that she generally thought that "missionaries and people who do charity work are not so very good themselves," and their activities are "rather terrible to see being done— or to have [them] done to oneself."[43] Elizabeth Sprigge maintains that Ivy Compton-Burnett "despised the disguise of social observances as divine ones," and maintained that religion was "man's most extraordinary aberration and an irresistible invitation to mockery."[44] In her novels family tyrants frequently use religion to legitimate their power, and they rule in their households like a wrathful and jealous god.

Duncan Edgeworth regularly invokes God and religion to intimidate the family and insists on observance of religious rituals to control their activities. At the end of the Christmas breakfast, he inquires into the New Year's resolutions of each of the family members and receives the disturbing answer from Nance that she resolves to be more independent;

Sibyl, on the other hand, affirms that she resolves nothing of the sort and says that she "shall always be dependent."[45] Both responses arise from his domestic tyranny; however, Duncan informs them that they "will both be dependent, whether or no you want it."[46] He turns to Grant, who at first demurs, but at Duncan's insistence—"make a resolve, when I order you, and tell us of it"—states that he resolves to become more involved with the managing of the estate. Duncan responds jealously: "You think that stage has come? So the place has so much to do with you? You are putting me in my grave."[47] Duncan's power rests on keeping the family dependent on him for as long as possible, and any attempt to come of age (all of the "children" are well into their twenties) or express an independent idea are a threat to his authority. "The egoist," remarks Polhemus, "is a monument to stasis. He hates change and finds it terrifying because it threatens him with loss and, implicitly, disintegration and death."[48] If everything and everyone is actual or potential property, which they are in Duncan's world, time menaces his possessions, and he must align himself with an eternal god. Duncan retaliates against Grant by demanding he attend church, despite his expressed desire not to go, to which Grant simply states, "I am in a simple position; I do not dare to remain at home,"[49] for though he wishes to assert some independence, he does not have any desire to jeopardize his inheritance.

Duncan requires the entire family attend church, despite his wife's increasingly frail health, both because it is important to his social position as lord of the manor and it allows him to claim divine right in his absolute control over his family. The duty to attend church is revealed to be a social one, not a spiritual one, and the hypocrisy of the family pew is made clear when the narrator informs us that Duncan and Ellen "proceeded to the church, unconscious that it was the only occasion in the week when they were seen abroad together."[50] Duncan reigns in the family pew as powerfully as at the family dining table, but this performance has a larger social function. The importance of appearing to be both social and moral superiors in the village church is not lost, even on Grant, who did not want to attend the Christmas service. Once there, however, Grant adopts "the bearing of his uncle," and contrives that Nance and Sibyl "appear to reproduce his aunt's."[51] In Grant's change of bearing, Compton-Burnett illustrates how the church conspires in reproducing and supporting officially sanctioned inequalities and has little or no bearing on the lives and morals of the village; indeed, in Grant's case, attendance at church functions to make him more like his uncle and less charitable toward his cousins. In the dark comedy of egoism, Polhemus notes, "the Christian God himself is a pattern of egoism; our notions of the highest good and the ethos of our whole civilization have been, and are, necessarily tainted by monomaniacal self-centeredness, by self-division and its inevitable contradictions, and by innate sexism (like God, the egoist is Father and Son, not Mother and Daughter)."[52]

Religious belief affords no safety from the effects of a badly ordered society—and indeed sustain it—and Compton-Burnett makes clear that intelligence and a wry sense of humor are better defenses against the traumas of life. Like other social structures that foster arbitrary privilege, religion has sunk into institutionalized oppression, and Compton-Burnett sees it as a fit object of derision. Freud's brief discussion of jokes that attack religion or the belief in God suggests that this type of humor can be seen as one of the most darkly funny forms of self-assertion. He narrates a joke about a man on his deathbed, who is reminded by a friendly priest that God is merciful and will forgive the man his sins if only he asks for forgiveness. The man responds, "*Bien sûr qu'il me pardonnera: c'est son métier*" (of course he will forgive me: that's his job).[53] Freud explains that this is a "disparaging comparison," based on condensation of the word *métier*, which is a trade or a profession, like that of a workman or a doctor, and God only has one *métier*. Thus, Freud argues, what the joke means to say is: "Of course he'll forgive me. That's what he's there for, and that's the only reason I've taken him on (as one engages one's doctor or one's lawyer)." The dying man's assertion of his inalienable self is profound and partakes of the grandeur and elevation that Freud speaks of in his essay "Humor"; it announces that there is nothing that the psyche can't transform into pleasure. It also cuts to the very heart of dark humor as the individual self confronts the end of its existence and makes a joke of it:

> So in the dying man, as he lay there powerless, a consciousness stirred that he had created God and equipped him with power so as to make use of him when the occasion arose. What was supposed to be the created being revealed itself just before its annihilation as the creator.[54]

Compton-Burnett viciously exposes the uses of creating a god in man's image, and disallows any comfort that religion might allow for. Even the parson, Oscar Jekyll, is a skeptic, who delivers sermons that are more like lectures and earns the comment, "faith as deep as his would hardly appear on the surface."[55] His shallow faith has not led him to "relinquish his living," with all that this statement implies, for there are few options available to men of his status, for the most part younger sons of slender means. He takes comfort in the belief that his job would be less well done by "a stupider man, as a believer would probably be; and his views, though of some inconvenience to himself, were of none to his congregation."[56] The intelligent characters in Compton-Burnett's novels are thorough-going skeptics, who hold an ironic view of life. On rare occasion she presents an intelligent character who is "a believer," as is the case with Oscar's mother, Gretchen Jekyll, but she is suspicious of her own faith and enthusiastically "gives her ear" to Oscar's "unguarded words," for "though a believer herself, she had a dislike for her beliefs."[57]

As is to be expected, Duncan is less than enthusiastic about Oscar Jekyll's church service and comments that it struck him as "an able discourse rather than a sermon."[58] Duncan's control of his household dependents requires him not only to adopt the aspect of a god-like figure but also to promote the belief in a deity above himself, whom he can claim to represent. Thus, Oscar's method of preaching, which "fancies we like exposition better than reproach,"[59] leaves Duncan's authority open to subversion. He retreats to the manor house where his rule is secure, proclaiming that "Christmas is a festival of family life."[60] In the family, Duncan can maintain order by a god-like surveillance and control of both the domestic space and the language used. He is always vaguely uncomfortable when the children are off on their own, out of sight and out of ear shot, and they are generally watched either by him or the servants, as they are assumed to be inclined toward an independence that would lead them from the path of righteousness.

Their one sanctuary is the schoolroom, which of course implies an enforced childhood on people who are clearly adults, but even this space is not free from Duncan's surveillance. When the young people retire there during a visit from their friends Dulcia and Almeric Bode, they fall into playful parody of the church service, with Grant caricaturing the performance of the preacher, Oscar Jekyll. As soon as all are overcome with mirth, there is a knock at the door and just as the maid is informing them that the master feels they are making too much noise for Christmas day, Duncan, with god-like omniscience, appears, putting an end to the "clamour." He interrogates each of them as to what they were doing and whether they thought it was humorous. With an end to the fun immediately brought about, Dulcia, a sanctimonious busybody, prone to the most egregious use of cliché, defends Duncan's actions, pronouncing, "We were making fun of serious things. I admit I was...Oh, yes, I went the whole hog...But that very circumstance helps me to see his point of view." To which Nance retorts, "Well, no one else's point of view has had any success."[61] A parody of religious authority—even that of Oscar Jekyll's—is tantamount to a parody of Duncan's authority, and as such cannot be tolerated.

Sunday breakfasts prove to be the most oppressive of the week, and throughout the novel traumatic events usually occur in the midst of controlled prandial conversation, darkened by the shadow of both God and Duncan. Ellen's death occurs on a Sunday, after a morning of whining and bad temper prompted by Duncan's inability to convince her that she is not too ill to attend church. Unable to have his way, he abruptly leaves the table, spilling the coffee and causing his wife to burst into tears: "I can't help what [your] Father says; I must stay at home to today. People must sometimes be ill."[62] Nance understands that Ellen's uncharacteristic defiance of Duncan's will indicates a serious illness and remarks, "Every Sunday breakfast seems the worst... But I imagine we have attained the climax now."[63] Duncan, unmoved, plays the role of an unpropitiated god, creating guilt and ill will in every member of the household: he castigates Ellen for not going to church and suggests she is feigning her illness; he harasses Nance for her decision to stay home with her mother but then accuses Sibyl of being a disloyal daughter for "feeling [she] could leave [her] mother," leaving Sibyl "at a loss for an answer"; and suggests that Grant's decision to call in the local Doctor Smollett, whom Duncan claims he would not consult if he thought there were something seriously wrong, evinces Grant's belief that Ellen is not seriously ill. Grant attempts to challenge him by demanding, "Which one would you choose?" However, Duncan's power over language is unassailable in the midst of the family grief, and he dismisses Grant's challenge: " 'The information would be of no good to you... If there is any ground for it [concern], Smollett is not the man. But if it is merely a show, as you seem to agree, it is well enough.' There was a silence."[64] The family silence in the face of Duncan's power and his demand for submission to his will align him with the god to whom he is off to pay homage.

Gods and their creators need each other and that shared need allows for the continuance of the power structure. Because of the nature of this complicitous relationship, Duncan feels Ellen's loss acutely. Though he hectored her into silence and kept her to a miserly household budget, Duncan plans an expensive funeral for her. He requires his daughters to continually reassure him of his tenderness and love for Ellen and manipulates them with histrionic displays of sorrow and grief that force them to comfort him and attest to his kindness as a husband. Nance becomes resentful of this new form of abuse and protects herself with grim humor from the psychological trauma inherent in this kind of dishonesty:

> "It is fortunate I am not a person who cannot tell a lie. I hardly remember the difference between truth and falsehood; and he is not in any way concerned with it."
>
> "Poor Father! It is the least we can do for him." [replies Sibyl]
>
> "It was the most I could do. You don't know how much virtue has gone out of me. The virtue was Father's, but I had to produce it."[65]

Duncan plays on his daughters' conflicting loyalties and, with the injustices done to Ellen now a thing of the past, forces them to ignore what they know was the truth in order to mollify him. His egotism denies the reality of their experience and regards them only as instruments for promoting self-esteem. Sibyl takes to the role with alacrity, deriving "her reward from his dependence on herself," which leaves her feeling all the more betrayed when he hastily marries the young and beautiful Alison. This pattern is not unusual in Compton-Burnett's fiction, and patriarchs who are sunk to the worst kind of self-absorbed sorrow often replace their departed wives with their daughters.[66] Upon remarrying, they attempt to return them to their "daughterly" role, as if nothing unusual had transpired. The psychological trauma inherent in this kind of role shift is clearly profound, and most daughters in the novels respond with some form of criminal activity, will tampering, or as in Sibyl's case, murder. However, Nance negotiates the demands and competing affiliations with a dark irony and a keen intelligence, remarking on Duncan's ability to play the roles of happy husband and sorrowing widower simultaneously, just as he is always ruler of the family and martyr to the various demands required of him by his rule.[67]

Duncan's need for new supplicants prompts in part his unexpected and hasty marriage to the young, vivacious Alison. He selfishly ignores his family's grief at seeing their mother replaced so swiftly and will brook no discussion of his actions despite the fact that he has used them terribly to assuage his guilt. He contrives to control Alison by continually reminding her that she is a second wife and moves Ellen's portrait from the landing on the stairs to the dining room as a constant reminder to Alison of her role. However, Alison is a woman of independent nature, and it becomes clear that she will not be easily managed. Her first breakfast with the family begins with her inquiring about the presence of the portrait, and she exposes Duncan's selfishness by commenting, "Oh,

I see. You wanted your consorts all around you."[68] Alison's brief stay in the household is marked by her refusal to be silenced and her defiance of Duncan's attempts to limit her access to language. Young and beautiful, she at first bolsters Duncan's ego, but her liveliness is an immediate threat as she does what Barreca says all dangerous women do—she makes a spectacle of herself.[69] She chides Nance for saying her "clever things so low" and believes witty words should be "shouted abroad."[70] She insists that everyone call her "Alison," a familiarity that torments Duncan both in its intimacy and in his inability to exercise god-like control over names. He rebukes Grant's use of her name: "Alison! Alison! You had to use her name, I suppose; there seemed no alternative. But you need not reiterate it every time you open your mouth, One would think you had never heard a name before."[71]

Duncan is aware that if he cannot control access to language, his position as head of the household is weakened, which of course happens in Alison's affair with Grant and her ultimate escape with Almeric Bode, and he derides Alison for allowing her "Christian name" to be "bandied about."[72] Sunday breakfasts are as oppressive as ever, despite Alison's tardy arrivals and easy manners, and Duncan insists on attending church as a way of reigning in her behavior and limiting her speech, admonishing her in a "harsh whisper, 'this is not the time for folly,'" and, in the face of her defiance, demanding, "Will you exhibit your wit at your own expense?"[73] Alison is the only one in the novel to exhibit her wit at her own expense; she cares little about the village gossip, or indeed her own child, as she risks her future well-being by abandoning the baby and running off with a relatively poor young man. While the advantages of throwing off the yoke of Duncan's oppression are many, the reality faced by a woman with a past like Alison's is bleak should events change and her "rescuer" grow tired of her. Several characters admire Alison, despite the fact that her behavior has caused gossip in the village. Aware of her misery and the precariousness of her new situation, the sympathy of some in the household is with her because they know full well that in the interest of maintaining patriarchal power, society will side with Duncan; "Your father has the power; the helpless person has the pity; and it is a poor substitute."[74]

The remainder of the melodramatic plot unfolds inevitably as Duncan's lust for power and "fear for the fame of his house" produce violence and pain.[75] The plot twists and crimes can be traced back to Duncan's towering ego as the first cause in this dark domestic universe. Nance comments, "He behaved like a god, and we simply treated him as one. It shows what it is never to have any criticism. Gods contrive to have nothing but praise; they definitely arrange it."[76] The personalities and behavior of every member of the household has been molded by Duncan's abuse of power, so there is little hope of things changing in the end. As Alison Light has noted about Compton-Burnett's families, "The taste for cruelty and the need to submit are necessarily tied up with the economic inequalities of the family."[77] No one is ready to risk their material being, so the transgressions of Grant and Sibyl are overlooked when Sibyl's inheritance and their marriage assure the estate's survival within the family. With grotesque clarity and calm, the characters discuss their motives and actions, aware that they "can get used to anything" and that Sibyl's lack of "a normal moral sense" is the result of "a life in which succession had loomed too large."[78] Of course, this is the case for all of the characters, and when there is the mention of shame attached to welcoming her back with her new fortune, despite her commission of murder, the practical, skeptical Parson Jekyll, who is now Nance's new husband, concedes, "it is natural to find a thing easier when we have compensation."[79] Nearly every character is implicated in the corruption that keeps the estate and the family together, and all are blighted by the greed, hypocrisy, and injustice of the family power structure by which they are defined and against which they attempt to protect themselves with only momentary victories. At the end of the novel, Duncan is still in power, and the young people find themselves united in the schoolroom, where the "old alliance in the face of Duncan's oppression rose between them" and the relationships continue much as they were in the beginning.[80]

The closing pages bristle with grim irony. The characters seemingly are aware of their participation in the structure that keeps Duncan in power, but they remain powerless—unable or unwilling—to do anything about it. The ambiguity of personal values and the lack of any unifying "normal moral sense," effectively bar them from enacting traditional ideals of "moral action," and the best defense against Duncan's oppression and the demands of competing loyalties and affiliations is a darkly humorous attitude.

Unlike earlier writers of social satire, such as Austen and Wilde, to whom she is frequently compared, Compton-Burnett offers no suggestion of an alternative way of ordering the world. Her humor is the dark humor of survival and has more in common with the early comedies of Waugh and Powell and with the drama of Beckett and Pinter—playwrights she particularly enjoyed—than with those who had come before her.[81] The stasis in her novels is a characteristic of her dark comedic vision, for her humor is not about the triumph of good but

about the "triumph of narcissism";[82] it is about carrying on in defiance
of those forces that threaten to overwhelm the individual and in spite of
the fact that carrying on may be the only victory. As Nance observes
about her mother's death, "We were fond enough of her, to want her to
have her life, even though it had to be lived with Father. It shows what
we think of life."[83] Compton-Burnett's resigned, distanced, and grimly
humorous fiction speaks directly to the changes in British cultural life
after World War I and unflinchingly confronts the fractured ideals of the
domestic family life, responsible uses of authority and power, and
religious morality. She does this not with the optimism of the reformer
but with the gallows humor of the condemned.

CHAPTER 4

THE TOO, TOO BOGUS WORLD: EVELYN WAUGH'S *VILE BODIES*

> "If I wasn't real," Alice said—half laughing through her tears, it all seemed so ridiculous—"I shouldn't be able to cry."
> "I hope you don't suppose those are *real* tears?" Tweedledum interrupted in a tone of great contempt.
>
> Lewis Carroll

The sense of stasis that pervades the enclosed domestic world in Ivy Compton-Burnett's *A House and Its Head* permeates all of society in Evelyn Waugh's *Vile Bodies*. As discussed in chapter 3, Compton-Burnett's novel offers only the victory available from hanging on, and the comedy is, as Alison Light has noted, "busy running fast in order to stand still,"[1] In Waugh the sense of busily going nowhere is a collective cultural condition, and he prefaces the novel with a quotation from *Through the Looking Glass*, which sets the tone of breathless futility: "It takes all the running you can do, to keep in the same place." Waugh felt that the effect of the novel rests on its "cumulative futility,"[2] and most of the novel's dark humor arises from the frenetic but meaningless activity of all the characters—from the prime minister to the feckless protagonist, Adam Fenwick-Symes—which preempts any chance of emotional release and prohibits opportunities for either tragic romances or heroic individualism. Waugh's novel, like Carroll's Alice books, "convey the feelings of living on the verge of hysteria and being in a dream or game whose form is constantly changing."[3]

Published in 1929, *Vile Bodies* engages most of the concerns, both narratively and thematically, explored in Modernist texts, and many have referred to the work as an experimental novel.[4] In the novel's evocation of the modern wasteland, its concern with the instability of individual identity, its use of montage, collage, and disjointed narrative, it has many similarities with the work of Eliot, Woolf, and Joyce; yet,

Waugh's riotous social satire and his refusal to examine the interior life of his characters have generally kept the novel from being included in discussions of literary Modernism.

Labeled a moralist and a satirist, Waugh has traditionally been read as a conservative novelist, and as such he has not generally been viewed as sharing the aims of Modernist writers. Even Waugh's darkly humorous view of the world has been judged as not quite dark enough, and scholars of black humor, such as D.J. Dooley and Max Schulz, have argued that Waugh's humor cannot be considered black humor because they read him as possessing a belief in a true and stable ordering of reality that is used to critique false orderings. Schulz suggests that for Waugh the "traditionalism identified with English country houses is the true ordering."[5] This view clearly overlooks the deeply ambivalent nature of Waugh's early fiction, as does the more commonly held notion of Waugh as a "Catholic" novelist, censoriously attacking Western culture for its deviation from Christian values.

Despite Waugh's later conversion to Catholicism, his early novels offer nothing salutary in their stinging satire, and religious values are represented as devoid of any real meaning as is every other societal value. Waugh's dark satire presents an absurdist world that makes ridiculous all authority, all doctrine, including the traditional Christian variety. It seems misguided to read the early novels through the lens of his later conversion; though Waugh does satirize the decadence of the modern world, he does not necessarily do so to the advantage of previous generations or alternative orderings of society, and in the early satires he suggests that Christianity, with its complicity in the transgressions of Western culture, has become as bankrupt as the societal, political, and familial institutions to which it has been historically linked. Christian virtues—Faith, Chastity, Fortitude, Humility, Prudence, and so on— exist only as showgirls and prostitutes in Mrs. Ape's traveling revival show who have no understanding at all of the qualities they are supposed to represent. The religious characters themselves, Mrs. Ape and Father Rothschild, are opportunistic and morally questionable, and though both have moments of insight, so too do the Bright Young Things, Agatha Runcible and Adam Fenwick-Symes, and the erstwhile illustrious scion of an ancient aristocratic family, now gossip columnist, Simon Balcairn. In *Vile Bodies* once vital religious ideals are as degraded as once meaningful aristocratic traditions, and neither offer any alternative to the "radical instability"[6] and moral decay that characterize the modern world of the novel. Though Waugh's later, "Catholic" novels will suggest that there are real religious values that transcend the material world's corruption of them and that God can and does work through even the most flawed and unlikely individuals, there is no evidence of this kind of faith in his darkly funny satires. With the disorientation and alienation that are the effects of the dizzying pace of modern life, stable religious values—if they exist—are unknowable, unavailable, and therefore, unhelpful, to all.

Instead, Waugh, like the other writers examined in this study, presents a modern world where traditional cultural systems and values no longer obtain and are shown to be meaningless and absurd. In *Vile Bodies* the modern world is synthetic and mechanized, and individuals are stripped of a useful cultural past, overwhelmed by chaotic and ceaseless change, and trapped in the frantic pursuit of meaningful experience in a culture where everything from individual identity and personal relationships to societal institutions and religious faith have become sham and "too bogus."[7] Caught in a cycle of infernal repetition, Waugh's characters, compelled by forces beyond their control to inhabit a series of improvised roles, exhaust themselves in the effort to stand still and are bewildered by the sense of social and personal dissolution. This potentially tragic situation, however, is never presented as such by the narrator. There are no lessons to be learned from the senseless deaths of Flossie, Simon Balcairn, or Agatha Runcible; rather, they and the other characters are presented by the narrator as the butts of a cosmically bad joke.

Waugh offers nothing comforting in his satire, and his raucous humor in the face of futility and despair left several reviewers nonplussed in their reaction to the novel when it first appeared. Rebecca West commented that "*Vile Bodies*, has, indeed, apart from its success in being really funny, a very considerable value as a further stage in the contemporary literature of disillusionment."[8] Unlike West, Richard Aldington seemed singularly annoyed with the making of comedy out of tragedy: "Personally, I see nothing to roar about in a book which seems to be based on complete despair. Of course, Mr. Waugh, is very high-spirited and amusing...but I cannot find his discouragement infectious."[9] And another contemporary of Waugh's, L.P. Hartley, managed the disjunction between form and content in the novel by assuming a similar disjunction within the character of Waugh himself: "Let us believe that Mr. Waugh's natural impulse to gaiety is as important as his intellectual conviction (if he holds it) that his gaiety is ill-founded."[10]

What is important in these early observations of *Vile Bodies* is the obvious ambivalence with which these readers respond to the work, and rather than feeling as though Waugh is attempting to correct the waywardness of modern society, these reviewers focus on the overwhelming sense of despair that haunts the novel, despite its humor. Aldington's remarks are especially interesting with his deft substitution of the word "discouragement" for the more expected word, "laughter," in a sentence describing Waugh's jocularity. Hartley's comments, too, with his apparent need to distinguish between Waugh's inclination to gaiety and his attitude toward gaiety, point to the disparity between form and content that is at the heart of dark comedy and suggest that Waugh's humorous approach to despair is every bit as important as the despair itself represented in the novel. These early comments reveal responses from readers that involve both humor and horror—they recognize humor because of a certain identification with the narrator's ironic presentation of tragic events and they feel horror because there is no apparent meaning attached to the hopelessness and suffering.

One thing readers do not feel is the comfort of a moral critique that presumes there is an alternative to the pain and chaos. Katharyn Crabbe has noted that some critics are reluctant to describe Waugh's work as satire because "it very often seems not to be interested in setting things right."[11] The uncertainty and ambivalence and a lack of forward movement are precisely what makes Waugh's satires so darkly humorous and so particularly modern, for the comfort of a stable critique is denied to the reader. Terry Eagleton sees these qualities as weaknesses in Waugh's satires and has argued that Waugh's early novels "criticise [the] social environment without taking up an identifiable alternative standpoint," and given the fundamental uncertainties that are inherent in both the thematic and structural elements of Waugh's novels, they are unable to offer "genuine criticism" of society.[12] In Eagleton's view, nothing useful can be made of Waugh's satire: society's values are exposed as "fraudulent and hollow, but there is really nowhere else to turn."[13] However, this is precisely the point of dark humor. Given Waugh's ambivalence and capriciousness in the face of tragedy and chaos, there is little for readers to do but laugh in the face of it, for they are presented with no other option from the narrator in the novel.

Indeed, contrary to Alain Blayac's claim that the reader comes to share Waugh's moralizing posture and humorous critique,[14] I argue that the reader really only comes to share the author's darkly humorous stance. Though humor does "presuppose the reader's collaboration,"[15] in *Vile Bodies* just what is being critiqued is never quite certain, and, like all the other works in this study, the comedy in the novel has more in common with the dynamics of gallows humor than it does with the didactic paradigm associated with traditional satire. Blayac and others, who would see Waugh as a "genuine moralist and satirist, who draws on all the forms of humour to propound . . . the moral, religious, and philosophical principles which he advocates for the saving of the individual and society," argue that Waugh's grim humor is in the service of his principles and generally functions to save his critique from the "cheap moralism and mawkishness" that Waugh so deeply mistrusted.[16] However, this view becomes problematic when one examines the ambivalence inherent in *Vile Bodies*.

Throughout the novel, whenever Waugh appears to be making a moral critique by juxtaposing the instability and decay of the modern world with the stability and traditional values of a previous era, he inevitably subverts any nostalgic notion that previous eras were ordered better, or, if they were, that lost values can be recaptured: Lottie Crump's establishment, Shepheard's Hotel, is referred to as a place where one, "parched with modernity," can go and "still draw up, cool and uncontaminated, great healing draughts from the well of Edwardian certainty,"[17] but this certainty is a sham, for in reality Lottie's place is awash in chaotic activity, and she keeps up with the erratic pace of people and events by dispensing with names altogether. Even those with the most illustrious of titles are reduced to a nameless anonymity, as she refers to her boarders as Lord Thingummy, Mr. What-d'you-call him, Judge What's-your-name, and simply The Major.[18] Her behavior is entirely appropriate, for anonymity is the most prominent feature in a world where identity corresponds merely to appearance and people and events are unloosed from their traditional moorings. Lottie's guests include the former king of a country that no longer exists and someone she refers to as the prime minister, because he held that post only the week before; however, he is no longer in office and only the butler can recall the name of this week's prime minister.

Even Father Rothschild's insight into the younger generation's "fatal hunger for permanence" and "radical instability"[19] offers no stable critique and can only be seen as reportage. He makes these comments to the prime minister (the very one who was out of office while at Lottie Crump's), a member of the older generation, who is in office one week, out the next, and then back in again. Prime Minister Outrage suffers from the same instability and lack of commitment that the younger set does; he credits his success to his ability to know "exactly how little effort each job is worth."[20] Rothschild himself is forced to admit that "it's all very difficult," and his position as what some have claimed as the bearer of the novel's "moral standard"[21] is undercut by his occasional and mysterious donning of a false beard, a description that refers to him as "too clever by half,"[22] and his plotting behind the scenes of Prime Minister Outrage's government, the nature of which is intimated when he curiously disappears into the night on his motorcycle, "for he had many people to see and much business to transact before he went to bed."[23] As Eagleton has charged, if Father Rothschild points to a moral center, it is a "centre which is necessarily suggestive rather than realised, alluding to some privileged access to significant truths and inside information,"[24] and it affords no useful alternative to the modern mayhem.

Likewise, the world of tradition and taste usually associated with country house values cannot confidently be seen as offering a firm reproof of the vulgar and mechanized modern world either. As George McCartney has pointed out, in all of Waugh's novels he consistently ridicules characters who "try to go on living as though the Great War had never happened, as though the achievement of true happiness were only a matter of perpetuating the attitudes and values of the previous age."[25] Their world is as laughably bogus as that of the Bright Young Things. After the very party at which Father Rothschild has made his pronouncements about radical instability, Lord Metroland returns to his posh London home at the same time as his stepson, Peter Pastmaster, to find that his wife is upstairs with a young man-about-town, Alastair Trumpington. Lord Metroland wants to assure himself that he has built his life around secure and stable values, musing to himself, "What a lot of nonsense Rothschild had talked."[26] However, in a carefully crafted scene, Waugh reveals the bankruptcy at the core of traditional constructions of value by focusing on the trappings and products of British cultural tradition:

> His stepson did not once look at him, but made straight for the stairs, walking unsteadily, his hat on the back of head, his umbrella still in his hand.
>
> "Good night, Peter," said Lord Metroland.
>
> "Oh, go to hell," said his stepson thickly, then, turning on the stairs, he added, "I'm going abroad tomorrow for a few weeks. Will you tell my mother?"
>
> "Have a good time," said Lord Metroland. "You'll find it just as cold everywhere, I'm afraid. Would you care to take the yacht? No one's using it."
>
> "Oh, go to hell."
>
> Lord Metroland went into the study to finish his cigar. It would be awkward if he met young Trumpington on the stairs. He sat in a very comfortable chair...A radical instability, Rothschild had said, radical instability...He looked round his study and saw shelves of books—the *Dictionary of National Biography*, the *Encyclopædia Britannica* in an early

and very bulky edition, *Who's Who*, Debrett, Burke, Whitaker, several volumes of Hansard, some Blue Books and Atlases—a safe in the corner painted green with a brass handle, his writing-table, his secretary's table, some very comfortable chairs and some very business-like chairs, a tray of decanters and a plate of sandwiches, his evening mail laid out on the table... radical instability, indeed. How like poor Outrage to let himself be taken in by that charlatan of a Jesuit.

He heard the front door open and shut behind Alastair Trumpington.

Then he rose and went quietly upstairs, leaving his cigar smouldering in the ash-tray, filling the study with fragrant smoke.[27]

Lord Metroland symbolizes the history and tradition of British cultural values, and he tries to convince himself that he is at the center of a coherent and manageable world. Waugh's careful enumeration of the objects and publications in Metroland's study subvert the nostalgic notion that these values allow for any control in the flux of the modern world. Though the reference books and publications of parliamentary proceedings, directories of peers, and maps of the world speak of an existence that is ordered by firm categories and comforting notions of stability, the hostility of his stepson and the presence of young Trumpington upstairs with his wife suggest that stability is as ephemeral as the cigar smoke that permeates the study. Metroland unconsciously speaks the truth when he tells his stepson, "it is cold everywhere"; not even his study, despite its reassuring ambiance, is warm and safe.

Undermining the usefulness of religion and tradition, Waugh never advocates any principles that would save the individual or society, and, as McCartney has rightly noted, "There is nothing to be done but gracefully [I would add humorously] report the futility of human existence in the twentieth century."[28] This state of affairs does not negate the idea of collaboration between the narrator and the reader, though it is no longer the collaboration of traditional satire. In dark humor the reader and the narrator are both in on the joke and collude in their defensive laughter in the face of futility and chaos and not in their moral judgment of the characters.

In *Vile Bodies*, the narrator and the reader share the same humorous response to the activities of the characters in the novel, for, unlike the works of Woolf, Compton-Burnett, and Powell, the characters in Waugh do not generally participate in the humor. Critical of solipsism and all social authority, Waugh's implied narrator acts as the joker, but, as Polhemus explains in his discussion of Thackeray's comedy, "the assumptions of authority—even narrative authority—need to be ridiculed and broken down."[29] Waugh's implied narrator is not exactly reliable, and, though he is always a distanced observer, his loyalties and sympathies shift; he doesn't mock with a stable set of values, and the only constant is that he is willing to make everything and everybody the butt of his joke. The implied narrator will allude to something and quickly move on—one jump ahead of despair—his comments a mix of transcendent knowing, caustic observation, and nostalgia born of his own participation in the social world he mocks. If the novel presents the world as an absurd game, then the narrator is a participant, not an objective player external to it. In his presentation of a disordered world, Waugh exposes the idea of order itself as illusion. If his humor seems outraged, it may be because of his "anger at the earlier efficacy of the illusion," as Barreca described similar rage in the fiction of Elizabeth Bowen.[30] The inadequacy of existence is clear, but one has no choice but to laugh at the horrors of living.

Laughter is the only defense available to the reader of Waugh's fiction because there is a certain identification with the characters and their desperate and futile search for meaning, despite their one dimensionality. This is why so many reviewers and readers comment on the feeling of despair—despite the comedy—that is at the heart of the novel rather than a feeling of censoriousness; however, as Freud describes in his discussion of gallows humor, the reader is able to protect himself from despair because the expected emotional responses to horrific circumstances, such as death, loss of personal identity, war on a massive scale, are not produced by the characters or the narrator.

Waugh's implied narrator remains unflappably aloof from the fast moving, chaotic activities he reports and, with the same detached, ironic distance, recounts the ordinary and the alarming—the collapse of governments, violent deaths, and world war are caught up in the same breathless whirl as are costume parties, frustrated courtships, and bets on horse races. There are moments in which the characters in the novel evince awareness of their terrifying circumstances, such as when Agatha Runcible learns that Simon Balcairn killed himself (by putting his head in an oven) and comments, "How people are disappearing," and then relates her dream of "driving round and round in a motor race," unable to stop, while the audience shouts at them to go faster until eventually all the cars crash, or when Adam repines to his on-again-off-again fiancé, Nina, that "things simply can't go on much longer," and he would "give anything in the world for something different."[31] However these moments are never allowed to last for very long, and the characters are never presented with any alternative to their existential angst. For the most part, they are doomed to keep up the pace of their hectic but empty lives and to be battered about by forces beyond their control, never uttering anything as forceful as a protest, while the narrator reports on their various tragedies from an amused distance.

The distance of the narrator and the one dimensionality of the characters are important characteristics of dark humor. In order for shocking events to remain comic, they cannot arouse too much sympathy in the reader, and this is achieved by presenting characters who cannot be known in any depth, whose fears, longings, and desires of the heart remain unexplored and unrevealed. In *Vile Bodies* Waugh gives us a hero, if the word can be attributed to a character so insubstantial, who reacts to any circumstance that comes his way, from his loss of 1000 pounds (and therefore his fiancé) to finding himself on the "biggest battlefield in the history of the world,"[32] with the same distracted response. The reader is able to laugh at the various circumstances the characters find themselves in because the characters themselves seem to see little that is dire in their circumstances. When Waugh first introduces Adam, he describes him as a sort of modern everyman, who, possessed of no past, a continually shifting present, and a very uncertain future, is so anonymous that it is really impossible to say anything unique about him: "There was nothing particularly remarkable about his appearance. He looked exactly as young men like him do look."[33] Standing on the deck of a boat as it returns from France, Adam is literally and figuratively at sea, queasy after a rather difficult Channel crossing, which is indicative of the general sense of existential nausea and despair engendered by modern society: it's all " 'Too, too sick-making,' said Agatha Runcible, with one of her rare flashes of accuracy."[34] As Adam enters England, the customs officer menacingly searches his belongings and unceremoniously strips him of the autobiography he has spent the last year writing, the money from which he was planning to use to marry Nina. He is also relieved of his copy of Dante's *Purgatorio*, for both books are considered to be decidedly subversive by the uniformed representative of monolithic and bureaucratic modern government. Curiously, Adam had been writing an autobiography rather than a novel, a somewhat audacious project for someone still in his twenties who hasn't really done anything, yet it suggests that Adam's claim to individuality is disallowed, and, in the burning of both his memoirs and his Dante, Waugh is satirizing the dehumanization of the individual in a modern *Inferno*, where there is no guide nor help to find the way out. As the Major utters to Adam at the end of the book, when he is back in France but this time in the wasteland of the battlefield, "Damned difficult country to find one's way about in. No landmarks...."[35] English society is as damned difficult as a French battlefield, and, upon his reentry into his homeland, Adam is effectively denied any personal or cultural history, as well as a future, since without money he cannot marry Nina.

Though Adam's "whole livelihood"[36] depends on his book, he offers little resistance when it is taken away from him. Most of Waugh's characters are hapless and helpless in the face of circumstances, left to drift aimlessly through the world without any hope of recourse to an effective social order. In the through-the-looking-glass world of the novel there is no longer any meaning attached to events, and the laws of cause and effect no longer seem to be in play; therefore, appeals to justice would be futile, and there are only appearances to contend with. Agatha Runcible, who has just been subjected to a "too, too shaming" strip search, is as unaffected by her experience as Adam is by his (though her ordeal will eventually, and out of all proportion, bring down the government) and urges, "Adam, angel, don't fuss or we shall miss the train," deciding instead to discuss the "lovely party that was going to happen that night."[37] Waugh's refusal to allow his characters any effective protest to the dehumanizing experience of modern life and his insistence that they respond trivially to threats against their emotional, psychological, and physical well-being has led Eagleton to argue that Waugh creates what is essentially a "morality of style," which ends up endorsing the very social system that abuses its members. As a result the characters, and indeed Waugh himself, are unable to belong to their own experience.[38] However, in dark humor, not belonging to your own experience is an important defensive gesture because it allows for the individual to retain a hold on his "customary self" and disregard what might overthrow that self and drive it to despair.[39] Eagleton is correct in his assessment, though, for dark humor is very much a "morality of style," in the sense that the making of a joke becomes the important action and not the correction of societal ills. What could evince more "style" than to make a joke in the face of absolute despair? Protest does not change the situation, so one may as well pour oneself a martini or request a scarf on the way to one's hanging. The world of *Vile Bodies* is characterized by such utter hopelessness that complaints would be beside the point. The narrator offers no remedies other than laughter because in a world lacking order and meaning, there is really no protest to be made.

Thus, Waugh presents us with characters that retain such "customary" reactions to the most absurd events that they appear almost blank in their lack of response, but their inability to adequately respond to their circumstances juxtaposed with the well-chosen comments of a narrator who seems more interested in a witty turn of phrase than with the minds of the characters accounts for much humor in the novel. If the characters were to belong to their experiences in the way Eagleton has suggested, there would be little opportunity for humor, as the reader would empathize too strongly with them and find their experiences painful rather than humorous. In addition, the humorous stylishness of the narrator structurally adumbrates Waugh's preoccupation with the utter hopelessness of existence in the modern world—there are no remedies or protests to be made, and the only recourses are a humorous stance and a well-crafted joke.

The almost mechanical behavior on the part of the characters also suggests a dark interpretation of Bergson's theory of the "mechanical encrusted on the living" for the source of the humor, as well as Freud's theory of gallows humor. The matter-of-factness with which Adam tells Nina that their wedding is off and the casual way in which she takes the news are typical of the kind of responses presented by Waugh. After an unemotional conversation about plans for dinner and a party that night, Adam offers:

> "Oh, I say. Nina there's one thing—I don't think I shall be able to marry you after all."
> "Oh, *Adam*, you are a bore. Why not?"
> "They burnt my book."
> "Beasts. Who did?"
> "I'll tell you about it tonight."
> "Yes, *do*. Good-bye, darling."
> "Good-bye, my sweet."[40]

Waugh's characters have little to say about the emotional consequences of their experiences, no matter how painful or disturbing, and rigidly maintain a comedic flexibility that allows them to adapt to whatever comes their way, almost to the point of total erasure of their identities. The result is a relentless shallowness—which is inevitable in the bogus modern world—that eliminates any possibility of true romance or heroic action and deals only with appearances, which are determined merely by saying they are so.

For example, when Adam and Nina do meet at the party, she is surprised by Adam's appearance: "I had quite made up my mind that your hair was dark."[41] When he asks if she is disappointed, one believes him to be referring to their inability to get married; however Nina responds, "Well no, but it's rather disconcerting getting engaged to someone with dark hair and finding it's fair."[42] Quite making up one's mind about someone substitutes for actual facts, and Adam, who presumably never was dark-haired, has to remind her that they aren't engaged anymore because he has no money, but he is unfazed at his beloved's misremembrance of his looks. Nina's inability to recognize Adam because she never apparently noticed what he looked like in the first place is not only a stinging comment on the kind of tragic love story befitting the modern world but also foreshadows Adam's experiences throughout the remainder of the novel. Bereft of personal or cultural moorings and forced to inhabit a series of roles determined by people who insist he is someone other than he is, though, of course, who he is is never stable, Adam hurriedly becomes one thing and then the next, performing the roles of writer, gossip columnist, Nina's husband, though she is married to someone else at the time, and, finally, war hero. This final performance is the work of his friend Van, who has "a divine job making up all the war news." Nina informs Adam that Van "invented a lovely story about you the other day, how you'd saved hundreds of people's lives, and there's what they call a popular agitation saying why haven't you got the V.C., so probably you will have one by now."[43] Van decided that Adam will be a war hero, just as Nina decided that he was her dark-haired lover; neither correspond to anything that Adam is or has done, but he will play both roles, as is expected of him, even if it means impersonating Nina's real husband for a weekend or costs him his life on the battlefield. Waugh's comedy of shifting identities mocks any notion of free will or self-determination and indicts a social world that reduces human behavior to mechanized performance.

In Waugh the modernist concerns over fractured identity and the "immense panorama of futility and anarchy which is contemporary history"[44] are refused their traditional gravity by a narrator who acknowledges the tragic circumstances of contemporary life but refuses to sink under the weight of them, though the characters sometimes do. His carefully crafted satire strikes the perfect pitch between tradition and innovation, evoking the major Modernist themes of social and personal dissolution without capitulating to it in his fictions. Waugh took great care to investigate the diminishment of the individual through an external approach, and throughout *Vile Bodies*, despite its obvious use of Modernist narrative techniques, he refuses to investigate modern society's threat to individual identity through what he considered the expressive fallacy of interior monologue and intense subjectivity.[45] Instead, Waugh engages Modernist experiment in just the kind of ambivalent way one would expect; he utilizes it in the form of disjointed narrative, collage, and cinematic montage to capture the riotous energy of a thoroughly indecorous age, and he parodies it as the desperate grasping after novelty that merely distracts victims of modernity from what he sees as the emptiness of modern art and culture. Essentially, Waugh draws on the strategies of modern art in order to make modernity and its devaluation of the individual the object of his joke.

One of the most important instances of Waugh's parodic modernity occurs when Adam, Agatha Runcible, Miles Malpractice, and Archie Schwert—"the *most* bogus man"—go to the motor races.[46] From the outset confusion reigns, as the Bright Young Things, rootless victims of modern flux, search for something to occupy their time. The entire party is inebriated almost from the beginning, and gender roles are confused, as Agatha is wearing trousers, and Miles gets the party thrown out of a hotel dining room because he touches up his eyelashes in public. They travel "miles in the wrong direction down a limitless bye-pass road," and not surprisingly, there is no place for them in the various hotels that symbolically take them through the British class system of "Old Established Family and Commercial, plain Commercial, High Class Board and Residence pension terms, Working Girls' Hostel, plain Pub. and Clean Beds: Gentlemen only."[47] They eventually find beds in a dreary inn, where they "were bitten by bugs all that night," which Miss Runcible had to kill with drops of face lotion.[48] Throughout the episode of the motor race, most modern philosophies, ideologies, and "isms" are ridiculed, and, in the description of the contents in Adam's revolting room at the inn, the narrator takes a swipe at modern psychology:

> There was also a rotund female bust covered in shiny red material, and chopped off short, as in primitive martyrdoms, at neck, waist and elbows; a thing known as a dressmaker's "dummy" (there had been one of these in Adam's home which they used to call "Jemima"—one day he stabbed "Jemima" with a chisel and scattered stuffing over the nursery floor and was punished. A more enlightened age would have seen a complex in this action and worried accordingly. Anyway he was made to sweep up all the stuffing himself).[49]

Like most of the narrator's parenthetical comments, this aside does nothing to further the action; however, it affords an opportunity to make a rather elaborate joke about Modernism's preoccupation with dark psychosexual motivations.

The motor race episode reveals Waugh's belief that modernity and its increasing mechanization and worship of the machine diminishes the individual in its perpetual quest for the new. In the age of the machine, people become as anonymous and expendable as car parts, and, in the flux of constant change, relativity replaces identity, so individuals can no longer make firm judgments about their experiences in the world or their place in it. From the overheard snippets of truncated conversations to the chaotic roaring of the engines as the Speed Kings prepare their cars for the race, the environment around the automobile garages, symbolic of the technology-enamored modern world, "shook with fruitless exertion."[50] In order to drive his point home, the narrator makes one of the most famous interruptions of the novel to expound upon the relationship between the drivers of cars and the cars themselves and the metaphysical implications of losing one's identity in the constant flux of "becoming":

> The truth is that motor cars offer a very happy illustration of the metaphysical distinction between "being" and "becoming." Some cars, mere vehicles with no purpose above bare locomotion, mechanical drudges such as Lady Metroland's Hispano-Suiza, or Mrs. Mouse's Rolls Royce, or Lady Circumference's 1912 Daimler, or the "general reader's" Austin Seven, these have definite "being" just as much as their occupants. They are bought all screwed up and numbered and painted, and there they stay through various declensions of ownership, brightened now and then with a lick of paint or temporarily rejuvenated by the addition of some minor organ, but still maintaining their essential identity to the scrap heap.
>
> Not so the *real* cars, that become masters of men; those vital creations of metal who exist solely for their own propulsion through space, for whom their drivers, clinging, precariously at the steering wheel, are as important as his stenographer to a stock-broker. These are in perpetual flux; a vortex of combing and disintegrating units; like the confluence of traffic at some spot where many roads meet, streams of mechanism come together, mingle and separate again.[51]

Many scholars have examined this passage with regard to Waugh's critique of Bergsonian Flux and Italian Futurism's deification of speed and the machine, and, clearly, Waugh uses this interpolation to parody the philosophical fascination during the decades of the 1920s and 1930s with ideas of relativity and technology, both of which he was deeply suspicious.[52] Unlike Modernists such as Woolf and Joyce, who shared a certain ambivalence toward the increasing technology of the age but who embraced ideas of flux and relativity, Waugh viewed the two ideas as related and saw in both the attenuation of individual autonomy and the lessening of the individual's ability to understand the world around him and to make choices. In the state of perpetual flux, everything is always "becoming" but never being itself, and technology aids this metaphysical confusion in the rapid pace of its advancement, which tends to outstrip human beings' mental, physical, and emotional ability to keep up with it. Waugh refuses to reproduce the flux of experience in his fiction, though he takes it as his subject, and there remains a humorous sense of control over the chaos of becoming, which the reader shares. Indeed, the "general reader," owner of one of the cars of being that the narrator privileges in the section, is decidedly in on the joke and can comfortably laugh at the chaos so elegantly presented by the narrator. It is no surprise that in the endless whirl of parties the most fashionable sort of invitation is the one adapted from the designs of *Blast* and Marinetti's *Futurist Manifesto*. Waugh informs the reader in a footnote:

> Perhaps it should be explained—there were at this time three sorts of formal invitation card: there was the nice sensible copy-book hand sort with a name and At Home and a date and a time and address; then there was the sort that came from Chelsea, Noel and Audrey are having a little whoopee on Saturday evening: do please come and bring a bottle too, if you can; and finally there was the sort that Johnnie Hoop used to adapt from Blast and Marinetti's Futurist Manifesto. These had two columns of close print; in one was a list of all the things Johnnie hated, and in the other all the things he thought he liked. Most parties which Miss Mouse financed had invitations written by Johnnie Hoop [33]

Of course, the fashionable "futurist" invitation leaves out any real information, such as the time, date, and place of the party, and Johnnie doesn't really *know* what he likes, he only *thinks* he knows.

In *Vile Bodies*, Waugh exposes the sickening side of the exhausting pursuit of the new, and none of the experiences involving new technology or faster modes of transportation produces a Marinettian sense of exhilaration but rather a debilitating sense of nausea. On the steamship over from France, every passenger is seasick, sporting complexions like "eau de Nil," and the party on the captive dirigible leaves everyone feeling queasy and bored. Though "it was the first time a party was given on an airship," the novelty is fleeting: "Inside the saloons were narrow and hot, communicating to each other by spiral staircases and metal alleys. There were protrusions at every corner, and Miss Runcible had made herself a mass of bruises in the first half hour... There were two people making love to each other... There was also a young woman he did not know holding one of the stays and breathing heavily; evidently she felt unwell."[54] When Nina takes her first ride in an aeroplane, her companion waxes poetic at the vastness of the landscape, quoting scraps of half-remembered Shakespeare: "This scepter'd isle, this earth of majesty, this something or other Eden": however, when Nina looks down her experience is altogether of another sort:

> Nina looked down and saw inclined at an odd angle a horizon of straggling red suburb; arterial roads dotted with little cars; factories, some of them working, others empty and decaying; a disused canal; some distant hills sown with bungalows; wireless masts and overhead power cables; men and women were indiscernible except as tiny spots; they were marrying and shopping and making money and having children. The scene lurched and tilted again as the aeroplane struck a current of air. "I think I'm going to be sick," said Nina.[55]

Technology does nothing to aid the progress of human history, and instead devastates the English countryside and contributes to the devolution of the human species, reducing them to the level of insects and robbing them of any individuality.

At the motor race, symbolic of what can arguably be considered one of the most meaningless uses of automotive technology, the Speed Kings compete for a trophy, "a silver gilt figure of odious design, symbolizing Fame embracing Speed."[56] Here, technology is dedicated to speed, but the cars only go round in circles, and the spectators are in thrall of the mysteries of machinery and velocity. As the narrator informs us, this is "no Derby day holiday making," perhaps alluding to William P. Firth's famous painting, which in a typical example of Victorian order presented carefully drawn figures from various walks of life enjoying the communal event in diverse but appropriate ways. At the modern race, the spectators "had not snatched a day from the office to squander it among gypsies and roundabouts and thimble-and-pea men. They were there for the race."[57] Though Waugh was no champion of Victorian culture, the modern, chaotic celebration of flux, in which the winners are those who most successfully embrace the relativity of speed and "becoming" at the expense of meaningful human interaction and any sense of identity, can have disastrous consequences for the individual.

Agatha Runcible's demise is as directly related to the confusion of identity that troubles all the characters in the novel as it is to the large quantities of alcohol she has imbibed. In order to be allowed in the drivers' pits, Agatha is given an armband that identifies her as a "Spare Driver," and, she, like Adam, becomes what she is called. After their friend has been hit in the shoulder by a spanner thrown by the Italian speed demon, Marino, he is unable to finish the race. The allusion to Marinetti and his paean to snorting, throbbing automobiles is unmistakable: "It's murder the way that Marino drives...a real artist and no mistake about it."[58] When the official appears in the pit and demands to know who is the spare driver, the following exchange ensues:

> "I'm spare driver," said Miss Runcible. "It's on my arm."
> "She's spare driver. Look, it's on her arm."
> "Well, do you want to scratch?"
> "Don't you scratch, Agatha."
> "No, I don't want to scratch."
> "All right. What's your name?"
> "Agatha. I'm the spare driver. It's on my arm."
> "I can see it is—all right, start off as soon as you like."
> "Agatha," repeated Miss Runcible firmly as she climbed into the car. "It's on my arm."[59]

When they later hear over the loudspeaker that Miss Runcible's car has driven off the course and was last seen "proceeding south on the bye-road, apparently out of control," no one seems particularly concerned. Lack of control is the one thing that can be expected from life in the twentieth century, and concern, like protest, is futile. By this time, everyone has come to see Agatha as a spare driver, a role in which accidents—by definition hazardous and unpredictable—are to be expected. After a good meal and more champagne, the rest of the party set out for the site where the car has been found wrecked against a large stone cross in the village market. A symbol of the past's religious belief stops her, but it is cold, unyielding, and deadly.

Agatha is found the next day, "staring fixedly at a model engine in the central hall at Euston Station. In answer to some gentle questions, she replied that to the best of her knowledge she had no name, pointing to the brassard on her arm, as if in confirmation. She had come in a motor car...which would not stop. It was full of bugs which she had tried to kill with drops of face lotion."[60] Caught up in the rapid change of the modern technological moment, Agatha has no defense against the overwhelming of her ego, as she and the rest of the characters are forced into performing various roles, with no recourse to anything stable, changing identities as frequently as the mechanics change car parts in the pits. Staring blankly at a model of the type of technology that has been her demise, she no longer even knows her name. As McCartney has noted, "Individuality is one the casualties of the dehumanizing speed of a technological society."[61] However, the humorous way Waugh presents her terrifying loss of identity and lack of control allows the reader to retain a feeling of both.

As Agatha lies in her hospital bed, she has a recurring nightmare in which she is driving round and round a race track while an enormous crowd of gossip columnists and gate-crashers shout at her to go faster and faster until she crashes. Agatha's dream is one of the darkest moments in the novel, though it is embedded in the midst of a very funny impromptu party in her hospital room. Speeding round and round a racetrack, like rushing from party to party, is a futile activity, all-consuming but, finally, going nowhere. In both its symbolism and its place in the novel, the dream comments on the futility of modern life with the uncomfortable realization that there is no escape except in death. Agatha dies in the midst of another hallucination, in which "There was rarely more than a quarter of a mile of the black road to be seen at one time. It unrolled like a length of cinema film. At the edges was confusion; a fog spinning past"; finally, the ambiguous words of a nurse are the last thing she hears: "There's nothing to worry about, dear. . . *nothing at all . . . nothing.*"[62]

As disconcerting as Agatha's death is—many scholars have referred to it as the central image in the novel[63]—her predicament is really no more tragic than anyone else's. All the characters are precariously poised on the brink of eternal nothingness and existential anonymity. Her deathbed scene abruptly follows Nina's nauseating aeroplane ride, and, in juxtaposing the filmlike quality of Agatha's final images with Nina's disorienting aerial experience of sprawling suburban blight and the reduction of human beings to indiscernible, tiny spots, Waugh emphasizes the difficulty—if not the impossibility—of retaining any sense of individuality or control in the flux and speed of modern life. Nina's vertiginous view of human activity, which has its own cinematic quality, frames the daily activities of people—"marrying and shopping and making money and having children"—in the most reductive and meaningless way. From her technologically superior vantage point, individuals have become indistinguishable and interchangeable, busily active, like so many ants, but viewed with enough speed and distance, indistinct and barely perceptible. The characters in the novel are almost as insubstantial as the people viewed from the aeroplane, and Waugh's point is not that they have diminished in worth, but they are dwarfed and degraded by the machine-like culture of the modern age.

The reference to the "length of cinema film" in Agatha's final hallucination and the unreal, filmic quality of Nina's view from the aeroplane, remind us of Waugh's fascination with the film medium, which, like most other products of modernity is used ambiguously in the work. Waugh appreciated the unique perspective of the camera's eye, and the capacity of a filmic approach to fiction to capture the fragmented and unreal quality of modern life, and yet he is scathing in his mockery of the confusion and disorientation that results from the bogus reality perpetuated in motion pictures. Throughout the novel, scenes and characters dissolve and are replaced by others, and the technique successfully depicts the hectic speed of modern culture. The two scenes just discussed effectively dissolve into each other, and the "nothing" of Agatha's death is immediately replaced by a new scene in the next chapter establishing the action back at Doubting Hall (referred to by all the servants as Doubting 'All), where Nina's father, Colonel Blount, has leased out his ancestral home to a film crew for the set of a historical film about the life of John Wesley.

The shooting of the film has been recounted earlier in the novel, hilariously described by the narrator as a nightmarish collapse of fact and fiction, with the identities of actors, historical figures, and landed gentry in an unsettling state of flux; Colonel Blount, a descendant of a land-owning family, begs to be allowed to play an extra stable hand, a role he wouldn't dream of inhabiting in "real" life. In the penultimate chapter, the film is finished, and the narrator informs us, in a curious blending of actors and real historical figures, that "everyone had gone away; Wesley and Whitehead, Bishop Philpotts and Miss La Touche, Mr. Issacs and all his pupils from the National Academy of Cinematographic Art."[64] The end result has a decidedly absurd quality to it, and like all machines or machine products in the novel, it ends up destroying all balance, proportion, and continuity with the past. The most telling characteristic of the film is the speed at which the film unfolds, which directly relates to the major themes of the novel:

> One of its peculiarities was that whenever the story reached a point of dramatic and significant action, the film seemed to get faster and faster. Villagers trotted to church as though galvanized; lovers shot in and out of windows; horses flashed past like motor cars; riots happened so quickly that they were hardly noticed. On the other hand, any scene of repose or inaction, a conversation in a garden between two clergymen, Mrs. Wesley at her prayers, Lady Huntingdon asleep, etc., seemed prolonged almost unendurably.[65]

The film version of Wesley's life parodies the modern infatuation with technology and speed and the resulting loss of stability and identity.

It holds up to ridicule the way we measure duration and equate time with meaning. "Historical consciousness," according to Polhemus, "particularly in modern times, has been a means by which people can appropriate racial and national experience to themselves and project themselves into a larger life."[66] Waugh mocks this idea of historical consciousness in the film, where activities and events become meaningless and individual characteristics become lost or blurred in the tumult of technological advancement.

Archie Loss argues that despite Waugh's ambivalent relationship to certain Modernist aesthetics, his concern for the individual is the most salient difference between Waugh's vision of the modern world and that of other "non-Bloomsbury" Modernists, such as Wyndham Lewis, whose work he admired but whose embracing of technology he suspected. Artists such as Lewis "are essentially idealists to whom individuals are far less important than the overriding principles they represent," and in promulgating their ideas they "make absurd overstatements and disregard important artistic and human subtleties."[67] In this respect, Waugh has more in common with high Modernists like Woolf and Joyce, though he disliked their style. As Loss and others have argued, in Waugh's view, the individual can never be subjugated to a "totalitarian ideal, political or aesthetic," and he approaches life from a more humane perspective: "Like all great satirists, he cannot resist seeing matters as they really are."[68]

Being lost in a senseless whirl of activity has become the general condition of society in *Vile Bodies*, and like other dark humor novels of the age, Waugh's comedy is the dark comedy of merely surviving. As Henri Bergson has argued, repeated activity uninformed with meaning is inherently funny because it is incongruous; it suggests a mechanical encrustation upon the organic.[69] Clearly, the comedy of *Vile Bodies* is the comedy of meaningless activity par excellence and takes as its joke the modern world that would turn individuals into machine parts. The senseless activity disallows any opportunity for meaningful experiences, as the characters are caught in a world of appearances and constantly shifting surfaces. However, unlike the characters, who are doomed to continually run in circles, the reader has the privileged position of viewing this busily useless activity from a distance. As Waugh's narrator guides us through the modern wasteland of London society, we are rarely brought to the position of judging the characters—their activities are merely an attempt to hang on in the face of a meaningless world. The humorous stance of the narrator allows for a feeling of control over the circumstances that is unavailable to the characters, even if that control is only as fleeting as laughter and darkly suggests the impossibility of altering the actual circumstances. Dark humor allows for a bit more than the black nihilism of merely muddling through; it allows for muddling through with a smile on your face.

Agatha Runcible and Simon Balcairn are just two of many characters in modern literature who die senseless deaths and who, afloat in a world that demands too many performances from them, sink from the exhaustion of trying to keep up; however, in the dark humor of Waugh's alternative Modernism, the reader is left with a certain sense of victory. Nothing in the plot warrants this response; Agatha dies, Nina marries the insipid Ginger Littlejohn, and Adam is lost among the rubble of a global conflagration the likes of which the world has never seen. There are no happy endings, in spite of the fact that the last chapter bears that title, but only the horrifying realities of loss and repetition. However, humor resists the anxieties and traumas that would threaten to swamp the ego, and it is the "highest of the defensive processes."[70] By making distressing circumstances the object of a joke, humor establishes its own kind of order in a disordered world. Waugh's originality does not lie in his denunciation of an insane society; it lies in his ability to make that insane society the object of his joke and therefore a source of pleasure, despite the unfailing conviction that nothing is going to change.

CHAPTER 5

ASTOLPHO MEETS SISYPHUS:
MELANCHOLY AND REPETITION IN
ANTHONY POWELL'S *AFTERNOON MEN*

If I laugh at any mortal thing, 'tis that I may not weep.

Byron

As Evelyn Waugh wryly noted in *A Handful of Dust*, "All over England people were waking up queasy and despondent."[1] It is precisely this combination of illness and melancholy that is captured in Anthony Powell's first novel, *Afternoon Men*. Both Waugh and Powell examine the social world of the disaffected, post–World War I generation; however, the tone with which they represent this world is radically different. Unlike the frenetic futility presented in *Vile Bodies*, *Afternoon Men* is marked by a crushing sense of despondency and dolor, and, rather than invoke the through-the-looking glass madness of *Alice in Wonderland*, Powell opens his novel with an epigraph from Robert Burton's *Anatomy of Melancholy*:

> . . . as if they had heard that enchanted horn of Astolpho, the English duke in Ariosto, which never sounded but all his auditors were mad, and for fear ready to make away with themselves . . . they are a company of giddy-heads, afternoon men . . .

However, melancholy is always close to comedy in Powell, and although the mania that distinguishes the world of *Afternoon Men* is not the riotous absurdity of *Vile Bodies*, the jaded weariness of his characters results in a grimly understated comedy. Cyril Connolly wrote that Anthony Powell's prewar novels deal "in nuances of boredom, seediness, and squalor [and] contain much of the purest comedy now being written."[2] Rather than present inept men of action, Powell gives us adept men of inaction and chooses to examine the period's "radical instability" and "hunger for permanence"[3] through the lens of the terminally bored. As Humphrey Carpenter has noted, *Afternoon Men* "sometimes seems like *Vile Bodies* with the camera moved to another position,"[4] for if the inebriated world of the Bright Young Things appeared the least bit glamorous in Waugh's novel, there is no such danger in Powell's work. History is a nightmare from which his characters try—unsuccessfully—to escape, and he portrays the social world of the younger set between the wars as monotonous and enervating. Dominated by a killing anomie, the characters are aware of the unfitness of things, but like all characters in dark humor novels, they are powerless to do anything about it; instead, they drift through their rootless lives battling the effects of bad food and drink and vague symptoms of infirmity, which function as outward signs of their disaffection and alienation.

The novel is haunted by the sense that contemporary life is moribund and diseased. The protagonist, William Atwater, is associated with a catalog of infirmities, ranging from headache and nausea to coma and poisoning, and refers to himself as a "dying man"[5] on a couple of occasions. From the opening lines of the novel the talk is of sickness:

> "When do you take it?" said Atwater.
> Pringle said: "You're supposed to take it after every meal, but I only take it after breakfast and dinner. I find that enough."[6]

The "it" refers to Pringle's medicine, discussions of which reappear in the novel at significant moments; however, the reader is never informed about the nature of Pringle's illness, though it seems to have something to do with his nerves. His suicide attempt later in the work suggests that he is one of the more damaged of the novel's characters, yet most of the characters suffer from a sense of affliction and ill-health: Nosworth is plagued with back spasms and is described as "rather diseased," Miller has varicose veins, Barlow shows up for tea having "just been sick in the mews" and is "always ill if [he] leaves London for short periods," Lola looks "inquisitive, but in low health," and Undershaft, the shadowy figure who appears to have escaped the vacuous social life of the afternoon men, is reported to be "palsied" upon his return from New York.[7]

Vaguely defined illness is an important metaphor throughout the novel, and the characters are cursed with an awareness of physical and cultural rot but withheld from the promise of anything as romantic or glamorous as violent death or apocalyptic world war. Echoing the melancholy of much late Modernist work, Powell's characters, like

T.S. Eliot's hollow men, are painfully aware that "Life is very long," and that things are more likely to end "Not with a bang but a whimper."[8] The dark humor in the novel turns on the tedium of the characters' lives and the disproportionate amount of time spent in inane conversations and in the doing of trivial tasks. These events, which neither produce real communication nor result in anything meaningful, are what mark the passage of time in a stagnant society, where the only movement is circular.

Powell's grimly humorous representation of the angst of living has a distinctly Modernist cast to it. The novel is frequently compared to Hemingway's *The Sun Also Rises*, and, in its themes and in its relentlessly superficial dialogue, which suggests more complicated depths, there are certain similarities. However, unlike Hemingway's Paris expatriates, Powell's lost generation of Londoners does not have recourse to hearty, satisfying meals and fortifying bottles of St-Emilion, which implies a certain vitality even in the face of the characters' disillusionment. In Powell's novel the food is uniformly bad and the drink worse, and, unlike Jake Barnes's salutary fishing trip in the country, Atwater's holiday in the country is disastrous and, despite Pringle's suicide attempt, as tedious as life in London. The denial of even trivial pleasures to the characters makes *Afternoon Men* a darker—and a darkly funnier—work than *The Sun Also Rises*. There are not even momentary sensual pleasures to be enjoyed; food, drink, and sex are merely things to be endured.

Powell's themes—alienation, disillusion, the inability to communicate or connect with others in any significant way—are presented by the Modernist techniques of montage, pared-down dialogue, and open ending. These techniques lend themselves to Powell's dark humor because his comedy of non sequitor, understatement, and anticlimax sets up the reader for one reaction to the depressing emptiness of the characters' lives but subverts those expectations by presenting a surprisingly unrelated or comically underplayed response from the characters within the novel or from the narrative text itself. Many of the chapters end in banality or farce, particularly chapters where something deep or meaningful has been hinted at, and, as a result, traumatic events and bleak futility are denied their traditional serious treatment. Powell's use of the techniques and themes of Modernism to create a comedy of melancholy allows the reader a defense against the impotence and repetition that characterize modern life in the novel. Feelings of ennui, boredom, and futility are often voiced in the literature of the interwar period, and Powell, with his coolly distanced comedic style, shows what it is like to suffer from these ailments at the same time he is amusing in his presentation of them, thereby rescuing the reader from the very condition plaguing the characters.

Freud has argued that we find things amusing when we are spared the anticipated response to traumatic situations when either the subject of the trauma or the joker "makes nothing of the situation."[9] Throughout *Afternoon Men*, Powell sets up carefully crafted social set pieces, many of which seem as if they will lead to a confrontation or a tragic situation; however, time and again these expectations are unfulfilled. The comic effect of Powell's understated humor arises from this very unfulfillment, and it is his representation of banality, triviality, and inaction that accounts for the novel's humor, for the characters repeatedly have inadequate or irrelevant responses to circumstances, diverting the reader's emotional expectations away from futility and melancholy into comedy. Freud has argued that inadequacy, when compared to "what ought to be effected" allows for meaninglessness and nonsense to become irresistibly comic.[10] To illustrate his point, Freud describes a joke:

> "What is it that hangs on the wall and that one can dry one's hands on?" It would be a stupid riddle if the answer were "a hand-towel." But that answer is rejected.—"No, a herring."—"But for heaven's sake," comes the protest, "a herring doesn't hang on the wall."—"You *can* hang it up there."—"But who in the world is going to dry his hands on a herring?"—"Well," is the soothing reply, "you don't *have* to."[11]

As Freud goes on to explain, the joker's explanation shows just how far the riddle falls short of a genuine joke, and "on account of its inadequacy it strikes us as being—instead of simply nonsensically stupid—irresistibly comic."[12] Throughout *Afternoon Men*, there are pages of inane conversation that generally end in the same sort of meaninglessness and non-sense as Freud's joke and which require a similar appreciation of the "meta-humor"—for the joke happens outside the text.[13] Conversations characterized by inadequacy, unfulfillment, and non-sense dominate the novel, and, in as much as modern life between the wars is characterized by these feelings, Powell's humor affords a useful psychological defense in the making of pleasure from these ostensibly frustrating and alienating exchanges.

Neil Brennan has argued that "the essence of Powell's meaning," in *Afternoon Men*, "is the apparent lack of meaning in life, or as rationally conceived, life's 'non-sense'."[14] Conversations frequently do not make "sense," and the conversations represent the society of which they are a part. For example, the boredom of inebriated party life is encapsulated in a brief exchange early in the novel, when Lola, a young woman Atwater has met at a party, spills her drink on his friend Pringle:

> The girl sat on the sofa next to Atwater. She said:
> "Is your friend angry?"
> "Yes."
> "I was looking for my bag."
> "Were you?"
> "It was suddenly knocked out my hand all over him."
> "He's very wet."
> "I expect he'll be able to dry himself somehow."
> "There must be some way."
> "Will you get me another drink," she said.
> "What?"
> "Anything."[15]

In a novel generally regarded as spare, it is somewhat surprising to find the lack of economy that is evinced in following the fatuous phrase, "I was looking for my bag," with the leaden line, "Were you?" However, in this and many other instances in the novel, Powell's purpose is to slow down the narrative, stretch out the emptiness, so that the torpid dialogue reveals the nature of the characters' lives. One would expect undistinguished talk like this to contain some subterranean meaning, to further the action, or reveal something as yet unknown about the characters; however, all of these expectations are left unfulfilled, and the inadequacy of the characters' responses becomes funny when we begin to realize just how short they fall from expected fictional conversations. Instead, boredom and apathy are the only qualities revealed, and it is in the illumination of those qualities that the importance and the humor of the conversation rests. For the small talk, seemingly a very pale imitation of real, meaningful communication, in fact manages to say everything about the lives of the characters.

The exchanges presented generally go nowhere and nothing momentous or profound happens in the novel: the characters go to parties, drink too much, and have casual sex; Atwater falls in love with Susan Nunnery but he only sees her a few times, none of which results in anything close to an intimate conversation; and Pringle attempts suicide but changes his mind. As Richard Vorhees has noted, "No other novelist has made party-going seem so dreary, and not even Aldous Huxley has made promiscuity seem so depressing."[16] Powell presents the facts of boredom and dissipation with a melancholy amusement, though he never openly condemns his characters or turns them into comic buffoons. Though he is concerned with the place of the individual in contemporary society and the possibility—or impossibility—of genuine feeling in a world that seems designed to thwart any attempt at meaningful communication, he examines these issues from a controlled distance. Like Ivy Compton-Burnett, Powell is neither cynical nor sentimental in the presentation of his characters or the disturbing situations they find themselves in; rather, he is a disinterested observer, attuned to life's absurdities and ambiguities and sustained by humor.

Powell's style is frequently defined by words such as distanced, detached, spare, classical, and as V.S. Pritchett stated, informed "by sense rather than outraged sensibility."[17] However, the "sense" in Pritchett's statement can only refer to Powell's controlled narrative style, for, as discussed earlier, Powell exploits the comedic possibilities of nonsense to examine the anxiety that lurks under the surface of postwar British life. Powell's humor—though understated—is aggressive, and it affords a defense against the disturbing feelings of alienation and powerlessness that prey on the characters. In a telling scene, Atwater is finally on a date with Susan Nunnery, but at the restaurant it is impossible to talk to her because drunken acquaintances continually join them at the table, drink their wine, prattle on about nothing, and flirt with Susan. As another inebriated fellow joins the table, Atwater responds,

> "Do you know everybody?" said Atwater. He hoped that lots more people would come and talk and drink and sit at the table and make assignations with Susan and give him good advice and argue with each other, because then it would become funny and he might feel less angry.[18]

Atwater's anger and impotence in the face of his frustrated desire to be alone with Susan is displaced into a conscious wish to find a distance from which he can find the situation humorous. Freud describes that in situations like this "the contributions of humor that we produce ourselves are as a rule made at the cost of anger instead of getting angry."[19] This is precisely the technique of the narrative itself; whenever characters are faced with potentially disturbing situations, Powell shifts the narrative to a distance where loneliness and futility can be regarded as funny and the trauma of pain and anger can be avoided.

The ennui and paralysis of interwar social life is captured in the amusing and exacting representation of some of the most boring conversations to be found in literature. Unlike the intensifiers used in the parlance of the party crowd in *Vile Bodies* (too, too shame making), the talk in *Afternoon Men* is so dull the characters hardly listen to each other, and the conversations proceed in non sequitors that reveal complete disinterest and inattention to what the speaker is saying and make clear to the reader the kinds of nonsense and absurdities that often characterize speech. Powell's characters are so bored they scarcely have anything to say, and yet their exchanges can run for pages, seemingly in slow motion, the inane and trivial subjects revealing the tediousness and conventionality of everyday life. For example, when Atwater calls on Lola at her flat, the anguishingly long exchange between him and Lola's roommate, Gwen Pound, is comedic in its vapidity, its repetition, and its length:

> "Is Lola in?"
> "She's out at the moment."
> "She'll be in soon, I suppose?"
> "Was she expecting you?"
> "Yes," said Atwater, "She rang me up."
> "Did she?"
> "Yes."
> "Come in," said Gwen Pound. "She'll be in soon." "Will you have a gasper?[20] I'm afraid there's nothing to drink."
> Atwater sat down. She said:
> "You haven't been here before, have you?"
> "No. Have you both lived here long?"
> "Nearly two years."
> She said: "I'm so sorry that we've got nothing here to give you to drink."
> "I don't want any drink, really."
> "We sometimes have drink here," she said. "But it seems to get drunk."
> "Oh yes, I know."
> "I always think it's so awful not to have a drink to offer people when they come in."
> "No, really."
> "Oh yes, I think it's awful."
> She said: "Lola will be in soon, I expect."
> Atwater said: "She should be in soon, because she told me to come about this time."
> "Did she ring you up?"
> "Yes she rang up."[21]

Capturing the awkwardness of a chance meeting between two people who don't particularly like each other, the exchange reveals Powell's unique approach to social satire. As Neil McEwan observes, Powell's slowed-down writing allows for the "wringing of comedy from very flat, commonplace talk, presented in painstaking completeness and without comment."[22] The unhurried pace allows for a comedic timing that adds to the amusement of the artless diction. The last, "Yes, she rang up," brings the characters and the readers right back to the beginning of the exchange, with nothing really having been said and the only result being the passage of time. The circular motion of the dialogue adroitly mirrors the circular motion of the novel and the characters' lives within it. With nothing meaningful to sustain them, the characters simply look for ways to fill the time. Powell's "ironic precision"[23] is perfectly suited to reveal the vacuity of mechanized, routine modern existence, and his social satire pierces the facade of false glamour and illusory freedom of the modern period.

The novel is divided into three sections: "Montage," "Perihelion," and "Palindrome," but as the name of the last section implies, the work could almost be read back to front, as the characters are exactly in the same spot at the end as they were at the beginning.[24] Powell offers no escape. Circularity and the metaphysical dilemma of "going round and round in circles" are common themes in dark humor novels of the twentieth century, and, as Patrick O'Neill has argued, much of the black humor of the century arises from the Sisyphean anxiety of endless repetition with nothing of meaning or value underpinning existence.[25] From a certain vantage point, this existential angst can be laughed at, and O'Neill credits Valéry with the darkly comic observation: "Sisyphus goes on rolling his stone, but at least he ends up with a remarkable set of muscles."[26] Though no one in *Afternoon Men* acquires anything as affirmative as a remarkable set of muscles, they do manage to endure, which from a darkly humorous perspective is as positive an outcome as one can expect.

In "Montage" Powell skillfully captures the social world of the bored and the boring. The story develops in a succession of scenes that seem casual and random and that reflect the same qualities in the characters' lives. The action appears to move in fits and starts, with some chapters stretching out in uninterrupted dialogue and other chapters occupying less than a page. Feelings of apathy and antipathy predominate as Powell introduces Atwater, who has obtained a position "through influence"[27] at a museum, and his circle of friends, a semi-bohemian group consisting of artists, models, publishers, and wealthy eccentrics. In a rather down-and-out club, which is stuffy and smells of ammonia, the group's conversation moves from talk of Pringle's medicine to difficulties with women, interrupted by Pringle reminding Atwater of the precise sum owed for the last round of drinks. The nickel and diming suggests a preoccupation with the trivial that pervades the novel, as well as the hostile nature of Atwater and Pringle's friendship, reinforced by a description of him as a "naturally bad painter," with "a dreadful veneer of slickness" and "a look of the traditional Judas."[28] The boredom is palpable, as Atwater ignores Pringle's caviling and dilatorily examines a newspaper someone had left behind on the table: "He read the comic strip and later the column headed 'Titled Woman in Motor Tragedy.'"[29] The modern blending of humor and suffering is already evident and displayed in the disjointed collage of a contemporary newspaper.

Powell wrote that he wanted to portray the world of "parties, nightclubs, pubs," and "a modicum of office life."[30] In "Montage" he juxtaposes the two parts of Atwater's life to examine the boredom and routine of both, for the round of parties and the daily office job combine to create a crushingly dull and repetitive existence. From the club at the novel's opening, the group is persuaded to crash a party by the novel's party girl, Harriet Twining, who, as a character falls somewhere between Agatha Runcible and Brett Ashley. At the party, the drink is bad, the room is cramped and hot, and Atwater develops a headache, none of which keep him from attempting the expected sexual advancements toward Lola. Atwater dispassionately pursues her, despite the fact that he is not particularly attracted to her because of her contrived bohemian persona; she has adopted the name Lola and is described as having the "look of a gnome or a prematurely vicious child. But underneath the suggestion of peculiar knowingness an apparent and immense credulity lurked."[31] In a wonderfully humorous example of the conversation of party seduction, Lola asks:

> "Do you read Bertrand Russell?"
> "Why?"
> "When I feel hopeless," she said, "I read Bertrand Russell."
> "My dear."
> "You know, when he talks about mental adventure. Then I feel reinspired."
> "Reinspired to do what?"
> "Just reinspired."
> Do you feel hopeless now?'
> "Rather hopeless."
> "Do you really?"
> "A bit."
> "Come back with me to my flat," said Atwater, "and have a drink there."[32]

Despite Lola's clichéd "liberalism" (which can be seen as a swipe at Bloomsbury) and the tawdriness of the encounter, there is something poignant in this scene, as Atwater, feeling rather hopeless himself, feels a moment of connection to Lola. However, as mentioned earlier, Powell never lets moments of poignancy last very long. As Atwater continues trying to inveigle Lola to return to his flat with him, red-faced drunks dance by them, murmuring intoxicated endearments, and the host of the party is informed that "two girls have fainted in the bathroom and can't get out." The chapter ends on a farcical note, as Lola and Atwater fade into the background and the host responds: "Nonsense, I don't believe it . . . There's no lock on the door . . . I took it off before the party started."[33]

Atwater has already made an impression on Lola when Susan Nunnery arrives at the party, and despite his obvious attraction to her, he and Lola will eventually leave together. The party is reduced to what Waugh sardonically refers to as "that hard kernel of gaiety that never breaks,"[34] and Powell paints a dark portrait of the almost suicidal determination to have a good time. A girl has fainted in the bathroom, and it took a member of the upper class, Naomi Race, her taxi driver, and "a policeman who was having a drink downstairs" to get her out, adroitly suggesting that all aspects of society have become "giddy-headed." Harriet Twining has left with a different man from the one she came with, the overweight American, Mr. Scheigan, has passed out on the floor. The concern shown by the afternoon men is illustrative of their boredom and apathy, and the non sequitur following the exchange captures their cynical disengagement:

> "He ought to be moved a bit," said Pringle. "People are tripping over his head. He's becoming a nuisance."
> Barlow said: "Nonsense. I like seeing him there. He gives the room a lived-in feel."
> "He lets down the tone of the party."
> "Not so much as when he's awake."
> "What do you think about Susan?"[35]

When Atwater arrives at his flat with Lola, they are both tired and sleepy and incapable of maintaining many pretenses to conversation. He is beginning "to be depressed" and "disinterested," hoping "she wasn't going to begin on Bertrand Russell again," and she is beginning to feel sick.[36] Boredom and illness prevent them from having even this momentary melancholy encounter, and Lola leaves as the sun is beginning to rise with a "curiously grey" light.[37]

Juxtaposed with the party scene, is the "modicum of office life" Powell was interested in portraying. Atwater's job at the museum is deadly dull, and he regards his position as "keeper of the national collection" with a large degree of irritation and cynicism. It is a running joke in the novel that whenever he tells someone he works in a museum, he usually receives the hackneyed response, "that must be very interesting work" (this is indeed Lola's response, but Susan responds with the more intriguing, "May I come visit you there?"). Atwater's work is portrayed as a more organized waste of time than a party but about as absurd. He and his colleague, Nosworth, spend most of their time discussing their ailments and pursuing their personal projects, if they do anything at all. Nosworth, like Atwater, is not a man without talents. The narrator informs us that "he was a good archaeologist,"[38] but most of his time is spent making notes in his pocket diary and "translating Danish poems for money."[39] Any talents or interests that either Nosworth or Atwater could bring to their positions appear decidedly irrelevant and, indeed, would prove to be a hindrance to effective non-running of the department.

Powell once described *Afternoon Men* as an "urban pastoral" and claimed to be surprised that the novel's reviewers treated it as a "savage attack on contemporary habits."[40] The remark smacks of a certain disin genuousness that is frequently present when Powell writes of his own works, for it is hard to see any sort of paean to urban life in the novel. In *Afternoon Men* London often evokes the "Unreal City," of T.S. Eliot's *Wasteland*, and the work-a-day world is full of absurdities and disturbing encounters for the novel's protagonist. To his request for a new office chair that revolves and tilts back, Atwater receives the ludicrous response from Nosworth, "I'll do my best. It took nine years to get mine."[41] Atwater, apparently conditioned to such absurdities, makes no reply, and there is absolutely no suggestion that there is something amiss in the fact that his superior spends his days doing freelance translations or that Atwater pays bills, writes letters, and reads books.

At the museum, Atwater's experiences are marked by a comedic, surreal quality and non-sense reigns. There is a comic grotesqueness to the people Atwater encounters throughout his day, a quality often found in dark humor novels that serves to alienate the characters from their environment and to further the notion that contemporary life is a nightmare world. When Nosworth first arrives at the office, he is described as looking "like something out of the Chamber of Horrors," with his "yellow face [standing] out against the buff distemper" of his collar and complaining of "shooting pains" in his back.[42] The office boy is "an ill-conditioned youth, overgrown and with a cauliflower ear and freckles," and there is something menacing in his presence, as he stands "farouchely clasping and unclasping his hands."[43] The boy delivers a message from a Dr. J. Crutch, which immediately and rather surprisingly frightens Atwater into action. The man's request to see "somebody" augurs work on Atwater's part, and "hop[ing] for the best," he attempts to put him off by sending the message that interviews are only given by appointment.[44] Dr. Crutch's desire to "see somebody about the exhibits in room 16," mark him as a "professional nuisance," and Atwater "felt rather angry. It seemed impossible ever to get any serious reading done, with Nosworth talking about his health and people bothering him all the time."[45] Dr. Crutch is another of the novel's grotesques, and like many of those who randomly fade in and out of Atwater's field of vision, they appear vaguely sinister.[46]

Neil Brennan has argued that Atwater "fears boredom,"[47] but clearly the novel does not bear out this assessment. Atwater does not fear boredom as much as he fears being roused from the state of boredom. Being invested in the world, leaves one open to pain and suffering, and a bemused apathy works to defend one from the anxieties of living in the modern world, which crushes the individual in its mechanized routine. Dark humor is not the humor of change; it is the humor of survival, the humor of getting through another day with as little trauma as possible, without committing suicide or dying of loneliness. It is not the most "moral" of humors, for as discussed in the previous chapters, traditional ideas of morality rarely obtain in dark comedy, and the distance required of a grimly comedic stance often requires certain amoral actions and attitudes from the characters. Atwater evinces many unpleasant characteristics, and Brennan has charged that Powell's "stringent detachment," may detach the reader too far: "That a 'hero' should be parasitic, lazy, and ambivalent about life tends to kill our sympathy," and "the reader . . . has some wrestling to do."[48] Bruce Janoff claims that the "sneering laughter" of dark humor suggests that it is ethically the opposite of altruistic satire, and "instead of appearing overly moral the black humorist leaves the impression of being excessively amoral."[49] As in the fiction of Waugh and Compton-Burnett, morality is a matter of perspective in *Afternoon Men*, and Atwater's negative virtues make him an effective dark comedic character. Though he has little or no ability—or even interest—to change the insane society he finds himself in, his frequently cold and wry demeanor protect him from the chaotic forces that drive Pringle to attempt suicide, and the ambivalence felt by the reader allows for enough distance from his character that he becomes the object of Powell's jokes on occasion.

Atwater's avoidance of work is a manifestation of his defensive inertia, and his treatment of Dr. Crutch, while hardly laudatory, is quite humorous. He has evidently come to the museum to inquire about possible employment and to examine some of the exhibits that are germane to his research, which does appear to be rather questionable. However, we only see him through Atwater's eyes, and through his eyes, Dr. Crutch is decidedly absurd, "a lunatic or some semi-serious nuisance and work-creator."[50] As Dr. Crutch relates his qualifications for employment, Atwater completely ignores him: "He achieved the complete detachment of thought of one who listens to the words of a schoolmaster."[51] As the old man continues, his outline becomes blurry, and "before Atwater's eyes he seemed to turn into one after another of the people who had been at the party and then back again."[52] As his image dissolves and recomposes into various guests at the previous night's party, the absurd and monotonous aspects of office life are linked with those of his party-going experiences. The surreal element in this scene is an important aspect of Powell's comment on contemporary social life. "Like all comic visions of life," explains Max Schulz, "black humor concerns itself with social realities. In this respect, it is not anti-realistic romance so much as realism forced to the extreme . . . and intensified, surrealistic, concentration on these details of contemporary existence illustrative of a disoriented world."[53] Atwater knows that "the best he could hope for was that he should avoid hearing it all more than once," but, of course, he never even hears it once in his distracted state.[54] Explaining to Dr. Crutch that there is nothing for him at the moment, he manages to get rid of him claiming that he is very busy and that his "duty to the State. *Pro bono publico* and so on," requires him to get back to work.[55] To his horror, he realizes that Crutch has left behind the copy of his treatise, which means he will be back for it, and Atwater will have to meet with "the bedlamite" again.[56]

Just who is the madder of the two remains open for debate— Dr. Crutch with his monomania concerning craniometric and cephalmometric calculations or Atwater with his desire to avoid any sort of trauma that may be associated with most engaged human intercourse. For part of the dark humor of the episode arises from the fact that Atwater's inertia and avoidance of unpleasant emotional experiences leave him terrifyingly isolated and jaded, and, even more disturbingly, he prefers these states to the trauma of any new encounter, a preference that runs the risk of exposing just how little in control of his life he really is. Atwater's wry humor protects him from most of the world's uncertainties; however, his humorous stance also keeps him disengaged from the world he inhabits. After Dr. Crutch leaves, Atwater returns to his desk with the rest of the morning "to be got through."[57]

He contemplates beginning a novel, answering some letters, and paying some bills, "but he did not feel much like either. Instead he sat and thought about existence and its difficulties."[58] His reverie is interrupted by a phone call from Lola, though he has a difficult time recognizing her voice at first. He unenthusiastically agrees to see her the following Tuesday, and we learn, "There was the world making itself felt again. Once more material things forced themselves forward . . . What was he going to do about her, he wondered, and thought of the gloomy intellectual affair he had with his dentist's wife soon after he had come to live in London."[59] Avoiding doing or feeling anything occupies so much of his energy that Atwater has little time for anything else.

Atwater is as implicated in the insanity of interwar society as he is a victim of it, and, while the humor of the novel is both aggressive and defensive in its response to the alienating aspects of modern life, it is often unclear just who or what is the object of the joke. We see the world from Atwater's perspective, and the reader is most often called upon to share his comedic distance when something is darkly funny; however, Atwater himself is frequently as absurd as the world around him, and when this is the case, in order to find humor in the situation, the reader is asked to join with the implied narrator to laugh at Atwater. Powell sometimes makes him the subject of the novel's humor, in which case we laugh at him; and he sometimes makes him the joker, in which case we join with him in his wryly dispassionate humor and laugh at someone or something else. Sometimes, he is both the joker and the subject of the joke, and he evinces a melancholy understanding of his existential dilemma. Therefore, the social satire is ambiguous, and just what is being critiqued is never quite certain. Regardless of who or what is the butt of the joke, the joke-work functions to defend the reader against the melancholia that pervades the novel, for as soon as it looks as though either the narrative or Atwater is about to be overcome, the perspective shifts and absurdity is revealed.

An important example of this occurs near the end of "Montage." Atwater has just met up with his friend Fotheringham, the one overtly comic character in the novel. Fotheringham is a subeditor of a spiritualist paper—"the aura of journalism's lower slopes hung round him like a vapour"[60]—and feels wasted in his job. He gives voice to many of the concerns and anxieties that burden most of the characters in the novel, but his clichéd articulation of them and his ostentatious sentimentalism undercut any usefulness his words may have. Like other characters in Modernist fiction who can see the problems vexing the modern world,

Fotheringham merely reports on the problems, for no one is capable of offering any viable alternative to the futility and meaningless of their lives. Complaining of the unfulfilling nature of his work, Fotheringham is challenged by Barlow, who demands to know what kind of job he would prefer. Fotheringham replies,

> What I should really like would be something in the open air. Somewhere where you'd wake up in the early morning feeling really fresh and go out and do something strenuous and come back about eleven and have a pint of beer at the pub and then go on working until lunch and spend the rest of the day rubbing up on the classics.[61]

The comic idealization of a way of life that not only no longer exists but probably never existed only serves to adumbrate the absurdity of looking to the past for an alternative to the weariness and alienation experienced in the modern world. The "vitality"[62] that Fotheringham looks for is always located somewhere else, either in a sentimentalized, bucolic past or a romanticized America, where the lucky Undershaft appears to have found success and excitement. Fotheringham effuses, "One of the reasons I want to go to America is that I hear everybody there has such wonderful vitality."[63] However, the idea of America as the land of promise is subverted as well. No one ever mentions what Undershaft is doing in America; he is reputed to be "doing very well" and living an exotic life with a "woman of colour," who is sometimes referred to as an "Annamite" and sometimes as a "High Yaller"—terms that play on notions of the foreign and the intriguing.[64] Undershaft is back in London at the end of the novel, living with Lola and caught in the endless routine of parties and drinking that characterizes the lives of the afternoon men, and Fotheringham, far from going to America, has to borrow ten bob from Atwater for a taxi. There is no hope and no alternative to the routine of modern existence.

Fotheringham evinces a comical awareness of the novel's melancholy and feelings of momento mori. In the saloon bar when he oafishly beseeches Atwater, "*Où sont les neiges d'antan?*" the rather grim awareness that the only release from the dullness of their life will be found in death becomes nothing more than a joke. Besotted, Fotheringham outlines the facts, while Atwater and the sympathies of the reader retreat to a wry distance:

> "It's times like this that I often think how little there is ahead of us, young men like you and I . . . A vista of ill-ventilated public houses. An army of unspeakably tipsy journalists."

"Put them from your mind."

"A million barmaids all saying the same thing."

Atwater nodded.

"Drink that is so nasty one can hardly get it down . . . Where is it all going to lead? I ask you that, Atwater."

"I don't know."

"No. You don't know. I don't know. None of us know. We just go on and on and on and on and on."

"We do."[65]

Fotheringham actually does go on and on, lamenting the "struggle, this mad, chaotic, armageddon, this frenzied, febrile striving which we, you and I, know life to be."[66] He stumbles upon the idea that the connection made with others is the only useful thing in an otherwise useless existence, but he comically loses his point in a mountain of fustian ramblings:

. . . "I suppose, the one and really only possible mitigation and excuse for the unbridled incoherence of this existence of ours, it is then, and only then, that we realise fully, that we shall realise in its entirety, that we shall in short come to know with any degree of accuracy—What was I saying? I seem to have lost the thread."

"Friendship."

"That was it, of course. I'm sorry. That we shall realise what friendship means to each one of us and all of us, and how it was that, and that only, that made it all worth while."

"Made what worth while?" . . .

"Everything," he said.

"As, for instance?"

"I'm not a religious sort of chap. I don't know anything about that sort of thing. But there must be something beyond all this sex business."

"Yes."

"You think so?"

"Oh yes. Quite likely. Why not?"

"But what?"

"I can't help."

"You can't?"

Atwater said: "But what has made you so depressed?"

"Depressed?"

"Yes, depressed."

Fotheringham finished his drink with a gulp. He said:

"I suppose I must have sounded rather depressed. You see, I had rather a heavy lunch."

"I see."

"You know how a heavy lunch always lets you down."

"About this time of the evening." . . .
"It's not the weather to eat and drink a lot in the middle of the day."[67]

Nothing could show more comically the importance of not being earnest, as Powell deftly puts the major themes of the novel into the mouth of an inebriated, clownish character. And just when it might be possible to see Fotheringham as a sort of wise fool, possessed of insights that are unavailable to the jaded Atwater, Powell undercuts any hope that Fotheringham's perceptions offer an alternative to modern anomie and reveals them to be only a case of indigestion. Atwater's skeptical humor protects him from the anxiety of living with doubt and from the kind of emotional exposure that leaves Fotheringham vulnerable to the disillusionment and disappointment of unfulfilled expectations. Atwater's humor is the humor of the condemned, and he protects himself from the trauma of emotional extremes with a darkly humorous view of his circumstances. Fotheringham's oration on the emptiness of their lives prepares the reader for feelings of pity and sorrow, but Atwater "makes nothing of it."[68] He retreats to a comic distance that saves both himself and the reader the trauma of these emotions and returns to more "customary concerns,"[69] inquiring, "Who were you lunching with?"[70] Thus, the conversation is redirected to more manageable, trivial topics.

The scene effectively bars any possibility that Atwater and the afternoon men will find engagement in the world, for, as presented in the Fotheringham exchange, that pursuit is loaded with emotional risk and destined to failure. However, in the next section, aptly entitled, "Perihelion," Atwater comes closest to feelings of powerful emotion in his attraction to Susan. Like the ostensible lovestory between Adam and Nina in *Vile Bodies*, Atwater's relationship with Susan is a bitter indictment of the possibilities for love in the modern world. They never have more than a superficial knowledge of each other, and because both are jaded and weary, neither is particularly willing to risk pursuing anything deeper. Atwater is taken with Susan from the moment he sees her, and his attraction to her is primarily physical; although, she does seem to symbolize an escape from his dreary, monotonous world. She appears to him "separate, like someone in another dimension,"[71] and unlike his refrain, "I'm a dying man," earlier in the novel, when he is out with Susan and orders a dish that takes twenty-five minutes to prepare, he rejoins, "I have my life before me."[72] However, he rarely manages to say anything more profound than, "You're so lovely," and, when he attempts to engage her in more penetrating conversation, they are routinely interrupted by others, usually other men whom she does not discourage.

The conversations that mark Atwater's meetings with Susan are a confusion of half-articulated sentences and weary non sequitor. In the restaurant scene noted earlier, they are prevented from getting to know each other by becoming engulfed in a fashionably inane conversation in which everyone is talking and no one is listening:

> "My dear, *I'm* so fat."
> "I shall have to bant."[73]
> The tall woman said: "There's a place one can go to just outside Munich.
> They say it's very good."
> "Didn't Mildred go there?"
> "It was Mildred's nerves."
> "Doesn't he do that too?"
> "Mildred went to the man at Versailles. He makes you scrub floors. It's a six-months' course and prohibitively expensive. Mildred said she felt quite different after it."
> "Then there are the readings from Croce in the evening. It's terrible if you don't understand Italian. You're made to listen just the same."
> Atwater said: "Is it for both sexes?"
> The tall woman said: "I could find that out from Mildred if you thought of going." She looked at him with no interest, through big watery eyes.
> "I don't think I will."
> Susan said: "Yes, you must."[74]

Though some scholars have argued that Susan is "fresh, individual, and free of cliché,"[75] there is little in the text to support this, and this view ignores the fact that we really only see her through Atwater's eyes. Susan is very much a part of Atwater's world; she is so bored she can hardly eat and is prone to the same sort of empty exchange and repetitive dialogue that pass for conversation with all of the characters in the novel. At dinner Atwater inquires,

> "What would you like to eat?"
> "Anything."
> "Anything?"
> "Oh, yes, anything."[76]

When he starts to press to see her more frequently, she consistently keeps him in check with the killing, "Don't be a bore"—fatal words in the fashionable set. They both appear to be diversions for each other, as both continue to see other people, and, in a world devoid of any real meaning and where life is merely something to be got through, one person is as good as another. Susan pursues whatever and whomever is more interesting to her at the moment, and Atwater pursues whatever or whomever is nearest to hand. One of the characteristics of the social life in the novel is the interchangeability of the couples. At the very least Harriet is involved with Mr. Scheigan, Arthur Gosling, and Pringle. Pringle moves from Olga to Harriet. Barlow has several women he continually jokes about marrying— Sophy, Miriam, and Julia—and he has an affair with Harriet. Susan moves from Gilbert to Atwater to Verelst, and Atwater has casual affairs with Lola and Harriet while he is in pursuit of Susan. Casual sex is emblematic of the emptiness of their lives, and Powell does not treat it with censoriousness but as a symptom of the rootlessness and disaffection that are the byproducts of modernity. In a parody of the modern celebration of the machine, Powell makes a grim comedy out of the sterility of modern seduction:

> "Don't," she said. "You're not allowed to do that."
> "Why not?"
> "Because you're not."
> "I shall."
> She said: "I'm glad we met. But you must behave."
> Slowly, but very deliberately, the brooding edifice of seduction, creaking and incongruous, came into being, a vast Heath Robinson mechanism, dually controlled by them and lumbering gloomily down vistas of triteness. With a sort of heavy-fisted dexterity the mutually adapted emotions of each of them became synchronised, until the unavoidable anticlimax was at hand. Later they dined at a restaurant quite near the flat.[77]

However, Atwater does seem willing to risk himself emotionally with Susan, despite the fact that she is far from encouraging, and, unlike Adam in *Vile Bodies*, Atwater is affected when she rejects him. When Susan stands him up for a date, she telephones the bar where they were supposed to meet:

> "I'm sorry I shan't be able to see you tonight. I'm in the country."
> "I see."
> "I can't get away."
> "Can't you?"
> "You don't mind, do you?"
> "Yes."
> She laughed.
> "No, you don't really."
> "All right, I don't."[78]

As in *Vile Bodies*, the telephone almost always conveys bad news, and its technology only makes conversations shorter and more difficult to understand. Though the conversation between Atwater and Susan has much in common with those of Adam and Nina, Atwater's emotional response is quite different. Later he visits Nosworth and relates what happened. To Nosworth's query, "Are you very angry?" Atwater replies, "Very."[79] No one is ever "very angry" in *Vile Bodies*; however, like Adam, Atwater does little to protest, and in the end of Perihelion, there is nothing he can do when Susan tells him she is going away but refuses to tell where or for how long. His relationship with Susan was brief and shallow, and his lament at losing her near the end of the novel strikes the reader as somewhat hollow, as he acknowledges, "he had only known her for about five minutes."[80] However, what really seems at issue is the loss of illusion—or the possibility of love—and this is at the heart of the melancholy in the novel:

> There had been meetings when he had felt that the whole thing had been a silly mistake and that she was not like what he thought she was like and he had not enjoyed being with her. But always when she had gone he had known that he was wrong and it was his imaginary picture of her that was real and her own reality an illusion . . . Or was it that filthy port that made him feel so ill?[81]

Feelings of disillusion and illness are again combined as the material world makes itself felt again, and Atwater realizes that his feelings of love were an illusion and his reality is one of loneliness and boredom.

After Susan goes away, Atwater leaves London in an attempt to avoid the melancholy of a London summer and the "smuts," which come through open windows and "lay thickly all over Atwater's desk and his papers."[82] The action in "Palindrome" takes place almost entirely at Pringle's cottage in the country, however Powell has a decidedly modern take on the traditional paradigm of the corrupt city versus the wholesome country. The sickness of modern urban life has contaminated country life as well. As Carpenter as noted, by the mid-1930s most writers saw the English countryside as "a mere extension of the city . . . investing English country life with an artificiality comparable to that of London."[83] Even the rural landscape is blighted, as Atwater and Pringle drive the five miles from the station to cottage, "There were wire fences and telegraph-poles along the roads and the grass beside them was covered with a white dust. The dust rose in the air as they passed and hung in a cloud over the gorse and on the downs in the distance was a pumping-station with domes and towers."[84]

Upon arrival at the cottage, the scene is of the same kind of disarray that Atwater has tried to leave behind in smut-covered London: "The room was in a mess and smelled of food and turpentine. Glasses with dregs in them were all over the place and someone had left a pair of trousers hanging over the piano."[85] The guests at the cottage include Harriet, Barlow, Sophy, and the imperious Naomi Race, Atwater only being invited after someone else couldn't make it. The boredom is palpable as the guests lie about, taking turns reading an old *Vogue* magazine, drinking, and bathing in the ocean. Harriet reveals to Atwater that she is Pringle's mistress "at the moment," and when asked what one does in the country, she replies, "Nothing."[86] On a walk with Atwater, Pringle discloses that he and Harriet "are probably going to get married"; however, when they return to the cottage, they interrupt Harriet and Barlow in the dark, on the sofa, and looking more than a little disheveled.[87] The episode is cheerlessly funny, as Pringle, "never very quick about taking things in," finally grasps what is happening, and Harriet, on hands and knees under the sofa, demands, "Where the hell is my shoe?"[88]

Oppressive boredom gives way to angry ranting; however, the tension of the scene is never allowed to fully develop as Pringle's accusations receive deflating responses from Barlow. When Pringle shouts, "I've seen this coming for some time," Barlow pauses while lighting his pipe and answers, "Well, why the hell didn't you warn me? I was never so surprised in my life," as though his participation in the affair was something beyond his control.[89] Naomi Race appears, a rather comic apparition "with a long cigarette-holder in her hand [and] wearing a curious green Chinese garment," requesting that they be quiet. To which Pringle, petulantly retorts: "It's my house, and I shall make as much noise as I like."[90] Her response makes his anger appear ridiculous:

> Mrs. Race shrugged her shoulders. She said:
> "You men have such bad tempers." . . .
> There was a pause. It was one of those situations when it did not make much difference whether you were in the right or in the wrong, if regarded purely from the point of view of development. That was how Atwater felt about it.[91]

Atwater's detached feelings become the reader's feelings, and from this distance, emotionally engaged questions of right or wrong appear almost silly. The thing has simply happened and the only decision to be made is how to respond to it. All the characters except Pringle treat the affair as a minor disturbance, and the narrative treats it as a farce, for the chapter ends with Pringle, slamming pots and pans around in the scullery and catching his coat on the handle of the water faucet. Atwater and Barlow find him "standing on the sink and twisted round at an angle" and must lift him into the air in order to free him from the levers and small wheels of the plumbing. Questions of honesty, betrayal, and love become objects of wry amusement. Though the reader may have sympathy for Pringle's frustrated feelings of anger and betrayal, the text refuses to take his anxiety seriously, and as Freud has stated, "We are entirely distracted from our pity" which he argues is "one of the most frequent sources of humorous pleasure."[92]

In his examination of the humorous displacement of feelings of pity, Freud relates a story by Mark Twain about a man who is working on a railroad. There is an unexpected explosion and the man is blown up into the air and lands far away from the place he is working. As Freud argues, the reader's immediate feelings are concern for the man's health, but when Twain ends the story by informing the reader that the man had "a half-day's wages deducted for being 'absent from his place of employment' we are entirely distracted from our pity and become almost as hard-hearted as the contractor and almost as indifferent to possible damage to the [man's] health."[93] We are set up to feel pity and concern, but the narrative diverts our attention, "often on to something of secondary importance,"[94] and we are given a defense against distressing feelings.

Powell's dark humor exploits the comedic possibilities available in distracting the reader by situations that are unexpected and ostensibly of less importance, and, in turn, the reader becomes as "hard-hearted" and distanced as Atwater, through whose eyes we generally see the characters' activities. Pringle's suicide attempt is quite disturbing, but it is farcical from start to finish, and because of the controlled narrative style the reader is never required to take it too seriously. Harriet and Atwater actually see him swim off into the ocean as they are making a feeble attempt at sex on the cliffs above, and he leaves the suicide note on the cold beef that is the main course at luncheon. As the guests assemble in the dining room, they are all hungry and rather at a loss as to what should be done. Mrs. Race responds practically:

> "I refuse to believe that this is not one of his heavy jokes. If we have lunch, I have no doubt he will turn up."
> Barlow said: "But, I mean, we can't have lunch."
> "Do you propose that we go without food indefinitely?"
> Harriet said: "The table is laid. We can eat the food now and call it lunch. Or we can eat it at half-past seven and call it supper."
> Mrs Race said: "When we've had some food we shall be more equal to coping with the situation. I feel confident of that."

They sat down and began to eat. There was very little conversation.
Atwater was hungry, but by putting the food into his mouth in a
disinterested way tried to appear as if he were not eating a lot.
Barlow said: "We must get something done about this after lunch."
"May I have the beetroot, Sophy," said Mrs Race.[95]

Pringle's suicide is seen as an annoying fact that indecorously interrupts
their tedious lives, and Mrs. Race is the first to complain about Pringle
being a bad host. Their response is horrifically funny in its apathy, as
they are all more concerned with the inconvenience to themselves than
they are with the fate of Pringle, and the tone is morbidly comic as they
weigh the importance of eating lunch with the bother of finding their
friend.

The trivial and serious have equal weight in Powell's novel, and as a
result the narrative refuses to be overwhelmed by the potential trauma
of Pringle's suicide attempt and insists on an absurdly comic view of the
situation. Having been rescued by fisherman after changing his mind
about killing himself, Pringle reappears at the cottage and is met by his
uncaring guests. He has gone to bed when the fisherman returns to
claim the clothes lent to Pringle after finding him naked in the sea. The
guests agree that they should give the man something for his trouble,
but they cannot agree on the amount he should receive. Mired in petty
bargaining that harks back to the beginning of the novel, the ridiculous
conversation runs for five pages. The guests cannot even agree on what
exactly the man did—or actually the men did, as there were two fisher-
men, and if one merely sat in the boat, he should receive nothing. If it
were merely a matter of the loan of some clothes, Mrs. Race decides a
half a crown is ample; however, Barlow argues that they lifted him out
of the water, as well:

> Mrs. Race said: "Why not make it up to ten shillings."
> Barlow said: "I'm not sure that seven or six is really enough for that."[96]

Atwater suggests a pound, as that is all he has on him, and the others
decide that a pound is far too much: "This sort of question is always so
difficult to settle. Afterward one always feels one has given either too
much or too little."[97] None of them give anything, and in the end, they
decide to awaken Pringle and make him decide. He compromises at
fifteen shillings, but he doesn't have any change, which sends them into
a frenzy of coin counting and quibbling. When the fisherman responds
to the money with the comparatively dignified "Tar," the self-satisfied
group decide, "That was obviously the right sum."[98]

The banality and flatness of their lives are presented with full force in these pages, and Powell skillfully illuminates the values of a social world where tipping the fisherman who pulled Pringle out of the sea presents the greatest difficulty arising from his attempted suicide. This darkly comic episode is haunted by a disturbing awareness of their bleak future, revealed rather offhandedly in an earlier exchange between Atwater and Harriet in which he asks: "Do you think one of these days everything will come right?" "No," she replies, and Atwater admits, "Neither do I," and laughs.[99] However, the trauma of examining the futility inherent in this belief is avoided by focusing on the comically trivial. Despair and death are diminished by "secondary" concerns—using Freud's terms— and tragedy gives way to comedy.

The novel ends with characters back in the same dreary club first introduced in the opening, and Atwater, though "not specially hungry,"[100] eats a kipper in order to have something to do. Harriet is with another man, whose name she doesn't know, "but he says a friend of his is giving a party and we can all come."[101] Thus, the action is effectively brought full circle and their Sisyphean exercise continues.

NOTES

Introduction

1. Evelyn Waugh, *Vile Bodies* (Boston: Little, Brown, 1930), 314, 317.
2. Virginia Woolf, "Friendship's Gallery," ed. and intro. Ellen Hawkes, *Twentieth Century Literature* 25: 3/4(1979): 299.
3. Lynne Hapgood and Nancy Paxton, eds., *Outside Modernism: In Pursuit of the English Novel, 1900–30* (New York: St. Martin's, 2000), 3.
4. Malcolm Bradbury and James McFarlane, eds., *Modernism: A Guide to European Literature, 1890–1930* (New York: Penguin, 1991), 28.
5. See Kirby Olson, *Comedy After Postmodernism: Rereading Comedy from Edward Lear to Charles Willeford* (Lubbock: Texas Tech University Press, 2001).
6. Patrick O'Neill, "The Comedy of Entropy: The Contexts of Black Humor," in *Black Humor: Critical Essays*, ed. Alan R. Pratt (New York: Garland, 1993), 75.
7. See Andy Croft, *Red Letter Days: British Fiction of the Thirties* (London: Lawrence and Wishart, 1990); Valentine Cunningham, *British Writers of the Thirties* (Oxford: Oxford University Press, 1989); and Samuel Hynes. *The Auden Generation: Literature and Politics in England in the 1930s* (Princeton: Princeton University Press, 1976).
8. Northrop Frye, *Anatomy of Criticism: Four Essays* (New Jersey: Princeton, 1957), 223.
9. Robert M. Polhemus, *Comic Faith: The Great Tradition from Austen to Joyce* (Chicago: University of Chicago Press, 1980), 5.
10. I. Compton-Burnett, *A House and Its Head* (London: Eyre & Spottiswoode, 1935), 276.
11. Bruce Janoff, "Black Humor: Beyond Satire," *The Ohio Review* 14.1 (1972): 5–20, 11.
12. Aldous Huxley, *Antic Hay* (Illinois: Dalkey Archive Press, 1997), 212.
13. Sigmund Freud, *Jokes and Their Relation to the Unconscious*, ed. James Strachey (New York: Norton, 1960), 285.
14. Sigmund Freud, "Humour," *The Standard Edition of the Complete Works of Sigmund Freud*, vol. 21 (1927–31), ed. James Strachey (London: Hogarth, 1961), 162.
15. Freud, "Humour," 162.
16. Freud, "Humour," 162.

17. Sigmund Freud, *Civilization and Its Discontents* (Garden City, NJ: Doubleday, 1958), 14.
18. Freud, *Civilization and Its Discontents*, 15.
19. See Mikhail Bakhtin, *Rabelais and His World* (Cambridge: MIT Press, 1968); Charles Baudelaire, "On the Essence of Laughter," and "On the Comic in the Plastic Arts," in *Comedy: Meaning and Form*, 2nd ed., ed. Robert Corrigan (San Francisco: Chandler, 1965); Andre Breton, *Anthologie de l'humour noir* (Paris: Jean-Jacques Pauvert, 1966); Immanuel Kant, *Critique of Judgment* (New York: Hafner Press, 1951); Friedrich Nietzsche, *Thus Spake Zarathustra* (New York: Penguin, 1978); Friedrich Schiller, *Naïve and Sentimental Poetry* and *On the Sublime* (New York: Ungar, 1966).
20. See Regina Barreca, *Untamed and Unabashed: Essays on Women and Humor in British Literature* (Detroit: Wayne State University Press, 1994); Regina Barreca, *They Used to Call Me Snow White ... But I Drifted* (New York: Penguin, 1991); Nancy Walker, *A Very Serious Thing: Women's Humor and American Culture* (Minneapolis: University of Minnesota Press, 1988); Nancy Walker, *What's So Funny? Humor in American Culture* (Wilmington: Scholarly Resources, Inc., 1998); and Nancy Walker, *Feminist Alternatives: Irony and Fantasy in the Contemporary Novel by Women* (Jackson and London: University Press of Mississippi, 1990).
21. Samuel Weber, *The Legend of Freud* (Minneapolis: University of Minnesota Press, 1982), 116.
22. For a further discussion of Freud's originality, see Jerry Keller Simon's *The Labyrinth of the Comic: Theory and Practice from Fielding to Freud* (Tallahassee: Florida State University, 1985).
23. Freud, "Humour," 163.
24. Matthew Winston, "The Ethics of Contemporary Black Humor," *Colorado Quarterly* 24 (1976): 275–88.
25. Winston, "The Ethics of Contemporary Black Humor," 285.
26. This will be dealt with more thoroughly in chapter 1.
27. Margaret Stetz, *British Women's Comic Fiction, 1890–1990: Not Drowning, But Laughing* (Aldershot, England: Ashgate, 2001), xii.
28. Kirby Olson, *Comedy after Postmodernism: Rereading Comedy from Edward Lear to Charles Willeford* (Lubbock: Texas Tech University Press, 2001), 4.
29. Olsen, 6.
30. Jean-François Lyotard, *Toward the Postmodern*, trans. Mira Kamdor et al. (New Jersey: Humanities Press, 1993), 83.
31. See Robert Kiernan, *Frivolity Unbound: Six Masters of the Camp Novel* (New York: Continuum, 1990) and Kirby Olsen, *Comedy after Postmodernism: Rereading Comedy from Edward Lear to Charles Willeford* (Lubbock: Texas Tech University Press, 2001) for interesting discussions of Wodehouse's humor. Also, Alison Light, *Forever England: Femininity, Literature, and Conservatism Between the Wars* (London: Routledge, 1991) and Alice Rayner, *Comic Persuasion: Moral Structure in British Comedy from Shakespeare to Stoppard* (Berkeley: University of California Press, 1987).
32. Virginia Woolf, *Mrs. Dalloway* (New York: Harcourt, 1953), 117.

33. Wylie Sypher, "The Meanings of Comedy," in *Comedy* (Baltimore and London: Johns Hopkins University Press, 1956), 194.
34. Sypher, *Comedy*, 195.
35. Sypher, *Comedy*, 195.
36. Freud, *Jokes*, 285.
37. Freud, "Humour," 162; and *Jokes*, 284.
38. Virginia Woolf, *Orlando* (New York: Harcourt, 1928), 199.
39. Freud, *Jokes*, 125.
40. George McCartney, "Satire Between the Wars: Evelyn Waugh and Others," in *The Columbia History of the British Novel*, ed. John Richetti et al. (New York: Columbia University Press, 1994), 876.
41. Henri Bergson, "Laughter," in *Comedy*, ed. and intro. Wylie Sypher (Baltimore and London: Johns Hopkins University Press, 1956), 82.
42. Bakhtin, *Rabelais*, 174.
43. Ibid., 401.

Chapter 1   Comedy Theory, the Social Novel, and Freud

1. Bergson, "Laughter," in *Comedy*, ed. by Wylie Sypher (Baltimore and London: Johns Hopkins University Press, 1956), 64.
2. Ibid., 180.
3. Ibid., 65.
4. Ibid., 72.
5. Ibid., 72.
6. Ibid., 67.
7. As Patrick O'Neill has argued, "All the major traditional theories of humour are, with various weighting, posited on the existence of an initial formal incongruity." See Patrick O'Neill, *The Comedy of Entropy* (Toronto: University of Toronto Press, 1990), 82.
8. Aristotle, *The Poetics*, trans. Hamilton Fyfe (London: Heinemann, 1927); Cicero, *De Oratore*, trans. E.W. Sutton (London: Heinemann, 1942); Plato, Philebus, ed. Harold N. Fowler (London: Heinemann, 1925).
9. O'Neill, *The Comedy of Entropy*, 25.
10. Thomas Hobbes, *The Leviathan* (London: Dent, 1914), 27.
11. Bergson, "Laughter," 89, 150.
12. Ibid., 88.
13. Ibid., 118.
14. Walter Benjamin, "The Work of Art in the Age of Mechanical Reproduction," in *Illuminations*, ed. and intro. Hannah Arendt (New York: Schoken Books, 1968), 221.
15. Ibid., 221.
16. Ibid., 221.
17. Ibid., 221.
18. Ibid., 221.
19. Robert Polhemus, *Comic Faith*, 4. Wylie Sypher also discusses the connections between religious faith and humor, arguing that comedy is essentially

a "carrying away of death," and that comedy like religious faith allows for the existence of contradiction and incongruity. See his essay "The Meanings of Comedy," in *Comedy*, ed. Wylie Sypher (Baltimore and London: Johns Hopkins University Press, 1956).

20. Polhemus, *Comic Faith*, 3.
21. Ibid., 269.
22. Ibid., 19.
23. See Trudi Tate, *Modernism, History, and the First World War* (Manchester: University of Manchester Press, 1998). Tate discusses the anxiety of post–World War I writers as they attempt to bear witness to events that are seen only partially, "through a fog of ignorance, fear, confusion, and lies" (1). Also, Paul Fussell, *The Great War and Modern Memory* (New York and London: Oxford University Press, 1975).
24. Bergson, "Laughter," 126.
25. Virginia Woolf, *Orlando* (New York: Harcourt, 1928), 310.
26. Mathew Winston, "*Humour noir* and Black Humor," in *Veins of Humor*, ed. Harry Levin (Cambridge: Harvard University Press, 1972), 270.
27. Freud, *Jokes*, 285.
28. Mary Douglas, *Purity and Danger* (New York: Frederick A. Drager, 1966), 121.
29. Regina Barreca notes that even critics who embrace the idea of comedy as subversive and gleefully threatening to the dominant order, such James Kincaid, Umberto Eco, Mikhail Bahktin, and Robert Polhemus, are "up against a central, longstanding, deeply-embedded, and ultimately, conservative belief" that the study of comedy does not concern women. Studies of dark humor, such as Patrick O'Neill's *The Comedy of Entropy* (Toronto: University of Toronto Press, 1990); *Black Humor: Critical Essays*, ed. Alan Pratt (New York: Garland, 1993); Douglas Davis, *The World of Black Humor* (New York: Dutton, 1967); and Max Schulz, *Black Humor Fiction of the Sixties: A Pluralistic Definition of Man and His World* (Athens: Ohio University Press, 1973) rarely, if ever, mention the writing of women, and certainly do not examine any dark humor writing by women in-depth.
30. See Regina Barreca, *Untamed and Unabashed: Essays on Women and Humor in the British Literature* (Detroit: Wayne State University Press, 1994); Regina Barreca, *They Used to Call Me Snow White ... But I Drifted* (New York: Penguin, 1991); Regina Barecca, ed., *Last Laughs: Perspectives on Women and Comedy* (Philadelphia, PA: Gordon and Breach, 1988); Regina Barecca, ed., *New Perspectives on Women and Comedy* (Philadelphia, PA: Gordon and Breach, 1992); Audrey Bilger, *Laughing Feminism: Subversive Comedy in Frances Burney, Maria Edgeworth, and Jane Austen* (Detroit: Wayne State University Press, 1998); Gail Finney, ed., *Look Who's Laughing: Gender and Comedy* (Philadelphia, PA: Gordon and Breach, 1994); Judy Little, *Comedy and the Woman Writer: Woolf, Spark, and Feminism* (Lincoln: University of Nebraska Press, 1983); June Sochen, ed., *Women's Comic Visions* (Detroit: Wayne State University Press, 1991); Nancy Walker, *A Very Serious Thing: Women's Humor and American Culture* (Minneapolis: University of Minnesota Press, 1988); Nancy Walker, *What's So Funny?*

Humor in American Culture (Wilmington: Scholarly Resources, Inc., 1998); and Nancy Walker, *Feminist Alternatives: Irony and Fantasy in the Contemporary Novel by Women* (Jackson and London: University Press of Mississippi, 1990).

31. Barreca, *Untamed and Unabashed*, 18.

32. Ibid., 21.

33. Ibid., 11.

34. In *A Very Serious Thing*, Walker observes: "[B]efore the 19702 women tended to write about being plagued by boxes of cereal as part of their domestic routine, they now write about the plague of junk mail that affects both women and men. The women's movement has not effected the radical changes that is seeks in political, economic, and social freedoms for women, but the entrance of large numbers of women into the labor force, the declining birth rate, and changes in family structure have brought both men and women into each others' worlds sufficiently that it is possible for women to write humor that lacks a specific gender consciousness" (14).

35. Helene Cixious, "The Laugh of the Medusa," trans. Keith Cohen and Paula Cohen, *Signs* 1, no. 4 (Summer 1976): 141–53.

36. For studies of this kind of dark humor, see Patrick O'Neill's *The Comedy of Entropy* (Toronto: University of Toronto Press, 1990); *Black Humor: Critical Essays*, ed. Alan Pratt (New York: Garland, 1993); Douglas Davis, *The World of Black Humor* (New York: Dutton, 1967); and Max Schulz, *Black Humor Fiction of the Sixties: A Pluralistic Definition of Man and His World* (Athens: Ohio University Press, 1973); Charles Baudelaire, "The Essence of Laughter," in *Comedy: Meaning and Form*, ed. Robert Corrigan (San Francisco: Chandler, 1965); André Breton, *Anthologie de l'humour noir* (Paris: Pauvert, 1966); Mireille Rosello, *L'Humour Noir Selon André Breton* (Paris: José Corti, 1987).

37. Mathew Winston, "Black Humor: To Weep with Laughing," in *Black Humor: Critical Essays*, ed. Allan Pratt (New York: Garland, 1993), 250.

38. O'Neill, *The Comedy of Entropy*, 34.

39. William Keough, "The Violence of American Humor," in *What's So Funny? Humor in America Culture*, ed. Nancy Walker (Wilmington, DE: Scholarly Resources, Inc., 1998), 134.

40. Ibid., 135.

41. Polhemus, *Comic Faith*, 165.

42. Freud, "Humour," 162.

43. Freud, "Humour," 162. This same example, among others, is discussed in *Jokes and Their Relation to the Unconscious* (284). Originally published in German in 1905 (the first English edition appeared in 1916), *Jokes* outlines Freud's appraisal of the defensive function of gallows humor, which is later expanded in "Humour" (published in 1927 in German and in 1928 in English translation) to include the suppressive nature of the super-ego on the ego, censoring it like a parent would a child. This discussion will draw from both texts, as the main argument in both is the defense of the ego through humor.

44. Freud, *Jokes*, 284–85.

45. Ibid., 285.
46. As Richard Keller Simon notes in *The Labyrinth of the Comic: Theory and Practice from Fielding to Freud* (Tallahassee: Florida State University Press, 1985), the idea of economy has been problematic for later critics of the comic, "for whom the laws of thermodynamics ... have no special charm or meaning" (214). However, its link to pleasure and play is important to the study of the comic because it frees theories of humor from arguments that would see it only in terms of aesthetic or social theory.
47. Ibid., 216.
48. Freud, *Jokes*, 285.
49. Ibid., 285.
50. Freud, "Humour," 162.
51. Mathew Winston, "Black Humor: To Weep with Laughing," 252.
52. Freud, "Humour," 162.
53. Freud, *Jokes*, 285.
54. Freud, "Humour," 161.
55. Ibid., 161.
56. Ibid., 161.
57. Condensation frequently involves wordplay, the multiple meanings, and the layered nature of language. One of his examples: "A doctor, as he came away from a lady's bedside, said to her husband with a shake of his head: 'I don't like her looks.' 'I've not liked her looks for a long time,' the husband hastened to agree" (*Jokes* 41). The joke turns on the multiple meanings of the "looks."
58. Freud, *Jokes*, 11.
59. Freud's example: "Two Jews meet in the neighborhood of the bath-house. 'Have you taken a bath?' asks one of them. 'What?' asked the other in return, 'is there one missing?' "(*Jokes* 55). The emphasis is displaced from "bath" to "taken."
60. Freud, *Jokes*, 114.
61. Ibid., 115.
62. Ibid., 120. These two categories are similar in some ways to Baudelaire's two comic categories, the referential and the absolute. According to Baudelaire, the referential comic has an object that is laughed at and aims at teaching a lesson or making a point; it is above all a comedy of superiority. The absolute comic emphasizes identification with the other; it unites rather than draws distinctions. See Charles Baudelaire, "On the Essence of Laughter," in *Comedy: Meaning and Form*, ed. Robert Corrigan (San Francisco: Chandler, 1965).
63. Freud, *Jokes*, 121, 162.
64. Ibid., 162.
65. Ibid., 163.
66. Ibid., 287.
67. Freud, "Humour," 162.
68. Ibid., 288.
69. Eugéne Ionesco, "La Démystification par l'humour noir," *Avant-Scène* (Paris) February 15, 1959, quoted in Patrick O'Neill, "The Comedy of Entropy: The Contexts of Black Humor," in *Black Humor*, 85.

70. See Koji Numasawa, "Black Humor: An American Aspect," in *Black Humor: Critical Essays*, ed. Alan Pratt (New York: Garland, 1993); Max Schulz, "Towards a Definition of Black Humor," in *Black Humor: Critical Essays*; D.J. Dooley, "Waugh and Black Humor," *The Evelyn Waugh Newsletter* 2 (Autumn 1968): 1–3. These works specifically comment on Waugh, but they suggest the same "conservative" role of comedy in other British satirists who follow in the tradition of "grotesque comedy of manners." Also, Alison Light examines the role of "conservatism" in the interwar British novel in *Forever England: Femininity, Literature and Conservatism Between the Wars* (New York and London: Routledge, 1991).

71. Terry Eagleton, *Exiles and Émigrés: Studies in Modern Fiction* (New York: Schocken Books, 1970), 11.

72. Ibid., 13.

73. Ibid., 13.

74. Ibid., 14. Eagleton argues that the outsider views of Eliot, Pound, Yeats, Joyce, and Lawrence (who is deemed an outsider because he is from the Midlands), writers who had access to alternative cultures and broader frameworks, were better able to examine the complex relations and the erosion of contemporary order within British society as a whole.

75. Ibid., 35, 43.

76. Sigmund Freud, *Civilization and Its Discontents*, trans. and ed., James Strachey (New York and London: Norton, 1961), 24.

77. Ibid., 24.

78. Ibid., 24.

79. Ibid., 25–26.

80. Sypher, "Our New Sense of the Comic, " in *Comedy*, ed. and intro. Wylie Sypher (Baltimore and London: Johns Hopkins University Press, 1956), 201.

81. Sypher's discussion of religion is limited to the Western traditions of Judeo-Christian religion and Greek paganism.

82. Sypher, "Our New Sense of the Comic," 213.

83. Ibid., 198.

84. Freud, "Humour," 163. These various methods of avoiding pain are discussed at length in chapter II of *Civilization and Its Discontents*.

85. Ibid., 163.

86. Bakhtin, *Rabelais and His World*, 401.

87. Mikhail Bakhtin, *The Dialogic Imagination*, ed. Michael Holquist, trans. Caryl Emerson and Michael Holquist (Austin: University of Texas Press, 1981).

88. Winston, "*Humour noir* and Black Humor," 270.

89. Sypher, "Our New Sense of the Comic," 197.

90. Polhemus, *Comic Faith*, 19.

91. Paul Lauter, ed., *Theories of Comedy* (Garden City, NY: Doubleday, 1964), 27.

92. Jean-Paul Sartre, *L'Idiot de la famille: Gustave Flaubert de 1831 à 1857* (Paris: Gallimard, 1971), I:681.

93. Thomas Mann, *Past Masters and Other Papers*, trans. H.T. Lowe-Porter (New York: Knopf, 1968), 240.

Chapter 2   Criticizing the Social System: *Mrs. Dalloway*, Virginia
Woolf's Dark Comedy of Manners

1. Her portrayal of Miss Kilman, as the name suggests, is typical of most of her portraits of reformers: "religious ecstasy made people callous (so did causes); dulled their feelings, for Miss Kilman would do anything for the Russians, starved herself for the Austrians, but in private inflicted positive torture, so insensitive was she, dressed in a green mackintosh coat" (*MD* 16).
2. Virginia Woolf, *A Writer's Diary*, ed. Leonard Woolf (New York: Harcourt, 1953), 17–18. The distinction between reformers and artists is interesting in light of the fact that many scholars have referred to Clarissa Dalloway as a kind of artist in the aesthetic creation of her party.
3. Freud, *Jokes*, 131.
4. Virginia Woolf, *Three Guineas* (New York: Harcourt, 1938), 80.
5. Alex Zwerdling, *Mrs. Dalloway* and the Social System, *PMLA* 92 (1977): 69–82.
6. Virginia Woolf, *A Writer's Diary*, ed. Leonard Woolf (New York: Harcourt, 1953), 56.
7. Ibid., 51.
8. Woolf, *Mrs. Dalloway*, 50.
9. Ibid., 133.
10. Ibid., 89.
11. Ibid., 17, 32.
12. Ibid., 17.
13. Ibid., 32.
14. Ibid., 100.
15. Ibid., 32.
16. Ibid., 17.
17. Ibid., 190.
18. Ibid., 190–91.
19. R.D. Laing, *The Politics of Experience* (New York: Random, 1967), 79.
20. Gloria Kaufman, "Feminist Humor as a Survival Device," *Regionalism and the Female Imagination* 3.2/3 (1977/78): 86.
21. Freud, "Humour," 162.
22. Suzette Henke, "Virginia Woolf's Septimus Smith: An Analysis of "Paraphrenia" and the Schizophrenic Use of Language," *Literature and Psychology* 31 (1981): 13–23.
23. Freud, "On Narcissism: An Introduction," in *A General Selection from the Works of Sigmund Freud*, ed. John Rickman (1914; rpt. New York: Doubleday, 1957), 105.
24. Woolf, *Mrs. Dalloway*, 100.
25. Laing, *The Politics of Experience*, 133, 139.
26. Woolf, *Mrs. Dalloway*, 118.
27. Ibid., 118, 93.
28. Woolf, *Mrs. Dalloway*, 39.
29. Ibid., 283.

30. Regina Barreca, *Untamed and Unabashed: Essays on Women and Humor in the British Literature* (Detroit: Wayne State University Press, 1994), 61.
31. Hermione Lee, *Virginia Woolf* (New York: Knopf, 1996), 107.
32. Ibid., 108.
33. Woolf, *Mrs. Dalloway*, 255, 266, 277, 261.
34. Ibid., 267.
35. Ibid., 117.
36. Ibid., 154.
37. Ibid., 273.
38. Ibid., 144.
39. Ibid., 142–43.
40. Melba Cuddy-Keane, "The Politics of Comic Modes in Virginia Woolf's *Between the Acts*," *PMLA* 105 (March 1990): 273–85.
41. Woolf, *Mrs. Dalloway*, 144.
42. Cuddy-Keane, "The Politics of Comic Modes," 276.
43. Ibid., 276.
44. Ibid., 57.
45. Nancy Walker, *Feminist Alternatives: Irony and Fantasy in the Contemporary Novel by Women* (Jackson and London: University Press of Mississippi, 1990), 4.
46. Woolf, *Mrs. Dalloway*, 57–58.
47. Ibid., 58.
48. Woolf, *Mrs. Dalloway*, 163.
49. Bruce Janoff, "Black Humor: Beyond Satire," *The Ohio Review* 14.1 (1972): 5–20.
50. Judy Little, *Comedy and the Woman Writer: Woolf, Spark, and Feminism* (Lincoln: University of Nebraska Press, 1982), 187.
51. Barreca, *Untamed and Unabashed*, 23.
52. Woolf, *Mrs. Dalloway*, 3.
53. Ibid., 11.
54. Ibid., 267.
55. Ibid., 282.
56. Ibid., 14.
57. Ibid., 23.
58. Ibid., 15.
59. Barreca, *Unabashed and Unashamed*, 20.
60. Virginia Woolf, "Modern Fiction," *The Common Reader*, ed. Andrew McNeille (New York: Harcourt, 1984), 146–54.
61. Virginia Woolf, *A Room of One's Own* (New York: Harcourt, Brace and Jovanovich, 1957), 76.
62. Woolf, *A Writer's Diary*, 59.
63. Elisabeth Bowen, *Collected Impressions* (New York: Alfred A. Knopf, 1950), 46.
64. Woolf, *Mrs. Dalloway*, 44.
65. Ibid., 43–44.
66. Ibid., 65.

67. Ibid., 65–66, my emphasis.
68. See Denise Marshal, "Slaying the Angel and the Patriarch: The Grinning Woolf," *Last Laughs: Perspectives on Women and Comedy*, ed. Regina Barreca (New York: Gordon and Breach, 1988), 149–78.
69. Barreca, *Untamed and Unabashed*, 20.
70. Woolf, *Mrs. Dalloway*, 155.
71. Ibid., 75.
72. Ibid., 229.
73. Ibid., 75–76.
74. Denise Marshall, *Intimate Alien: Virginia Woolf and the Comedy of Knowledge and the Comedy of Power* (Ann Arbor: Dissertation Abstracts International, 1985), 26.
75. Marshall, *Intimate Alien*, 17.
76. Gail Finney, *Look Who's Laughing: Gender and Comedy* (Longhorne, PA: Gordon and Breach, 1994), 9.
77. Kenneth White, ed., *Savage Comedy: Structures of Humor* (Amsterdam: Rodopi, 1978), 11.
78. Virginia Woolf, "Friendship's Gallery," ed. and intro. Ellen Hawkes, *Twentieth Century Literature* 25: 3/4 (1979): 299.
79. Woolf, *Letters*, 76.
80. Mark Hussey, *Virginia Woolf and War: Fiction, Reality, and Myth* (Syracuse: Syracuse University Press, 1991), 17.
81. For an interesting discussion of this see Sue Thomas, "Virginia Woolf's Septimus Smith and Contemporary Perceptions of Shell Shock," *English Language Notes* 25 (December 1987): 49–57.
82. Woolf, *Mrs. Dalloway*, 279.
83. Thomas, "Virginia Woolf," 49.
84. Woolf, *Mrs. Dalloway*, 263.
85. Robert M. Polhemus, *Comic Faith: The Great Tradition from Austen to Joyce* (Chicago: University of Chicago Press, 1980), 137–41.
86. Woolf, *Mrs. Dalloway*, 5.
87. Ibid., 187.
88. Ibid., 16.
89. Woolf, *Letters*, 71.
90. Woolf, *Mrs. Dalloway*, 16.
91. Patrick O'Neill, *The Comedy of Entropy* (Toronto: University of Toronto Press, 1990), 20.
92. Ibid., 20.

Chapter 3   The Dark Domestic Vision of Ivy Compton-Burnett:
A House and Its Head

1. Angus Wilson, "Ivy Compton-Burnett," in *Diversity and Depth in Fiction: Selected Critical Writings* (New York: Viking, 1983), 196.
2. See Anthony Powell's obituary notice for Ivy Compton-Burnett, *Spectator* (September 6, 1969), 304.

3. James Lees-Milne, "Major/Minor," *Twentieth Century Literature Ivy Compton-Burnett Issue* 25 (Summer 1979): 132.
4. Regina Barreca, *Untamed and Unabashed: Essays on Women and Humor in the British Literature* (Detroit: Wayne State University Press, 1994), 117–18.
5. Victoria Glendinning, *Elizabeth Bowen: A Biography* (New York: Alfred A. Knopf, 1978), xv.
6. Barreca, *Untamed and Unabashed,* 110.
7. "Ivy Compton-Burnett and Margaret Jourdain: A Conversation," in *The Art of I. Compton-Burnett: A Collection of Critical Essays,* ed. Charles Burkhart (London: Gollancz, 1972), 27.
8. Ibid., 23.
9. John Bowen, "An Interview with Miss Compton-Burnett," in *Twentieth Century Literature Ivy Compton-Burnett Issue* 25 (Summer 1979): 169.
10. Maurice Cranston, "The Writer in His Age," *London Magazine* 4.5 (May 1957): 38–40.
11. Elizabeth Bowen, "Parents and Children," *Art of I. Compton-Burnett: A Collection of Critical Essays,* ed. Charles Burkhart (London: Gollancz, 1972), 55.
12. Ivy Compton-Burnett, *Daughters and Sons* (London: Gollancz, 1954), 159. Characteristic of Compton-Burnett's condensed style and veiled aggression, the brother's response can be seen as both agreeing with his sister's statements or mocking them. It depends on how one reads the reference to the pronoun "they."
13. Burkhart, "A Conversation," 26.
14. Wilson, "Ivy Compton-Burnett," 196–97.
15. Michael Millgate, "An Interview with Miss Compton-Burnett," in *The Art of I. Compton-Burnett: A Collection of Critical Essays,* ed. Charles Burkhart (London: Gollancz, 1972), 30, 43.
16. Ibid., 41.
17. Wilson, "Ivy Compton-Burnett," 201.
18. See Charles Burkhart *The Art of I. Compton-Burnett,* 163; Frank Baldanza, *Ivy Compton-Burnett* (New York: Twayne Publishers, 1964), 53; Robert Liddell, *The Novels of I. Compton-Burnett* (London: Gollancz, 1955), 43.
19. Millgate, "An Interview," 43.
20. Ivy Compton-Burnett, *A House and Its Head* (London: Eyre & Spottiswoode, 1931), 11.
21. Ibid., 11.
22. Ibid., 11.
23. Ibid., 11.
24. Ibid., 12.
25. Ibid., 12.
26. Ibid., 13.
27. Ibid., 57.
28. Ibid., 22–23.
29. Barreca, *They Used to Call me Snow White ... But I Drifted: Women's Strategic Use of Humor* (New York: Penguin, 1991), 11.

30. Andrzej Gasiorek, *Post-War British Fiction: Realism and After* (London: Edward, Arnold, 1995), 30–31.
31. Compton-Burnett, *A House and Its Head*, 15–16.
32. Barreca, *Untamed and Unabashed*, 75.
33. Ibid., 61.
34. Compton-Burnett, *A House and Its Head*, 17.
35. Ibid., 17.
36. Freud, *Jokes*, 125.
37. Ibid., 124.
38. Ibid., 124.
39. Alison Light, *Forever England: Feminity, Literature, and Conservatism Between the Wars* (London: Routledge, 1991), 23.
40. Light, *Forever England*, 40, 42.
41. Robert M. Polhemus, *Comic Faith: The Great Tradition from Austen to Joyce* (Chicago: University of Chicago Press, 1980), 216.
42. Compton-Burnett (CB) makes some interesting comments on this subject when her interview with Michael Millgate veered off into a political discussion. Millgate inquires whether CB ever thought that the forces that emerge as domestic tyranny are "precisely those which on a larger scale have recently produced wars and revolutions and totalitarian regimes." CB responds that this is probably so, but that the "tremendous impetus that came from Germany arose from the presence of the forces inside millions of people—not only in Hitler." Millgate, uncomfortable with this line, wants to insist that Hitler is the primary cause and instigator of German aggression and genocide: "Yes, Except that Hitler was surely a very important instigating factor ... without his personality the movement wouldn't have taken quite that course." CB refuses to dismiss the complicity of society, though, and responds, "It might not have taken it at all, but that would be because people hadn't the leader to give things the specific shape. I think they would have been smouldering there just the same" (Millgate, "An Interview," 46).
43. Ibid., 44.
44. Elizabeth Sprigge, *The Life of Ivy Compton-Burnett* (New York, George Braziller, 1973), 40.
45. Compton-Burnett, *A House and Its Head*, 21.
46. Ibid., 21.
47. Ibid., 21.
48. Polhemus, *Comic Faith*, 237.
49. Compton-Burnett, *A House and Its Head*, 22.
50. Ibid., 24.
51. Ibid., 24.
52. Polhemus, *Comic Faith*, 208.
53. Freud, *Jokes*, 137.
54. Ibid., 137.
55. Compton-Burnett, *A House and Its Head*, 24.
56. Ibid., 24.
57. Ibid., 24.

58. Ibid., 34.
59. Ibid., 35.
60. Ibid., 35.
61. Ibid., 38.
62. Ibid., 59.
63. Ibid., 59.
64. Ibid., 60.
65. Ibid., 83.
66. See Compton-Burnett's *The Mighty and Their Fall*, and *Daughters and Sons*.
67. Compton-Burnett, *A House and Its Head*, 268.
68. Ibid., 129.
69. Barreca, *Untamed and Unabashed*, 31.
70. Compton-Burnett, *A House and Its Head*, 129.
71. Ibid., 130.
72. Ibid., 158.
73. Ibid., 158.
74. Ibid., 175.
75. Ibid., 175.
76. Ibid., 179.
77. Light, *Forever England*, 42.
78. Ibid., 267.
79. Ibid., 267.
80. Ibid., 275.
81. Sprigge, *The Life of Ivy Compton-Burnett*, 157.
82. Freud, "Humour," 162.
83. Compton-Burnett, *A House and Its Head*, 276.

Chapter 4   The Too, Too Bogus World: Evelyn Waugh's *Vile Bodies*

1. Alison Light, *Forever England: Feminity, Literature, and Conservatism Between the Wars* (London: Routledge, 1991), 52.
2. Humphrey Carpenter, *The Brideshead Generation: Evelyn Waugh and His Friends* (Boston: Houghton Mifflin, 1990), 202.
3. Robert M. Polhemus, *Comic Faith: The Great Tradition from Austen to Joyce* (Chicago: University of Chicago Press, 1980), 246.
4. See Stephen Jay Greenblatt, *Three Modern Satirists: Waugh, Orwell, and Huxley* (New Haven and London: Yale University Press, 1965); Brooke Allen, "*Vile Bodies*: A Futurist Fantasy," in *Twentieth Century Literature* 40 (Fall 1994): 318–28; Archie Loss, "*Vile Bodies*, Vorticism, and Italian Futurism," in *Journal of Modern Literature* 18 (Winter 1992): 155–64; and George McCartney, *Confused Roaring: Evelyn Waugh and the Modernist Tradition* (Bloomington and Indianapolis: Indiana University Press, 1987).
5. Max Schulz, "Towards a Definition of Black Humor," in *Black Humor: Critical Essays*, ed. Alan R. Pratt (New York: Garland, 1993), 165. See also

D.J. Dooley, "Waugh and Black Humor," *The Evelyn Waugh Newsletter* 2 (Autumn 1968): 1–3.

6. Evelyn Waugh, *Vile Bodies* (Boston: Little, Brown, 1930), 185.
7. As George McCartney has pointed out in "Satire between the Wars: Evelyn Waugh and Others" (*The Columbia History of the British Novel*, ed. John Richetti et al. (New York: Columbia University Press, 1994), The bogus theme is a commonplace in the fiction of the period, and Waugh and his fellow novelists of the time—Aldous Huxley, George Orwell, and Graham Greene—are characterized by their "attack on a world that seemed to them increasingly synthetic" (867–68).
8. Rebecca West, review of *Vile Bodies*, in *Evelyn Waugh: The Critical Heritage*, ed. Martin Stannard (London: Routledge & Kegan Paul, 1984), 106.
9. Martin Stannard, ed., *Evelyn Waugh: The Critical Heritage* (London: Routledge, 1984), 103.
10. Ibid., 89.
11. Katharyn Crabbe, *Evelyn Waugh* (New York: Continuum, 1988), 71–72.
12. Terry Eagleton, *Exile and Émigrés: Studies in Modern Literature* (Oxford: Oxford University Press, 1970), 41, 48.
13. Ibid., 49.
14. Alain Blayac, "Evelyn Waugh and Humor," in *Evelyn Waugh: New Directions*, ed. Alain Blayac (Hong Kong: Macmillan, 1992), 121.
15. Ibid., 122.
16. Ibid., 114, 116.
17. Waugh, *Vile Bodies*, 40–41.
18. Ibid., 44–45.
19. Ibid., 183, 185.
20. Ibid., 184.
21. Blayac, "Evelyn Waugh and Humor," 116.
22. Waugh, *Vile Bodies*, 42.
23. Ibid., 186.
24. Eagleton, *Exile and Émigrés*, 51.
25. McCartney, *Confused Roaring*, 4.
26. Waugh, *Vile Bodies*, 186.
27. Ibid., 186–87.
28. McCartney, *Confused Roaring*, 78.
29. Polhemus, *Comic Faith*, 151.
30. *Untamed and Unabashed: Essays on Women and Humor in the British Literature* (Detroit: Wayne State University Press, 1994), 110.
31. Waugh, *Vile Bodies*, 266, 273.
32. Ibid., 314.
33. Ibid., 7.
34. Ibid., 9.
35. Ibid., 317.
36. Ibid., 25.
37. Ibid., 25.
38. Eagleton, *Exile and Émigrés*, 34, 50.
39. Freud, *Jokes*, 285.

40. Waugh, *Vile Bodies*, 38.
41. Ibid., 67.
42. Ibid., 67.
43. Ibid., 314. These types of exchanges occur throughout the novel, and, in addition to commenting on the shifting nature of identity, they suggest Freud's comment that "usage of language itself is unreliable and is itself in need of examination for its authority" (qtd, in Polhemus, *Comic Faith*, 283, who uses a different translation than the Standard Edition).
44. T.S. Eliot, "*Ulysses, Order, and Myth*," in *Selected Prose of T.S. Eliot*, ed. Frank Kermode (New York: Harcourt Brace, 1975), 177.
45. McCartney notes that Waugh "argued that the pursuit of truth in the subjective was not only self-indulgent but, worse, uninteresting. To exalt the interior feelings above an intellectual engagement with history was to betray one's artistic duty; and to suppose that truth lay in 'the dark places of psychology,' as Woolf had put it, was to be either criminally self-indulgent or culpably misled." See Satire between the Wars: Evelyn Waugh and Others" (*The Columbia History of the British Novel*, ed. John Richetti et al. (New York: Columbia University Press, 1994), 880.
46. Waugh, *Vile Bodies*, 29.
47. Ibid., 216–17.
48. Ibid., 220.
49. Ibid., 221.
50. Ibid., 225.
51. Ibid., 227–28.
52. For a thorough discussion of Waugh's engagement with both Bergson and Marinetti and the Italian Futurists, see chapter three in George McCartney's *Confused Roaring*. See also, Allen, "*Vile Bodies*" 318–28; Loss, "*Vile Bodies*," 155–64.
53. Waugh, *Vile Bodies*, 65.
54. Ibid., 168–69.
55. Ibid., 284.
56. Ibid., 230.
57. Ibid., 23.
58. Ibid., 238.
59. Ibid., 246.
60. Ibid., 258.
61. McCartney, *Confused Roaring*, 49.
62. Waugh, *Vile Bodies*, 284–85, emphasis in the original.
63. See Stephen Jay Greenblatt, *Three Modern Satirists: Waugh, Orwell, and Huxley* (New Haven and London: Yale University Press, 1965), 14; Charles E. Linck, Jr. and Robert Murray Davis, "The Bright Young People in *Vile Bodies*," in *Papers on Language and Literature* 5 (1969): 80–90; and Loss, "*Vile Bodies*," 155–64.
64. Waugh, *Vile Bodies*, 286.
65. Ibid., 300–01.
66. Polhemus, *Comic Faith*, 159.
67. Loss, "*Vile Bodies*," 164.

68. Ibid. See also, Blayac, "Evelyn Waugh and Humor," 122.
69. Bergson, "Laughter," 66.
70. Freud, *Jokes*, 290.

Chapter 5   Astolpho Meets Sisyphus: Melancholy and Repetition in Anthony Powell's *Afternoon Men*

1. Evelyn Waugh, *A Handful of Dust* (Boston: Little, Brown, 1934), 16.
2. Qtd. in Humphrey Carpenter, *The Brideshead Generation: Evelyn Waugh and His Friends* (Boston: Houghton Mifflin, 1990), 290.
3. Waugh, *Vile Bodies*, 183, 185.
4. Carpenter, *The Brideshead Generation*, 245.
5. Anthony Powell, *Afternoon Men* (London: Heineman, 1952), 4, 7. All subsequent references are to this edition.
6. Ibid., 1.
7. Ibid., 70, 37, 49, 55, 32, 219.
8. T.S. Eliot "The Hollow Men," *The Collected Poems* (New York, Harcourt, 1991), 82.
9. Freud, *Jokes,* 286.
10. Ibid., 267.
11. Ibid., 267.
12. Ibid., 267.
13. In *The Comedy of Entropy* (Toronto: University of Toronto Press, 1990), Patrick O'Neill describes this as "self-reflective humor ... that moves from the rejection of all norms to the celebration of parodied norms" (51).
14. Neil Brennan, *Anthony Powell* (New York: Twayne, 1995), 30.
15. Powell, *Afternoon Men*, 18–19.
16. Richard Vorhees, "The Music of Time: These and Variations," *Dalhousie Review* 42 (Autumn 1962), 313.
17. V.S. Pritchett, "London Letter," *New York Times Book Review* (January 12, 1958), 22. It is interesting that these adjectives are frequently attributed to the fiction of Ivy Compton-Burnett, a writer Powell very much admired, according to Neil McEwan (10).
18. Powell, *Afternoon Men*, 96.
19. Freud, *Jokes*, 287.
20. Slang for a cheap or inferior cigarette (*OED*).
21. Powell, *Afternoon Men*, 78–79.
22. Neil McEwan, *Anthony Powell* (New York: St. Martin's Press, 1991), 17.
23. Ibid., 22.
24. The anonymous reviewer for *The Times Literary Supplement*, September 17, 1931, suggested that "Palindrome" applies to the whole novel.
25. Patrick O'Neill, "The Comedy of Entropy: The Contexts of Black Humor," in *Black Humor: Critical Essays*, ed. Alan R. Pratt (New York: Garland, 1993), 85.
26. Ibid., 85.
27. Powell, *Afternoon Men*, 2.

28. Ibid., 3.
29. Ibid., 2.
30. Powell, *Messengers of Day* (New York: Holt Rinehart, 1978), 109.
31. Powell, *Afternoon Men*, 18.
32. Ibid., 21.
33. Ibid., 22.
34. Waugh, *Vile Bodies*, 69.
35. Powell, *Afternoon Men*, 25.
36. Ibid., 30, 31.
37. Ibid., 33.
38. Ibid., 34.
39. Ibid., 45.
40. Powell, *Messengers of Day*, 155.
41. Powell, *Afternoon Men*, 35.
42. Ibid., 34.
43. Ibid., 35.
44. Ibid., 36.
45. Ibid., 36.
46. Another of these is the doorman at the art gallery, where Atwater views Pringle's show. He is described as an "ape-faced dotard in uniform, who fussed unsteadily towards them as they came in, bent on causing some petty annoyance" (101). The porter at the country station near Pringle's cottage is "very old," "deaf and partly mad" (147). James Tucker has argued that representatives of the working classes "come in for some very rough handling" in Powell, but this appraisal ignores the fact that most of the characters have an element of the grotesque —no matter their social class— and, for the purposes of dark humor, the grotesquerie of these minor characters work to make Atwater feel that the world is indeed a menacing place and survival in it requires a defensive posture.
47. Brennan, *Anthony Powell*, 40.
48. Ibid., 31.
49. Janoff, "Black Humor," 10.
50. Powell, *Afternoon Men*, 39.
51. Ibid., 39.
52. Powell, *Afternoon Men*, 39.
53. Schulz, "Toward a Definition of Black Humor," in *Black Humor: Critical Essays*, ed. Alan R. Pratt (New York: Garland, 1993), 158.
54. Powell, *Afternoon Men*, 39.
55. Ibid., 41.
56. Ibid., 41.
57. Powell, *Afternoon Men*, 42.
58. Ibid., 43.
59. Ibid., 43.
60. Powell, *Afternoon Men*, 53.
61. Ibid., 55.
62. Ibid., 55.
63. Ibid., 55.

64. Ibid., 54, 9, 43, 10.
65. Ibid., 59–60.
66. Ibid., 63.
67. Ibid., 62–63.
68. Freud, *Jokes*, 286.
69. Ibid., 285.
70. Powell, *Afternoon Men*, 63.
71. Ibid., 73.
72. Ibid., 88.
73. Slang for diet.
74. Powell, *Afternoon Men*, 93.
75. Brennan, *Anthony Powell*, 34.
76. Powell, *Afternoon Men*, 88.
77. Ibid., 83.
78. Ibid., 117.
79. Ibid., 119.
80. Ibid., 216.
81. Ibid., 215–16.
82. Ibid., 145.
83. Carpenter, 245.
84. Powell, *Afternoon Men*, 147–48.
85. Ibid., 149.
86. Ibid., 153.
87. Ibid., 171–72.
88. Ibid., 173.
89. Ibid., 174.
90. Ibid., 175.
91. Ibid., 176.
92. Freud, *Jokes,* 286.
93. Ibid., 286.
94. Ibid., 289.
95. Powell, *Afternoon Men*, 188.
96. Ibid., 201.
97. Ibid., 203.
98. Ibid., 205.
99. Ibid., 182.
100. Ibid., 219.
101. Ibid., 221.

Bibliography

Allen, Brooke. *"Vile Bodies*: A Futurist Fantasy," in *Twentieth Century Literature* 40 (Fall 1994): 318–28.

Anonymous, Review of *Afternoon Men* in *The Times Literary Supplement*, September 17, 1931.

Aristotle. *The Poetics*, trans. Hamilton Fyfe (London: Heinemann, 1927).

Auden, W.H. "Notes on the Comic" in *Comedy: Meaning and Form*, ed. Robert Corrigan (San Francisco: Chandler, 1965).

Bakhtin, Mikhail. *The Dialogic Imagination*, ed. Michael Holquist, trans. Caryl Emerson and Michael Holquist (Austin: University of Texas Press, 1981).

———. *Rabelais and His World*, trans Helene Iswolsky (Cambridge: MIT Press, 1968).

Baldanza, Frank. *Ivy Compton-Burnett* (New York: Twayne Publishers, 1964).

Barreca, Regina. *Untamed and Unabashed: Essays on Women and Humor in the British Literature* (Detroit: Wayne State University Press, 1994).

———, ed. *New Perspectives on Women and Comedy* (Philadelphia: Gordon and Breach, 1992).

———. *They Used to Call Me Snow White . . . But I Drifted* (New York: Penguin, 1991).

———, ed. *Last Laughs: Perspectives on Women and Comedy* (Philadelphia: Gordon and Breach, 1988).

Baudelaire, Charles. "On the Comic in the Plastic Arts," in *Comedy: Meaning and Form*, ed. Robert Corrigan (New York: Harper & Row, 1981).

———. "On the Essence of Laughter," in *Comedy: Meaning and Form*, ed. Robert Corrigan (New York: Harper & Row, 1981).

Benjamin, Walter. "The Work of Art in the Age of Mechanical Reproduction," in *Illuminations*, edited and introduced by Hannah Arendt (New York: Schoken Books, 1968).

Bergson, Henri. "Laughter," in *Comedy*, ed. Wylie Sypher (Baltimore and London: Johns Hopkins University Press, 1956).

Bilger, Audrey. *Laughing Feminism: Subversive Comedy in Frances Burney, Maria Edgeworth, and Jane Austen* (Detroit: Wayne State University Press, 1998).

Blayac, Alain, ed. "Evelyn Waugh and Humor," *Evelyn Waugh: New Directions* (Hong Kong: Macmillan, 1992).

Bowen, Elizabeth. "Parents and Children," *Art of I. Compton-Burnett A Collection of Critical Essays*, ed. Charles Burkhart (London: Gollancz, 1972).

———. *Collected Impressions* (New York: Alfred A. Knopf, 1950).

Bowen, John. "An Interview with Miss Compton-Burnett," in *Twentieth Century Literature Ivy Compton-Burnett Issue* 25 (Summer 1979): 169.

Bradbury, Malcolm and James McFarlane, eds. *Modernism: A Guide to European Literature, 1890–1930* (New York: Penguin, 1991).

Brennan, Neil. *Anthony Powell* (New York: Twayne, 1995).

Breton, Andre. *Anthologie de l'humour noir* (Paris: Jean-Jacques Pauvert, 1966).

Burkhart, Charles ed. "Ivy Compton-Burnett and Margaret Jourdain: A Conversation," in *The Art of I. Compton-Burnett: A Collection of Critical Essays* (London: Gollancz, 1972).

Carpenter, Humphrey. *The Brideshead Generation: Evelyn Waugh and His Friends* (Boston: Houghton Mifflin, 1990).

Chapman, Antony J. and Hugh C. Foot, eds. *It's a Funny Thing, Humour, International Conference on Humour and Laughter, Cardiff, Wales, 1976* (Oxford: Pergamon, 1977).

——, eds. *Humor and Laughter: Theory, Research, and Applications* (New York: John Wiley, 1976).

Clark, John. *The Modern Satiric Grotesque and Its Traditions* (Lexington: University Press of Kentucky, 1991).

Cicero. *De Oratore*, trans. E.W. Sutton (London: Heinemann, 1942).

Cixious, Helene. "The Laugh of the Medusa," trans. Keith Cohen and Paula Cohen. *Signs* 1, no. 4 (Summer 1976): 141–53.

Clark, Suzanne. *Sentimental Modernism: Women Writers and the Revolution of the Word* (Bloomington: Indiana University Press, 1991).

Compton-Burnett, Ivy. The Mighty and Their Fall (London: Virago, 1990).

——. *Daughters and Sons* (London: Gollancz, 1954).

——. *A House and Its Head* (London: Eyre & Spottiswoode, 1935).

Cordner, Michael, Peter Holland, and John Kerrigan. *English Comedy* (Cambridge and New York: Cambridge University Press, 1994).

Corrigan, Robert, ed. *Comedy: Meaning and Form* (San Francisco: Chandler, 1965).

Crabbe, Katharyn. *Evelyn Waugh* (New York: Continuum, 1988).

Cranston, Maurice. "The Writer in His Age," *London Magazine* 4.5 (May 1957): 38–40.

Cuddy-Keane, Melba. "The Politics of Comic Modes in Virginia Woolf's *Between the Acts*," *PMLA* 105: 2 (March 1990): 273–85.

Davis, Douglas. *The World of Black Humor* (New York: Dutton, 1967).

Dooley, D.J. "Waugh and Black Humor," *The Evelyn Waugh Newsletter* 2 (Autumn 1968) 1–3.

Eagleton, Terry. *Exiles and Émigrés: Studies in Modern Fiction* (New York: Schocken Books, 1970).

Eliot, T.S. "The Hollow Men," in *The Collected Poems* (New York, Harcourt, 1991).

——. "Ulysses, Order, and Myth," *Selected Prose of T.S. Eliot*, ed. Frank Kermode (New York: Harcourt Brace, 1975).

Emerson, J.P. "Negotiating the Serious Import of Humor," *Sociometry* 32 (1969): 169–81.

Engels, Frederick. *The Condition of the Working Class in England*, eds. and trans. W.O. Henderson and W.H. Chaloner (New York: Macmillan, 1958).

English, James. *Comic Transactions: Literature, Humor, and the Politics of Community in Twentieth-Century* (Ithaca: Cornell University Press, 1994).

Finney, Gail, ed. *Look Who's Laughing: Gender and Comedy* (Longhorne, PA: Gordon and Breach, 1994).

Flieger, Jerry Aline. *The Purloined Punchline: Freud's Comic Theory and the Postmodern Text* (Baltimore and London: Johns Hopkins University Press, 1991).

Freud, Sigmund. *Civilization and Its Discontents*, translated and edited, James Strachey (New York and London: Norton, 1961).

———. "Humour," in *The Standard Edition of the Complete Works of Sigmund Freud*, vol. 21 (1927–31), ed. James Strachey (London: Hogarth, 1961).

———. *Jokes and Their Relation to the Unconscious*, ed. James Strachey (New York: Norton, 1960).

——— . "On Narcissism: An Introduction," in *A General Selection from the Works of Sigmund Freud*, ed. John Rickman (1914; rpt. New York: Doubleday, 1957)

Frye, Northrop. *Anatomy of Criticism: Four Essays* (New Jersey: Princeton, 1957).

Fussell, Paul. *The Great War and Modern Memory* (New York and London: Oxford University Press, 1975).

Gasiorek, Andrzej. *Post-War British Fiction: Realism and After* (London: Edward, Arnold, 1995).

Glendinning, Victoria. *Elizabeth Bowen: A Biography* (New York: Alfred A. Knopf, 1978).

Goldstein, Jeffrey H. and Paul McGhee, eds. *The Psychology of Humor* (New York: Academic Press, 1972).

Gorra, Michael. "Through Comedy Toward Catholicism: A Reading of Evelyn Waugh's Early Novels," *Contemporary Literature* 29.2 (Summer 1988). 201–20.

Greenblatt, Stephen Jay. *Three Modern Satirists: Waugh, Orwell, and Huxley* (New Haven and London: Yale University Press, 1965).

Gurewitch, Morton. *The Ironic Temper and the Comic Imagination* (Detroit: Wayne State University Press, 1994).

Hapgood, Lynne and Nancy Paxton, eds. *Outside Modernism: In Pursuit of the English Novel, 1900–30* (New York: St. Martin's, 2000).

Heller, Terry. "Notes on Technique in Black Humor," *Thalia: Studies in Literary Humor* 2.3 (1979): 15–21.

Henke, Suzette. "Virginia Woolf's Septimus Smith: An Analysis of 'Paraphrenia' and the Schizophrenic Use of Language," *Literature and Psychology* 31 (1981): 13–23.

Hewison, Robert. *In Anger: British Culture in the Cold War, 1945–1960* (New York: Oxford University Press, 1981).

Hobbes, Thomas. *The Leviathan* (London: Dent, 1914).

Hussey, Mark. *Virginia Woolf and War: Fiction, Reality, and Myth* (Syracuse: Syracuse University Press, 1991).

Ionesco, Eugéne. "La Démystification par l'humour noir," *Avant-Scène* (Paris) February 15, 1959.

Janoff, Bruce. "Black Humor: Beyond Satire," *The Ohio Review* 14.1 (1972): 5–20.

Kant, Immanuel. *Critique of Judgment* (New York: Hafner Press, 1951).

Kaufman, Gloria. "Feminist Humor as a Survival Device," *Regionalism and the Female Imagination* 3.2/3 (1977/78): 86.

Keough, William. "The Violence of American Humor," in *What's So Funny? Humor in American Culture*, ed. Nancy Walker (Wilmington: Scholarly Resources, 1998).

Kiernan, Robert F. *Frivolity Unbound: Six Masters of the Camp Novel* (New York: Continuum, 1990).

Kincaid, James R. *Annoying the Victorians* (New York and London: Routledge, 1995).

Laing, R.D. *The Politics of Experience* (New York: Random, 1967).

Lauter, Paul, ed. *Theories of Comedy* (Garden City, NY: Doubleday, 1964).

LeClair, Thomas. "Death and Black Humor," *Critique: Studies in Modern Fiction* 17.1 (1975): 5–40.

Lee, Hermione. *Virginia Woolf* (New York: Knopf, 1996).

Lees-Milne, James. "Major/Minor," *Twentieth Century Literature Ivy Compton-Burnett Issue* 25 (Summer 1979): 132.

Liddell, Robert. *The Novels of I. Compton-Burnett* (London: Gollancz, 1955).

Light, Alison. *Forever England: Feminity, Literature, and Conservatism Between the Wars* (London: Routledge, 1991).

Linck, Charles E. and Robert Murray Davis. "The Bright Young People in *Vile Bodies*," *Papers on Language and Literature* 5 (1969).

Little, Judy. "(En)Gendering Laughter: Woolf's *Orlando* as Contraband in the Age of Joyce," *Last Laughs: Perspectives on Women and Comedy*, ed. Regina Barreca (New York: Gordon and Breach, 1988).

———. *Comedy and the Woman Writers: Woolf, Spark, and Feminism* (Lincoln: University of Nebraska Press, 1983).

Loss, Archie. "*Vile Bodies*, Vorticism, and Italian Futurism," *Journal of Modern Literature* 18 (Winter 1992).

Lyotard, Jean-François. *Toward the Postmodern*, trans. Mira Kamdor et al. (New Jersey: Humanities Press, 1993).

Mann, Thomas. *Past Masters and Other Papers*, trans. H.T. Lowe-Porter (New York: Knopf, 1968).

Marshall, Denise. "Slaying the Angel and the Patriarch: The Grinning Woolf," in *Last Laughs: Perspectives on Women and Comedy*, ed. Regina Barreca (New York: Gordon and Breach, 1988).

———. *Intimate Alien: Virginia Woolf and the Comedy of Knowledge and the Comedy of Power* (Ann Arbor: Dissertation Abstracts International, 1985).

Marx, Karl and Friedrich Engels. "The Eighteenth Brumaire of Louis Bonaparte," in *Basic Writings on Politics and Philosophy*, ed. Louis Feuer (New York, 1959).

McCartney, George. "Satire Between the Wars: Evelyn Waugh and Others," in *The Columbia History of the British Novel*, ed. John Richetti et al. (New York: Columbia University Press, 1994).

———. *Confused Roaring: Evelyn Waugh and the Modernist Tradition* (Bloomington and Indianapolis: Indiana University Press, 1987).

McEwan, Neil. *Anthony Powell* (New York: St. Martin's Press, 1991).

McWhirter, David. "Feminism/Gender/Comedy: Meredith, Woolf, and the Reconfiguration of Comic Distance," in *Look Who's Laughing: Gender and Comedy*, ed. Gail Finney (New York: Gordon and Breach, 1994).

Millgate, Michael. "An Interview with Miss Compton-Burnett," in *The Art of I. Compton-Burnett: A Collection of Critical Essays*, ed. Charles Burkhart (London: Gollancz, 1972).

Nietzsche, Friedrich. *Thus Spake Zarathustra* (New York: Penguin, 1978).

Numasawa, Koji. "Black Humor: An American Aspect," in *Black Humor: Critical Essays*, ed. Alan Pratt (New York: Garland, 1993).

O'Neill, Patrick. "The Comedy of Entropy: The Contexts of Black Humor," in *Black Humor: Critical Essays*, ed. Alan R. Pratt (New York: Garland, 1993).

———. *The Comedy of Entropy* (Toronto: University of Toronto Press, 1990).

Olson, Kirby. *Comedy After Postmodernism: Rereading Comedy from Edward Lear to Charles Willeford* (Lubbock: Texas Tech University Press, 2001).

Ostrovsky, Erika. "Black Humor and the Modern Sensibility," *Modern Language Studies* 2.1 (1972): 13–16.

Plato. *Philebus*, ed. Harold N. Fowler (London: Heinemann, 1925).

Polhemus, Robert M. *Comic Faith: The Great Tradition from Austen to Joyce* (Chicago: University of Chicago Press, 1980).

Powell, Anthony. *Messengers of Day* (New York: Holt, Rinehart, and Winston, 1978).

———. *Afternoon Men* (London: Heineman, 1952).

Pratt, Alan R., ed. *Black Humor: Critical Essays* (New York: Garland, 1993).

Pritchett, V.S. "London Letter," *New York Times Book Review* (January 12, 1958), 22.

Pugh, Martin. *Women and the Women's Movement in Britain, 1914–1945* (New York: Paragon, 1993).

Purvis, June, ed. *Women's History: Britain, 1805–1945* (London: UCL Press, 1995).

Rayner, Alice. *Comic Persuasion: Moral Structure in British Comedy from Shakespeare to Stoppard* (Berkeley: University of California Press, 1987).

Rado, Lisa, ed. *Rereading Modernism: New Directions in Feminist Criticism* (New York and London: Garland, 1994).

Rosello, Mireille. *L'Humour Noir Selon André Breton* (Paris: José Corti, 1987).

Sanders, Barry. *Sudden Glory: Laughter as Subversive History* (Boston: Beacon, 1995).

Satre, Jean-Paul. *L'Idiot de la famille: Gustave Flaubert de 1831 à 1857* (Paris: Gallimard, 1971).

Schiller, Friedrich. *Naïve and Sentimental Poetry and On the Sublime* (New York: Ungar, 1966).

Schulz, Max. "Towards a Definition of Black Humor," in *Black Humor: Critical Essays*, ed. Alan R. Pratt. (New York: Garland, 1993).

———. *Black Humor Fiction of the Sixties: A Pluralistic Definition of Man and His World* (Athen: Ohio University Press, 1973).

Simon, Richard Keller. *The Labyrinth of the Comic: Theory and Practice from Fielding to Freud* (Tallahassee: Florida State University Press, 1985).

Sinfield, Alan. *Literature, Politics, and Culture in Postwar Britain* (Berkeley: University of California Press, 1989).

Sochen, June, ed. *Women's Comic Visions* (Detroit: Wayne State University Press, 1991).

Sprigge, Elizabeth. *The Life of Ivy Compton-Burnett* (New York: George Braziller, 1973).

Stannard, Martin, ed. *Evelyn Waugh: The Critical Heritage* (London: Routledge, 1984).

Stetz, Margaret. *British Women's Comic Fiction, 1890–1990: Not Drowning, But Laughing* (Aldershot, England: Ashgate, 2001).

Swindon, Patrick. *The English Novel of History and Society, 1940–80* (London: Macmillan, 1984).

Sypher, Wylie. *Loss of Self in Modern Literature and Art* (New York, 1962).

———. "The Meanings of Comedy," in *Comedy* (Baltimore and London: Johns Hopkins University Press, 1956).

Tate, Trudi. *Modernism, History and the First World War* (Manchester: Manchester University Press, 1998).

Thomas, Sue. "Virginia Woolf's Septimus Smith and Contemporary Perceptions of Shell Shock," *English Language Notes* 25 (December 1987): 49–57.

Vorhees, Richard. "The Music of Time: Theme and Variations," *Dalhousie Review* 42 (Autumn 1962).

Walker, Nancy. *What's So Funny? Humor in American Culture* (Wilmington: Scholarly Resources, Inc., 1998).

———. *Feminist Alternatives: Irony and Fantasy in the Contemporary Novel by Women* (Jackson & London: University Press of Mississippi, 1990).

———. *A Very Serious Thing: Women's Humor and American Culture* (Minneapolis: University of Minnesota Press, 1988).

Waugh, Evelyn. *A Handful of Dust* (Boston: Little, Brown, 1934).

———. *Vile Bodies* (Boston: Little, Brown, 1930).

Weber, Samuel. *The Legend of Freud* (Minneapolis: University of Minnesota Press, 1982).

Weisenburger, Steven. *Fables of Subversion: Satire and the American Novel, 1930–1980* (Athens: University Press of Georgia, 1995).

West, Rebecca, Review of *Vile Bodies*, in *Evelyn Waugh: The Critical Heritage*, ed. Martin Stannard (London: Routledge & Kegan Paul, 1984).

White, Kenneth, ed. *Savage Comedy: Structures of Humor* (Amsterdam: Rodopi, 1978).

Wilde, Alan. *Horizons of Assent: Modernism, Postmodernism, and the Ironic Imagination* (Baltimore: Johns Hopkins University Press, 1981).

Wilson, Angus. "Ivy Compton-Burnett," in *Diversity and Depth in Fiction: Selected Critical Writings* (New York: Viking, 1983).

Winston, Mathew. "Black Humor: To Weep with Laughing," in *Black Humor: Critical Essays*, ed. Alan Pratt (New York: Garland, 1993).

———. *"Humour noir* and Black Humor," in *Veins of Humor*, ed. Harry Levin (Cambridge: Harvard University Press, 1972).

Woolf, Virginia. "Modern Fiction," *The Common Reader*, ed. Andrew McNeille (New York: Harcourt, 1984).

———. "Friendship's Gallery," ed. and intro. Ellen Hawkes. *Twentieth Century Literature* 25: 3/4 (1979), 299.

———. *Between the Acts* (New York, Harcourt, 1969).

———. *A Writer's Diary*, ed. Leonard Woolf (New York: Harcourt, 1953).

———. *Three Guineas* (New York: Harcourt 1938).

———. *Orlando* (New York: Harcourt, 1928).

Zwerdling, Alex. *"Mrs. Dalloway* and the Social System," *PMLA* 92 (1977): 69–82.

INDEX